PRAISE FOR GE

**Praise for *Harry Harambee's Kenyan Sundowner***

"The convincing, well-rounded characters offer a few stereotypical barbs about African culture, which is realistic considering their perspectives, but otherwise the Kenyan backdrop offers an inviting element for readers to explore with the protagonist. Readers looking for engaging contemporary fiction with an emotionally available adult male lead. Great for fans of: Graham Greene's *The Heart of the Matter*, Eric Jerome Dickey's *Thieves' Paradise*." - **BookLife Reviews,** *Publisher's Weekly*

**Praise for *Preacher Finds a Corpse***

**NYC Big Book Awards 2020 Winner in Mystery, IPA 2020 Distinguished Favorite in Mystery, Eric Hoffer 2020 Finalist in Mystery**

"This is literature masquerading as a mystery. Carefully yet powerfully, Gerald Jones creates a small, stunning world in a tiny midwestern town, infusing each character with not just life but wit, charm, and occasionally menace. This is the kind of writing one expects from John Irving or Jane Smiley." - **Marvin J. Wolf, author of the Rabbi Ben Mysteries, including** *A Scribe Dies in Brooklyn*

**Praise for *Clifford's Spiral***

**Independent Press Awards 2020 Distinguished Favorite in Literary Fiction**

"We've seen and noted the comparison of this author by other reviewers to literary giants like Roth and Vonnegut. And we can't disagree. Yet we feel there may be yet another strata for Gerald Everett Jones, who arguably is doing the best work of his career. We predict that he lacks only a mention in the *The New York Review of Books* or, better yet, *Oprah,* to become a nationwide best-selling author. Five-plus stars to *Clifford's Spiral,* a true literary novel if ever there was one. We say in all seriousness that if you only read one novel this year, this should be it." - **Don Sloan,** ***Publishers Daily Reviews***

# Jonathan's Journal

# Jonathan's Journal
## A Novel

## Gerald Everett Jones

LaPuerta
Books and Media
www.lapuerta.tv

Copyright © 2026 by Gerald Everett Jones

All rights reserved. No part of this book may be reproduced in any form or by any electronic or mechanical means, including information storage and retrieval systems, without written permission from the author, except for the use of brief quotations in a book review. LaPuerta Books and Media www.lapuerta.tv Email: bookstore@lapuerta.tv

Trade paperback ISBN 979-8-9907273-4-2; Kindle ISBN 979-8-9907273-5-9; ASIN B0GHBG19HT; EPUB ISBN: 979-8-9907273-6-6

Library of Congress Control Number: 2026903273

The novel in this book is a work of fiction. Names, characters, places, and incidents either are products of the author's imagination or are used fictitiously. Any resemblance to actual events or locales or persons, living or dead, is entirely coincidental. The author has attempted throughout this book to distinguish proprietary trademarks from descriptive terms by following the capitalization style used by the manufacturer.

The person shown on the front cover is a photographer's model. This image does not depict or represent any character in this book.

Contains public sector information licensed under the Open Government Licence v3.0. Portions of the fiction narrative are based on a true story, an anonymous unpublished work created in the UK in 1919, "Memoirs of My Travels East 1916 - 1919," by RFW. Orphan Works Licence Issued under UK orphan licensing scheme: Licence number: OWLS000456, Licensee: Gerald Everett Jones, Date of issue: 29/07/2025. Persons mentioned in the memoir other than public figures are cited with fictitious names.

Book cover photo credits: Still image from the film *The Battle of the Somme* showing a staged attack. Believed to be shot before the opening of the battle on 1 July 1916, possibly at a trench mortar school behind the lines, Geoffrey Malins [PD 1916]; "Writing in My Diary" Canva Pro; "E Indian Woman" Canva Pro.

Book design: La Puerta Productions
Editorial associate: Adero Joan Cate
Research team lead: Anna Tjeltveit
Diary transcription: Robin Levey
Copyeditor: Jason Letts
Author photo: Runkee Productions

*To Magdalena Fuchs,*
*whose courage is an inspiration*

# The Found Diary

*Russia will always covet warm-water ports.*
  Anonymous World History Teacher

*War is never a solution. It's an aggravation.*
  Benjamin Disraeli

---

If I hadn't found that soldier's diary, I wouldn't have much to tell you.

I might have stayed locked up in this apartment like a musty winter coat in a beachcomber's closet.

I can tell from flipping through its meticulously handwritten pages that it is a war story.

The question why we fight is fundamental and therefore broad in scope.

The reasons we are given are never the root causes.

- Jonathan Frederick Worthington, Ph.D.
  Santa Monica, California
  September 6, 2025

# Memoirs of My Travels East

## A Soldier's Diary

My enthusiasm to join the Colours was roused by the sight of the Territorials passing through Exeter en route for Salisbury Plain following the outbreak of war in August 1914.

In November 1914, I joined the Royal 1st Devon Yeomanry, and I was posted to the Second Line then in course of formation at Teignmouth. The following spring we moved to Woodbury Common, and in the autumn, we went on the East Coast defenses, where we did mounted patrol work until November 1916. At that time most of the cavalry regiments were being dismounted and turned into infantry on account of the fighting on the Western Front having developed into trench warfare.

I then forwarded to France and joined the 8th Devons, which was holding a portion of the line in the Beaumont Hamel Sector. Here I met with an accident to my elbow and was invalided home in the early spring of 1917. After convalescence, I was sent to Raglan Barracks Devonport (the depot of the Devonshire Regiment). A large number of troops stationed there were being sent to Mesopotamia as the Germans, under General von Falkenhayn, intended to endeavour to take Baghdad.

With my ambition to see the East, I succeeded in joining one of these drafts. This gave me an opportunity of seeing several countries, and the following gives a brief account of my recollections, aided by a small pocket diary, which I carried during my travels.

# Reading Between the Lines

## Prof. Jonathan Frederick Worthington

He watched a parade and decided to *enlist?*

Didn't he have friends or relatives who'd already been lost? Any loves — or at least responsibilities — he'd regret leaving? And was his sense of honor or duty so compelling that he needed to justify it in writing? Was it to memorialize his valor?

Or was his life at home so uninspiring? A perfectly plausible motive would be that he was simply bored and purposeless, like me, and too unimaginative to have pictured other alternatives.

*A small pocket diary?* That's not what I hold in my hands. It's leather-bound with meticulous cursive handwriting in India ink, no doubt transcribed by a professional calligrapher, the handsome volume intended as a memento and keepsake.

I've read enough of his memoir to know that it's not some intimate confession. This is not a fellow who dwells on his thoughts. Disappointing, that. Because my understanding of the events of World War I is at about the prep-school level, I will need some background and context.

By profession, I'm an art historian. I have capable research skills, whether online or in the stacks, but even a slacker graduate student knows when it's time to get some expert help. I might need to dig through arcane troves such as card catalogs, fiche, crumbling and yellowed acid paper, and musty boxes of ephemera.

But I'm afraid of people.

---

I turned forty last month. I'm middle-aged, at least by actuarial standards. All during my childhood, Mum often quipped I was *born* forty, either reminding me I was too sullen for my young age or saying I was already old enough to know better than to do whatever I'd done to vex her.

If you saw me on the street, you might wonder what I was upset about. The right side of my face is set in a permanent scowl. That's from a sudden onset of Bell's palsy when I was a boy of ten.

But when I look in the mirror, I don't see the deformity that betrays my usual lightness of being. I see salvation. You see, at Torquay Boys' Grammar School, I was always the shortest kid in the class. I was also — no reason not to brag now — always the smartest. And mocking my diminutive stature, my head was disproportionately big for my body, and my oversized ears stuck out. They still do, but I wear my hair long enough to comb it back on the sides. And my body has filled out until I'm downright stocky, as if swelling to support my brain. Because I was scrawny back then, I was always last to be picked on the playground for any team sport, put front and center in any class photo, and proved an irresistibly vulnerable target for bullies.

My facial deformity changed all that overnight. I awoke one morning (during Christmas break, can you imagine?) to feel a numbness in my cheek accompanied by a paralysis of those muscles caused by impairment of the seventh cranial nerve. When I presented myself to my mother at breakfast, she was aghast, not only from the sudden transformation in my usually grinning countenance but also because her brother, Nathan, had been similarly afflicted. In his case, it was paralysis from childhood polio; he died from the disease in his teens. I hadn't been sick, but she worried the cause must be inherited and dire, if not contagious. She rushed me to the emergency clinic, where another common cause of the condition, stroke, was promptly ruled out.

To this day, the causes of Bell's palsy are still not fully understood, although viruses and stress top the list. Now they treat the condition with corticosteroids and antiviral drugs. No one knew what to do about it back then. Mum felt the attending physician's bedside manner was hardly serious enough. His pasted-on smile was meant to be reassuring to both of us, telling her that in most of these cases the paralysis and disfigurement would disappear in a few days.

I was sent home without even advice to rest lazily in bed.

My condition did not disappear. During the incident, Dad had been away on business, as he was often, even on holidays. He returned from that trip on Boxing Day, when the three of us enjoyed a deferred and gloriously catered family feast. There being no other guests, Mum need not have offered explanations about my scowl.

Dad's reaction was sympathetic but terse. "We buck up and carry on, don't we? Could well be a passing thing. Time will tell, and meanwhile we do our bit."

Since that time, I've worn a menacing sneer, which rarely matches my habitually less threatening moods.

When I returned to school after the New Year, Dad hired a car to take me, possibly at Mum's urging and despite his sanguine advice. No need to deal with strangers on a train.

My new face became my salvation though, because the bullies must have thought I was one mean son of a bitch, which was only partly true. Looking back on my difficulties then, I realize I might have started carrying a jackknife, pulling it from the pocket of my jeans and brandishing it at odd times. They'd have run the other way!

These days, the set of my face is as much a part of me as my rinse-in herbal hair color and my dwindling crop. But on first encounters, I remain shy about my bit of a lisp, owing to partial paralysis of the upper lip.

From the onset of my condition until the end of her life, my mother referred to me as her "Southern gentleman" because of my inability to pronounce certain consonants. She must've felt it endearing, but to me it always felt like teasing, as if to say, "Don't worry about your defect. I'll always love you." It implied she might well be the only one.

---

Not only do I not know who the other J.F.W. might have been or why my mother had his book, but also Uncle Ted was a puzzle to me. About my father's family, I was told almost nothing at all. She didn't speak of her parents or her ancestry. I assume none of those relatives are now alive. She was downright stingy with family lore on both sides, and she let it be known she wanted it that way. I have my birth certificate, but among Mum's things I could find no family records.

Unless this mysterious diary is one.

I know enough about genealogical research to know I don't want to do it as a hobby. I could hire a professional, I suppose. But until I found the soldier's story, I had no interest in researching my roots. I could send a DNA sample to one of those family heritage services, but I don't want to be deluged with queries from third or fourth cousins.

My parents were an odd couple, and I was their only — and unexpected — child. They were married in 1980 when he was sixty and she was twenty-eight. Five years later, I was born. For her, it was a late-term pregnancy. For him, not quite a miracle. Years later, when classmates would tease me that I must've been some other man's love child, Mum coached me to remind them that Cary Grant was sixty-two when his then wife, Dyan Cannon, had their daughter Jennifer.

I was born in London, sent to an all-male boarding school in Torquay, then left England for college at Brown and Rhode Island School of Design in Provincetown.

At Brown, attending a coeducational school was a novelty for me. Before then, I let my deformed face justify my shyness, and then my defensiveness kept potential friends of either sex at a distance. In college though, it's not much of an exaggeration to say that I discovered women. My face was intriguing to them in ways I'd not yet experienced. For some, in my early encounters, I'd play the sympathy card. Then, as I gained confidence, I found I could leverage my "mean streak" as a bad-boy persona, which was even more successful. But ultimately, because authentic meanness is not in my nature, convincing nastiness was impossible for me to sustain.

Those relationships were trivial compared to the genuine affection I discovered with another instructor in the MFA program. As for me, that relationship might have lasted a lifetime, but she decided she'd rather live with a musclebound smoke jumper in Portland and make artisanal pottery.

Since leaving, I'd return to the UK only rarely to visit Mum, most often at Christmas when she had the best possible excuse to indulge herself at Harrods. We'd see a show in the West End and have a lavish, catered dinner at home, then I'd jet back to LAX, breathing sighs of relief she had neither prevailed on me to move back nor provide her with grandchildren.

Besides shopping routinely, she sat on the boards of philanthropies, got invited to cocktail receptions, and attended couturier fashion shows. If she had male friends, I didn't hear about them, and they didn't get invited to our outings or dinners.

I did my graduate work at UCLA, which is where I teach now. I live on the sixteenth floor of the Azzura condos in Marina Del Rey, where my suite is below the three penthouse levels, all with much the same views of the Pacific.

I haven't given up on the idea of marriage or even committed relationships. Let's say I've been cautious. Among my students today, polyamory seems to be a thing, and it's not that I'm judgmental. I don't understand it, but if I did, I doubt it's sustainable.

Then of course the challenges of Mum coming to live with me and then Covid confinement put my thoughts of companionship recruitment on hold.

---

My mother was a collector, and I have her collectibles. Or at least most of them. I sold the ones that held no fond memories along with some that reminded me of times I'd rather forget. She lived with me here during her last years, having joined me just before the pandemic and challenging me to endure her company during lockdown. The virus didn't kill her. Bugs of any strain didn't stand a chance. One morning, after masks were no longer mandatory, and I planned to urge her to take a healthful stroll with me, I couldn't rouse her from her bed.

I hadn't been a doting caregiver, but I did help her as much as she'd let me. When she finally let go, we'd been together for five years.

The alternative would have been assisted living, which she abhorred. Convincing her to move in had been a chore in itself. At that point, she was forgetful at times but not yet in the throes of dementia. For twenty years since my father died, she'd been alone in their seven-room Victorian flat in Kensington. He'd failed to live out the twentieth century.

During their years together in London, Mother's avocation was furnishing their place with antiques. When we haggled over her conditions for joining me, she refused to part with her precious things, and she had the wherewithal, so I contracted to bring her favorite pieces over via air cargo, filling two containers. Among her prized furniture, I still have her breakfront, sideboard, Davenport escritoire, chairs, settee, and dining room suite. There are fine crystal decanters, goblets, and highball glasses. There is a full set of Wedgwood bone china, along with a Spode tea service, complete with a knitted cozy for the pot. The Sterling service and trays bear suitably impressive hallmarks.

I didn't curate any of it until she'd passed. I didn't dare, but later I sorted the last items – sell, donate, keep, store. Even when she was with me, many of her things had to be put in storage already. Among the items she prized and kept here were a few rare books, some of them first editions. However, she was not a reader. I presume she'd purchased them for the stunning appearance of the spines, all red leather with gilt lettering and filigreed ornamentation.

None of these tomes touched on topics remotely interesting to me, so once arranged neatly on my shelves, they remained in place.

I had one clue she coveted that soldier's diary for its appearance rather than its content. Among the books she'd had shipped over were some hardcovers of Dad's. I dutifully shelved them along with her collectible volumes. One morning, I found she'd removed all the dust covers and then rearranged the books by color. I found the jackets in the recycling bin, fortunately not wadded up, so I saved them.

I hold a professorship, and my salary is sufficient for my needs, but one day I became curious about whether any of those gorgeous volumes would fetch a handsome price. I knew none had been her bedside favorites, but if any had rarity value, I was curious to know how much.

I was hoping this artifact would prove valuable, if not as an antique *objet d'art*. Rather, I was expecting that the author of the diary might be some notable person or at least his firsthand account of momentous events. A signed early Churchill, that kind of thing. Something that would command a dear price from a museum or a collector.

Something that, from a literary standpoint, would be a find.

---

When I began to read, I understood so little of the world situation at the time. Nevertheless, I skimmed ahead. It was also difficult because the old cursive is almost illegible in places, difficult to focus on for extended periods. His narrative is dense with facts but not context, episodic but devoid of feeling. Reading this left me perplexed. I needed to immerse myself in his world, if that were at all possible. I present this first section to give you an overview, and I apologize in advance if I'm leading you into befuddlement. You'll see why I had to return to it later for careful study and reflection.

As a documentarian, I must disclose my process here. I have transcribed the diary much as I found it, which is to say with British spellings and stylings, including no doubt some errors that would not otherwise escape an editor's red pen. Authenticity was my goal. As an expat Englishman working for so long now with American institutions, I have come to adopt American usage, and my speech has pretty much adapted to the local argot.

In poring over this soldier's story, it struck me how much proper names have changed. Among these, the names of many cities in India now more closely approximate transliterations of the original local tongue. For example, the place Brits called Trimulgherry is now Tirumalagiri, as Calcutta is now Kolkata. I flag these for the reader on first instance by enclosing the newer version in brackets.

Fred is no enraptured raconteur. As a military man, he strives to give us only the facts, as if in a field report, but occasionally, he lets some juicy bits slip through.

I invite you to learn with me to read between the lines.

# Outward Bound

## Fred's Diary

On Saturday, the 11th August 1917, our draft, comprising two officers and sixty-four other ranks, paraded at 4:30 a.m. and proceeded to Southampton, where we embarked with 400 other troops on the transport *King Edward* in the afternoon. The anchor was weighed at 7:30 a.m. In the stormy southwesterly weather, I gazed on the fast-fading shores of Old England. Everyone wore a lifebelt in case of a submarine attack or our ship striking an enemy mine. I spent the night on top of my kit in the ship's hold.

Rising at 5 a.m. the following morning, I found we were entering Cherbourg Harbour, a scene familiar to me, having visited Cherbourg on two occasions before the war. We disembarked at 7 a.m. and marched about four miles out to a rest camp in the beautiful grounds of the Chateau Trouville.

After forty-eight hours' rest, we entrained on a ten-day rail journey through France and Italy. Two days travelling through France brought us to a rest camp at St. Germain Mont d'Or. This journey gave me a different impression of

France and its people from my experiences in Northern France.

The vineyards were in their glory, and the scenery of the valley of the Golden Mountains was delightful. Leaving this rest camp, we ran through Lyons and Aire les Bains and reached the Franco-Italian frontier on Friday the 14th of August at 7 a.m. After a cold morning ablution in a nearby mountain stream, we entered the Electric Mountain Railway and crossed the Italian Alps, where the rear portion of the train in which I was travelling separated from the remainder. It was some time before the couplings were repaired and we were again linked up. We made use of our time by getting a supply of fruit from the inhabitants. This is a wonderful railroad, having a succession of viaducts and tunnels. We ran through a tunnel which is fifteen miles long.

Leaving the Italian Alps, we entered the plains of northern Italy where the principal crops were vineyards and maize. We reached our third rest camp at Faenza, which was well laid out. An abundance of fruit was available, especially peaches, and I was impressed with the fine taste of first berries.

We left Faenza on Sunday morning and reached Rimini on the Adriatic Coast in the evening. The following morning, we arrived at Castella Marc Adriatico, where we had a four-hour stay and bathed in the warm, deep-blue waters of the Adriatic. Continuing along the coastline to Brindisi, we made for Taranto, which we reached at 1 p.m. on Tuesday, the 21st of August.

The country along the latter part of our journey was flat and principally cultivated with olive groves and fruit farms. Quantities of peaches and figs were being sun-dried on mats.

The camp at Taranto was very hot and deep in dust. But our stay here was short, as at 7 p.m. that evening, we embarked on the troop ship *Saxon* (Union Castle Line), which was lying in the harbour. The second-class salon was allotted for the sergeants' mess, and I had a comfortable second-class berth. We lay here for two days, weighing anchor at 6 p.m. on Thursday the 23$^{rd}$ of August. As we made way, all troops were summoned on deck at their respective posts, and greetings were exchanged with the Italian Grand Fleet, which was an impressive sight. The populace of Taranto also gave us a hearty farewell from the Promenade on the seafront as we made for the open sea.

We entered the Adriatic escorted by three Japanese and four Italian destroyers, an airship, and a hydroplane. It was a lovely evening. The rich red sunset made a striking effect on the deep-blue waters.

At 12:30, whilst I was in a dead sleep, our ship received a crushing blow. An alarm was immediately sounded, and everyone took up his position on deck without any sign of panic. The S.O.S. was signaled, which gave our position and rendered us subject to attack by any enemy submarine lurking in the vicinity. The searchlight of one of our escorts also played around us. It transpired that the other escort, mistaking the signal to change course, accidentally rammed us in the bow, piercing the plates above the waterline. The damage was not serious, and we were soon dismissed from our posts, and we proceeded full steam ahead. We afterwards heard that the destroyer, although badly damaged, returned safely to Taranto.

The morning brought us off the island of Corfu. We anchored close to the shore in a delightful bay. The ships, boats, and rafts were lowered, and we bathed most of the day. I swam around the ship's bows and saw the damage done during the night. The inhabitants of the island flocked around us in small boats. Their chief mission appeared to be collecting the empty boxes and tins, which were thrown overboard. The island looked mountainous and barren.

The following day, heavy gunfire was heard at sea. There was compulsory bathing for all the troops; those who could not swim had to wear lifebelts. It was a sight to see 2,000 men in the water around the ship's sides. It was difficult to get out of one another's way.

On Saturday evening at 6:30, we sighted the approach of our fresh escort of two other Japanese destroyers, and at 7 p.m. we started for our next halting place. After an uneventful night's voyage, we entered the Bay of Navarino. Church parade was held on deck, and then gangways and boats were lowered for bathing. On our right, the tower of Navarino nestled under the mountains of Greece.

We moved off again that evening. It was a moonlit night, and our escorts riding out on our flanks in the moon-speckled water were a pretty sight.

Monday found us running through some of the Greek island waters, then Crete appeared on our port side, where we expected another halt but found we were making a dash for Port Said. A call was made for volunteers for the stokehole, for which there was a ready response, and during the night we travelled full steam ahead.

The next day we ran through dangerous waters, and a fire broke out in the coal bunkers with which the crew fought all day. At 10 p.m. we were safely piloted into Port Said. This brought us through the only dangerous part of our voyage.

# Just Who Was This Man?

## Jonathan's Journal

THE AUTHOR of the diary was anonymous, or nearly so. If I could identify this fellow, give a name and heritage to him, research sources might provide biographical information, family history, or perhaps genealogical traces. The scant information on the flyleaf was:

By J. F. W.
W. Pollard and Co. Ltd. Exeter, Bradford, and London
Reg. No. S.2050 diary

It did disconcert me at first that this fellow's initials were the same as mine. I am pretty sure he was not a forebear because Mum would no doubt have mentioned him. She would have been proud she'd found a family heirloom. Lest he also be a Jonathan (and why not?), my given name for him in these pages will be "Fred."

At the outset, I wasn't curious about this fellow's story. I was eager to learn how much I might get for the thing from a bookseller. Or it might be a news item I could share with a podcaster whose niche audience includes history geeks like me.

Perhaps from the sales record I could uncover the identity of J.F.W., if he was indeed the purchaser, look him up in the war records, and then prove his celebrity or contribution to the annals of empire. I dared to imagine that his use of the initials might be a device to deliberately hide his notoriety.

The old-line firm of W. Pollard proved to be diligent, as you might expect, but the curator informed me in his prompt reply via email that their documentation from that period had been lost in the destruction of their head office by the V-2 bombing of London in World War II.

This musty book survived the War to End All Wars and the next big one, which happened mostly because of, not despite, the first.

Given the profuse and detailed military records available online, I assumed it would be quick work to identify this fellow. There were a few possible matches on those initials in various divisions of the Royal Devonshire Yeomanry, but crucial factors such as enlistment date, age, or marital status didn't fit J F.W.'s version of the facts.

Partly because Fred gave such scant information about his early wartime postings, I wondered whether discovering his identity and possibly his service record might yield some telling background. It also frustrated me that he'd been so coy about disclosing his name, but he couldn't have known that a century later curious chaps like me could search military archives from the comfort of an easy chair.

I hadn't pursued the task too far before I realized, despite having so much data at my fingertips, narrowing the possibilities to a single individual would be a challenge. When I approached W. Pollard booksellers, I assumed finding the name of the purchaser of the blank journal would be a straightforward lookup, even if there might be a delay as some obliging storekeeper rummaged through dusty boxes. Learning that their records no longer existed was a surprise and a disappointment. Still, even if they'd found the sales record, the purchaser might have been the calligrapher and not the client.

A service record, if found, was bound to be specific. However, even in Fred's brief description, I hoped I had enough clues to flush him out.

I'm not uncomfortable with the paper chase, and I'm a diligent researcher, but I'm easily frustrated if I hit too many dead ends in a labyrinthine rabbit hole.

I decided to seek professional help.

# Library Reference Desk

## Jonathan's Journal

It's not that I'm an agoraphobic, nor am I a misanthrope. When I say I'm afraid of people, it's that I'm afraid of *being seen* by people.

As a teacher, I'm fond of my students. I find the few bright, motivated ones refreshing. even at times entertaining. And I give extra attention to the challenged ones. But frankly, if they are slacking off and I suspect they can do better, I might not remember their names. And I'm good with names, dates, and events. When you teach history, it's an essential skill.

Given the gaps between generations, I expect many of my students to regard me as an old crank, though I'm neither white-haired nor dyspeptic. For the slackers who don't bother to know me beyond my appearance, the permanent scowl on my face can be useful. I may be having a pleasant day and in a generous mood and yet be perceived as angry and mean, no acting skill or effort required.

Braving my infirmities, one portentous day I ventured out and met Elena Russikova in the Santa Monica Public Library. On this day, she sat at the information desk in the reference section. Accosting her would be the expected thing for a clueless patron to do.

She was charming on first sight, if a bit aloof. Neither new nor old school. Perhaps around my age. Prettier than I expected for a bookish type. Not at all my stereotype of a prudish librarian. She was outwardly cool, yes, even cold. Because she was so attractive, I fantasized there was smoldering desire underneath. She had my attention from the first glance. Maybe it was the cocked eyebrow in her deliberate glance and the hint of a sneer.

I asked, "Do you have anything on British military engagements in the Middle East?"

She looked up from her display screen. "Rows and rows on the shelves. And if you want to get into microfilm, probably miles and miles." Her English was flawless, with the trace of an accent, like one of those sultry expat stars in old Hollywood movies. Long, dark hair. Big black eyes. Ivory skin with a hint of blush. Garbo? Dietrich? Lamar? Enchanting!

She huffed, "Have you tried genealogy websites? Military records? That's the quickest way, if you happen to hit on anything." Taking another glance at me, perhaps deciding I had nothing better to do, she added, "For British and Irish, there's Findmypast dot com. Eight million British Army records. Attestation papers, medical forms, discharge documents, pension claims…"

She was promising a quick fix, probably thought she'd be rid of me.

I could have guessed, but still I asked, "What's an attestation record?"

She feigned boredom. Perhaps her lunch break was overdue. "First document in their service file. A contract of service, personal details such as name, age, residence, and trade. Also the oath of allegiance, results of medical examination, and physical appearance, including any remarkable features such as missing teeth or scars or tattoos." Off my blank stare of amazement, she said, "You know, helps to ID the remains."

"I don't even have a name. Just his initials, regiment, dates and locations of postings," I said, to her surprise.

"Some relative?"

I didn't have much of an accent myself anymore. Unless you were attuned, mine could be the Cambridge of Boston and not of East Anglia.

I explained, "I don't think so. I have an old handwritten diary I got from my mother. World War One." I paused for a reaction, and none came. I continued with a wry smile, "Might have been her boyfriend. That would be a treat."

"Your *mother?*"

"Yes," I said. "Like an onion, she was. So many layers and often gave me a good cry."

She smiled. "Your grandmother, you mean. Or did some kindly old folks adopt you?"

"Oh, of course. My father was almost old enough to have been *her* father. She did have me late, for her. It was far from a miracle. Perhaps not all that wanted. She was cold and I guess you'd say clever, but she always gave me everything I asked for. I'm a spoiled child. What can I say? I am certain she didn't tell me everything, even after Dad had passed."

What I didn't say was how alike Elena seemed in this

way, teasing with a straight face, along with the fleeting thought I'd happily let her discipline me.

She smirked. "You can say, 'Thank you, Mother. I never appreciated you. Not nearly enough.' What about this aged father?"

"He's been gone for decades now, years before she went," I muttered. "Died when I was away at school." I quickly changed the subject, hardly hiding my agenda. "So, are you a mother?"

She answered, "Only to little lost souls like you, and only because I'm paid decently."

Despite my reluctance to show my face to strangers, I have long since given up on worrying about what people think when I do manage to speak. I give myself permission to let whatever thought passes through my brain come out through my mouth. I am shameless and can't be embarrassed because I assume my question might be met with a sneer, mirroring their mistaking my appearance for nastiness, so I blurt it out anyway and let it fall where it will.

Before I could check the impulse, I risked suggesting, "There's a wine bar down the block…"

She countered with a smirk that implied I was suggesting we have a quickie in the utility room.

When she didn't answer, I flashed my best winning smile, which lit up only half my face and might be interpreted as smirking back. Assuming her look was a polite rejection, I walked away, consulted the online catalog, and exited the library with a musty tome that hadn't been dusted in a long while.

## JONATHAN'S JOURNAL

Having strolled down the block from the library, I gave up on the wine bar and stopped in at the tea shop next door. Elena wouldn't be coming, I was sure. I took my strong black tea with oat milk to a table farthest away from the few other patrons and the buzz of their conversations.

I'd intended to have the diary transcribed, forsaking the chore myself. I had yet to get it done. I wanted to dive back into Fred's story, but I hadn't brought the volume with me. I could have dug into the history book I'd found, yet I was still bewildered by what I'd read so far in the diary. As I said, I knew little enough about the battles on the Western Front but almost nothing about the place names and geography Fred describes once he's on the troop ship. To complicate matters, I had to bear in mind that southern parts of Ottoman Turkey are now Syria, Armenia, and Lebanon. Palestine is now Israel, Persia is Iran, and the mashup of Mosul, Baghdad, and Basra is today Iraq.

Basra was crucial, then as now.

As I sipped my cuppa, I tried to relax and think about how much I remembered.

Fred compresses years of his early wartime experiences into a few opening paragraphs. He may have kept a diary of his time on the Western Front, but titling this journal *Memoirs of My Travels East* suggests he won't be preoccupied with grim dispatches from the European battlefield. It would be understandable if he didn't want to reflect on those experiences, but there was another reason. He might never have made it into the fight.

Fred's narrative only truly begins when he undertakes what he expects to be his adventure. I assumed — hoped — the lessons of his life would prove to be exceptional, thrilling, and inspiring. I suppose he did too. Why else take the trouble to write it all down and to memorialize it in such a fine volume?

He joined the cavalry and patrolled the beaches on horseback for two years, which got little more than a wink and a nod in his text. I suspect that the likelihood of an invasion from across the English Channel would have been remote at that time. Did he, coward that he may have been, assume it was a safe gig? If you had to serve, it might have been a pleasant posting. He probably looked as dashing in his uniform as he'd hoped, especially in the dress crimson provided for ceremonial occasions.

I rather think he knew little or nothing of the risks. In this latter-day age, we've seen vivid, graphic depictions of that war as reenacted in movies. But in his day, newspaper reports were not so detailed. Reports from the field of battle stressed gains and losses, much as we now recap the scores of sporting events. Certainly, even early in the war, the returning wounded might have shared their stories. But in bloody battles, then and now, soldiers typically don't want to talk about it at all.

Was there something driving Fred away from home that he desperately wanted to escape? Had he impregnated a lass and refused to step up? Had he filched some funds from an employer and feared getting caught? Had he taken out a huge loan he couldn't hope to repay?

Was he joining for king and country or fleeing a burdensome family, a tedious job, or simple boredom? He claimed he was eager to go. For the sake of my story-telling, I was hoping something nasty in his past was thrusting him onward.

Curious that it took the British High Command so long to decide to make foot soldiers of these horsemen. Trench warfare was a particularly useless form of deadly stalemate that steadily ground men to suppurating meat on both sides. Perhaps he did not appreciate this grim reality the day he saw that parade. Through the retrospective lens surveying history, we bring the context of having seen war movies depicting the bloody chaos of barbed-wire killing fields, land mines, barrages of shelling, and machine-gun fire. But back when Fred was considering whether to enlist, his notions of trench warfare would have been no more vivid than terse, censored descriptions in a newspaper, often written by reporters who were nowhere near the battlefield.

I thought the Great War was fought in France. I've seen those grisly scenes of trench warfare in the movies. I don't recall any movie or school history lesson covering other theaters in that war. Sure, they called it a *world* war, but I assumed it was because the conflict engaged major world powers.

I had drawn my notions of World War I from old movies, which focused on the muck and mire of those killing fields in France. The idea that there had been any fighting outside of Europe seemed oddly beside the point, if not inconsequential. And the possibility that the Kaiser had any designs on Baghdad seemed remotely perilous, if not groundless.

I skimmed a few more pages of Fred's dense prose, but I could find no reasons for his eagerness to go. He either didn't understand or wouldn't say. Thinking that the army would send him on an extended vacation would have been impossibly naïve.

Dispatched from the heady stink on horseback for the safety of the beaches to slog through the cold muck of the muddy ditch on the front lines, the unsuspecting Fred was being sent to die in a deadly game that was numbered in corpses.

Did he understand this before he was sent?

Nothing in his prose suggested he feared going. Or, like so many twentysomethings, he may have simply assumed death was something that happens to other people. Even in wartime, it's astounding that such hubris can prevail.

He describes the wound he suffered at the Western Front as an "injury."

To his *elbow?* How did this injury happen? An accident? Cleaning his gun? Hoisting a pint? It didn't seem particularly heroic. If he'd been wounded, I'm sure he'd have boasted about it. It was no gunshot, I was sure. More likely he got drunk, passed out, and hit his funny bone on the bar as he fell.

I didn't wonder how much he'd embellished. I continued to fret about what he'd left out.

I'm not a believer in the afterlife, and I'd say the only spirits that speak to us are manifestations of our own subconscious thoughts.

Reading between the lines would be my challenge. I'd hoped he would prove to be a scoundrel.

I won't claim that Fred spoke to me. Suffice it to say, I must have a vivid imagination.

# The Past Responds

## Fred Speaks

I must interrupt!

I admit I genuinely feared the prospect of jumping into a muddy trench. Before my enlistment, we'd had one letter from Henry. His duty in the forests of Bulgaria was open-field fighting, trees for cover rather than trenches. I could imagine being hunkered down with him, shoulder to shoulder in a trench in France, terrified to climb out, waiting for the dreaded whistle calling us to go over the top and die. Thankfully, it was not to happen that way for either of us.

Clever chap, this Jon. Yes, the "accident" was not a combat wound. I suffered a dislocation of my shoulder. The mishap was a fall I took when ordered to jump from a troop transport lorry. With the heavy kit on my back, I lost my balance. When I fell, I landed on my elbow, enduring the snap and the pain. I thought I had fractured my collarbone. The sergeant helped me get up then grabbed that arm by the wrist and jerked it upward as if in salute. The joint snapped back, but the pain was so sharp I nearly fainted. He insisted I had no broken bones, that I'd be right by morning, and he ordered me onto a cot in the medic's tent for the rest of the day. Come morning, I could not lift the least weight without excruciating pain. I insisted bravely that I could well carry my rifle in my right arm. The chief pointed out sarcastically that aiming carefully also required a steady left, so they sent me home.

He's right. I had yet to see a day of battle.

I did not discuss my injury with mates or family at home, hence the omission from my diary. I worried Sarah would think me a coward. She had joined a sewing circle patching uniforms, and gossip was the order of the day. On occasion in the public house, as if in explanation, I would clutch my shoulder, some old fellow would mutter, "Shrapnel," and I would do no more than wince, my sin one of omission.

As to the question of the Germans' designs on the Near East, all I will say at this point is that poor Jon and his generation have a lot to learn.

# Priscilla's British Tea Room

## Jonathan's Journal

The little bell on the door of the shop tinkled, and in walked Elena. My table was in the back, some distance from the storefront window, so I had no reason to think she'd come in because she'd seen me. I was sure she hadn't when she didn't look in my direction as she approached the counter to give the barista her order.

I held my attention on her with a sidelong glance. If she happened to look my way, I didn't want her to think I was staring at her. When she turned around, she held a paper coffee cup and a bakery sack. She had the handle of a brief bag slung over the arm that held the sack. As she took a step toward the door, she glanced in my direction, recognized me, smiled, hesitated a moment, and then walked over.

"I thought our date was for wine," she scolded, as if correcting an errant pupil.

I managed a crooked smile. "If you're going to drink

alone, there is no social stigma in tea. Now I regret I didn't wait for you."

She softened. Her smile was demure but not to be missed. "I'm the one to say I'm sorry. I let you walk away from my desk without saying yes."

"Do sit."

She remained standing and explained, "I can't stay. We're updating to the new BISAC categories, and my team is stickering spines on the night shift."

"I don't understand any of that, but perhaps for you it beats discussing military history."

When she set her cup on my table, I thought she'd changed her mind.

"Not at all," she muttered and used her free hand to reach into her bag to pull out a book. She clutched it to her chest as if hiding the paperback's cover. She straightened to assume a pose I knew well — the teacher's challenge — and prompted, "Tell me the cause of World War One."

Was the book to be my prize for the right answer or a punishment for the wrong one?

The question was second-form world history. I didn't sleep through that course, but I was no star pupil. The trick question would have a confusing answer on a multiple-choice quiz. It would have to be D, meaning *both* A and C. My confident answer was, "The assassination of Archduke Ferdinand *and* interlocking directorates, whatever those were."

With a cheerful "gotcha" grin, she thrust the book at me, *The Train that Disappeared into History: The Berlin-to-Baghdad Railway and How It Led to the Great War*.

I thumbed it. "Three hundred and forty-four pages?" I looked up to give her my wincing smile. I hoped a slight nod of my head would let her know mine was a serious question. "Assuming I can speed read, when can I see you next?"

Her head tilt was a no, and she replied, "Jon, you checked out two books today, Townshend's *Desert Hell* and *this* one. Your personal information is in your library record. Don't let them be overdue!"

She turned away and hastened out the door.

# THE RESEARCH DEEPENS

## JONATHAN'S JOURNAL

NOW I HAD TWO BOOKS, each of them as thick as an old dictionary and almost as factually dense. Yes, I'm supposed to love that stuff, but curiosity and the intriguing memory of Elena's coy smile urged me to prompt action.

*Attestation records.* She'd given me a valuable clue, even told me where to look. But it didn't take me long with the laptop unhinged to appreciate this would be no quick task. Without the fellow's name, I was confronted with a myriad of correlations and inferences.

The library website gave a catchall email address for the reference desk. Preceding the Subject line with "ATTN: Elena R.," I sent her a query.

I assumed she was an ambitious scholar. I hoped she'd be eager to take on work to make her rent money. She might find this task more appealing if stickering spines was not her idea of fun. Perhaps they got overtime pay. If she were single and had no social life, I could worry she had trouble with relationships. Presumptuous of me, I know. I should take my own advice and get out more.

Giving her this research assignment might also get her interested in the project, and perhaps in me. She'd presumed to check out that book on my behalf. Her stopping by the tea shop was no coincidence!

Her accent sounded Eastern European. If she knew languages, that would indeed be a plus.

Almost as soon as I'd clicked send, her reply came back.

How can I help, Jon?

For my description of the assignment, she quoted an hourly rate I thought was modest. More than an intern but probably considerably less than her municipal employee labor rate.

I emailed her the excerpts of Fred's narrative that I've shared so far with you. I wasn't concerned about confidentiality, either mine or Fred's. But even if I'd been able to attach the full transcript, I wouldn't want her reading ahead. Perhaps it was selfish of me, but her speculations might be spoilers. This was to be my quest, and I didn't want her to be done with me any time soon. I might refrain from calling it a hobby, but I looked forward to unraveling a mystery worthy of at least a white paper, if not an auction item at Sotheby's. The little I'd studied so far suggested that Fred was a private, taciturn person. He was neither an adventurer nor an engaging storyteller. He may have thought of himself as a loyal subject of the crown.

As I said, I doubted Fred was a relative, but if there were family secrets, I wanted to be the first to discover them.

## The Research Deepens

Elena spent two weeks on the service-records assignment, for which we'd budgeted ten hours. She returned four documents that she suspected referred to the same person. These were official forms, filled in with hastily scrawled handwriting, microfilmed years later, and then scanned more recently to create files in the online archive. After studying them, I replied:

Elena,

I agree all four records you found seem to describe the same person. The question is whether this is our guy.

Service dates 1914 - 1920 in the archive record heading agree with the diary. The discharge date of April 30, 1917, is the same in two of the records and agrees with the diary (Spring 1917). However, that discharge date is from the service record of the soldier's first tour only (Western Front, France). Drafts from the 8th Devons were deployed to the Near East, but after this fellow's discharge date. And there's no indication of reenlistment. I suppose it's possible he volunteered, but according to the diary he enlisted as regular army for deployment to the Near East and India when he was presented with the opportunity.

The wound that ended his time on the Western Front is shown on the service certificate as GSW (gunshot wound), right side of abdomen, with the notation "No Longer Physically Fit for War Service." His diary mentions only an "accident" to his left elbow. Odd that he doesn't call it a wound. It's certainly possible that a bullet grazed his elbow and then entered the stomach, or perhaps he suffered two wounds, one not recorded. By the "unfit" assessment, you would think he would not be able to reenlist.

One service record does show first and second postings, but this fellow's rank shows "private" in both tours. Again, there is no enlistment or discharge dates shown for the second posting. The third document you sent shows "lance corporal" and a variation on the spelling of the surname. It's so similar to the others that it could be the same person. These records could be far from perfect. In the diary, he doesn't give his rank in the cavalry or at the Western Front.

All this considered, I don't think we have a match. We're at a dead end unless a close reading of the rest of the diary yields more particulars.

Jon

We refrained from exchanging personal greetings or news. I wondered whether she was using staff time for this. How would anyone know? Would it matter to me whether she was ethical?

Fred's not showing up in the searchable service records seemed to be a dead end. Our search, after all, was limited to the records that still exist. His might have been shoved into a box that was destroyed before its papers could be entered into the archive. The lack of information from Pollards was a reminder of the inevitable gaps in our collective memory.

It chills me to think that digital records may prove to

be more quickly perishable than paper — or parchment or papyrus.

One other line of inquiry occurred to me, but I didn't follow up on it at the time. Although the family records I had from Mum were scant, running some queries in genealogical databases might turn up a cousin in that timeframe with those initials. The coincidence of his being a JFW might be telling, but this clue wasn't much to go on. When she bought the thing, Mum might have thought it simply charming, as though she'd found a necktie that matched my favorite striped dress shirt.

Some further digging might discover bits of his story. The facts and circumstances he gave did seem real enough. His was no work of fiction, I was sure.

Elena offered, and I readily agreed, to budget more of her time. She was more successful generating summaries of the military units Fred mentions and their campaigns. Although he'd provided almost no details about what he actually did in his postings after the outbreak, having her descriptions provided context and helped me read between his lines. I still fully intended to digest those references, but her concise summaries provided enough background for me not to feel lost as I read through Fred's narrative.

# The Man I Was

## Fred Speaks

Jonathan dubs me "Fred." It's not a name I would have chosen. I knew a Fred Stewart at school. Stewie, we called him. Perfect rotter back then, but one presumes he mellowed with age, as do most of us who are fortunate enough to grow old. But for our purposes here, I will accept the fictitious nickname. If I'd wanted you or anyone to know my real name, I would have put it on the title page instead of those initials.

He reads through my journal and learns dates, locations, events, and consequences, especially as notable for myself. And as he says, he endeavors to read between the lines. In many instances, he misses it by a mile. Such, I suppose, are the inevitable fallacies of interpreting history.

I will now explain in a more fulsome manner what should have gone in the white space.

Jon remarks on the coincidence of our initials. But beyond those few letters, there is little resemblance. Oh, male vanity, but what ounce of courage did this Jon ever need to muster? Look before crossing the street? Granted, looking into oneself requires a kind of boldness. He may do a better job of it than I did. He is more introspective and cerebral than I was back then, perhaps because he is unburdened and unoccupied. My fellows and I had a war to fight. Granted, there were some long stretches during which I had little to do, but then my thoughts would inevitably turn to whatever creature comforts could be sought straightaway. I was hungry and uncomfortable most of the time.

A scoundrel? Hardly. Sorry to disappoint. Rather it was my wife Sarah's lover who was the scoundrel, although I had no proof. That day watching the guard bobbing proudly on their cantering horses, it occurred to me that new honor could be found separate and apart from the mundane trials of daily life among the stay-at-homes in Exeter.

Like this author chap, when I began writing (and he began reading), my mates and I hoped it would be an adventure. I have a second chance here to tell you how it was.

I had no pretensions to greatness, certainly. I was proud of both my service and the few adventures I could fit in. I did expect to share my missive with family and friends. The handsome volume would have an honored place on my shelf, next to my pipe rack and war memorabilia. I fancied I might pull it down over a convivial brandy after dinner. Impress the guest, you know. Use it as an excuse to ramble on about the old times, muck about in memories.

As to the attribution of my work, this fellow has overlooked a key factor in my decision. As an officer of His Majesty's forces, I was sworn to secrecy about the details of any campaign or engagement. Granted that I didn't hold the bound volume until considerably after the armistice was signed, one appreciates that one's obligations persist for a lifetime.

Hence, my anonymity.

No doubt many of my young mates anticipated they would return as heroes and that beautiful women would fall at their feet. The romantic thrall of military bearing was a popular and admirable thing before the war, but not after.

A safe posting? Hardly. During my service in the cavalry, an invasion across the Channel was the likely scenario. In the beginning of the conflict, aerial attack was not the concern, nor did we expect a flotilla of warships. From the start and throughout the war, penetration by stealth was assumed to be a significant vulnerability, saboteurs alighting on the beaches under cover of darkness. They might not bring war materiel with them. They would instead meet up with agent provocateurs who delivered caches of explosives and perhaps even the rumored new evil, poison gas.

Patrolling on horseback gave the advantage of being able to surveil long stretches of the coast with modest deployments of men. Civilian spotters were also recruited, but one had to beware of loyalties.

I actually thought I would get a distant posting. I did not manage to leave home until later. Teignmouth is sixteen miles from Exeter, so for the first few months of my service, command ordered us locals to be billeted and fed much of the time at home. Many of us rode our own horses. We were conducting night patrols along the coast, so army life was still a rude adjustment. Nevertheless, we did not expect the conflict to last, least of all that killing would ever come to our shores.

The beach at the mouth of the River Teign is long and sandy, stretching south toward Holcombe. No doubt command thought it a more likely landing place than the rocky cliffs farther south in Cornwall.

The challenge of the posting was not the boredom but nagging unease. We were as worried about whatever it was we did not see.

I understood my service experiences would be no lark. One goes where one's orders specify. As to trench warfare, there were news reports, but the visible testimony of the returning wounded spoke volumes. My brother Henry had been dispatched to the Bulgarian front a year before I received my orders. I avoided mentioning him. We didn't communicate during the conflict, both because of difficult logistics and secrecy of locations. News about him, even rarer than my own letters home, was relayed from family in Exeter.

I admit that following him into the service was a factor in my decision to enlist. There was the risk we might both perish, but my deployment with the coastal troops seemed far less dangerous. Telling Sarah I'd be honoring him and the family name might have made my going off seem unavoidable. I hoped she would pray for my safe return. Later, as I say, orders were orders.

Even before war broke out, the editorial pieces in the newspapers as well as the recounting of debates in Parliament stirred public opinion powerfully. The glory of the British Empire suffered much more from the pens of historians than from any U-boat. Without question, Germany and Austria-Hungary lusted for their own global empire, necessitating, they no doubt believed, the decline of our own. Britons had been aware of the growing threat from the east for decades. Prussian forces had very nearly taken Paris in 1871, twenty years before I was born. They ringed the city and shelled the civilian population. This mode of battle in itself was a new outrage. The French resisted admirably, even though their Commune was abusive and unjust, and it was not so much that the French won but that Kaiser Wilhelm grew weary of the standoff and the expense. Ever since that time, the consolidation and the continued buildup of those enemy forces was a fearsome prospect for us.

Before, during, and after the Great War, this was "the Eastern Question."

# HISTORY REIMAGINED

## JONATHAN'S JOURNAL

ELENA'S SUMMARIES helped me imagine what Fred was doing in those early years. By the time he was deployed to France, trench warfare there had become the primary order of battle.

Engagements were exchanges bullets from rifles and machine guns. Troops charging at each other across the field of battle were maimed or killed by shrapnel flying from explosions of land mines and artillery shells. Horses and mules were used mostly in supply lines, and the new technology of motorized vehicles, including fearsome German tanks, had taken over.

Fred's unit was sent to France after the War Office realized this conflict would not be open-field fighting on the plains of England with horse-mounted troops. By this time, late 1916, the Devons already been on the Continent for two years.

From facts he discloses later, I get that Fred's proficiency with a rifle was exceptional. Because of his time in the cavalry, his rank may have been lance corporal, ranking above private and below corporal. My guess is that he was an instructor in riflery at the time of his reenlistment, so perhaps he'd made sergeant by then or soon after. Besides marksmanship and maintenance of the weapon, British military discipline at the time included training in *musketry,* which focused on tactics of coordinated attack, covering fire, and reloading.

---

In the Spring of 1917, having served at Raglan Barracks in Eastern England for some months, Fred was presented with the opportunity of reenlisting. Was he disappointed he hadn't seen much if any action in France? Or was he experiencing survivors' guilt? He implies he thought this new posting would be an adventure, and whatever he had going at home obviously didn't make him hesitate long enough to change his mind.

He felt he had something to contribute. His horsemanship would be of almost no use where he was going.

Take Baghdad?

---

I feared investing my time if I didn't understand the historical context of Fred's situation. This was the main reason I'd asked Elena to help me. We shared the preoccupations of historians. When I did my thesis, the research was more fun than the writing, and scholars risk becoming so enthralled with the paper chase that they don't know when to quit. And now I worried that the data drilling might be more fun than reading Fred's story. In some ways, delegating work to Elena might help me from becoming mired in it.

The passage following Fred's reference to Baghdad made it clear he regarded this as the beginning of his adventure. Depending on his degree of disability, he may have had the option of staying home.

I've traveled in France, and my studies in art history familiarized me especially with locations that attracted *plein-air* painters, including Impressionists such as Camille Pissarro and Claude Monet. On a trip through Normandy in the north, where Parisian families go in late summer to escape the humid heatwaves, I visited the seacoast resort at Trouville. The town is at the mouth of the Toque River, less than a hundred miles east of Omaha Beach, the Allied military designation where troops landed on D-Day in the next World War.

For Fred's narrative to make any sense, I realized I'd be consulting maps online as I read. St. Germain Mont d'Or is near Lyon, which is about a hundred miles southwest of the Swiss border at Geneva. Another quick search showed me that the westernmost line of the Western Front was an almost continuous trench stretching from the seacoast in northern Belgium for 250 miles southward to the Swiss border. Fred's train trip through France must have kept him well outside the line of battle and the range of enemy mortar shells.

Odd to me that Fred's trek thorough France should seem so uneventful. At the time, trench warfare was raging in parts of that country, which presumably he'd experienced firsthand until his fateful elbow injury.

The British Command must have been well aware of the possible dangers traveling through France, but the demarcations of battle zones must have been clear. These

Jonathan's Journal

guys were not headed for the front, and the trains that carried them were no different from the lines that carried civilians to and fro, not that so many could afford it — or risk it — at this time. Lines of passage for troops apparently were not disrupted. The idea back then that warfare could be contained to designated fields of battle is remarkable. Early in the war, the conflict focused mainly on military targets.

He'd made it through France. If there were risks and fears along the way, he hadn't mentioned them.

It was reading like a travelogue. I wished he'd have shared more about whatever was going through his mind on that journey about his troop's mission and his sense of what his role would be in it. He strikes me as a rather plain fellow. I don't think of myself that way, but if I were to set down the straightforward facts of my own existence so far, you might think me downright dull as well.

# My Fateful Decision

## Fred Speaks

My injury had not disqualified me from service. At Raglan, I was an instructor in riflery and by behaving myself and minding my sums, I rose to drill sergeant. Men I trained were deployed throughout the duration. Many did not return. Others did, some maimed badly, and one wondered whether those survivors were the less fortunate.

I had some letters from Henry during this time. The fighting in the Balkans was continual and intense. The enemy were mostly Turks. They used land mines and artillery in the shooting, but they were not mechanized with tanks and transport vehicles as their comrades were to the west. Owing to lack of horses on both sides, they were foot soldiers, not cavalry. Henry felt those chaps had not the spirit of the Huns. They were defending the sultan's empire in a long, losing strife. The Germans and Austrians were out for conquest, eager to build a new empire to achieve Kaiser Bill's promise, their "place in the sun."

I read the newspapers. I chatted with the returning

fellows. I was faithful in my duties. Devon is twenty-seven miles inland from Exeter, not nearly far enough away to have suited me.

My tour would extend for the duration, and many of the bloodiest battles had yet to be fought. The perils of deployment to the Continent were known to me. I wasn't shirking my duties or running from danger. However, when the draft for Mespot was ordered, I wasn't selected at random.

I enlisted for a second tour.

Kaiser Bill planned to take Baghdad. I read the newspapers diligently whenever I could get them. For years, even leading up to the war, the editorial pages were filled with debate in Parliament as well as among the public about the Eastern Question. No one questioned the necessity of preventing the Central Powers from grabbing Southern Mespot and hence threatening the Persian Gulf, which we resolved must remain a British protectorate, patrolled by the Royal Navy.

# THE BERLIN-TO-BAGHDAD RAILWAY

## JONATHAN'S JOURNAL

I STAYED up most of the night digesting the railway history, which was scholar Kathie Somerwil-Ayerton's master's thesis.

I fretted about what I might have said to Elena instead of my textbook answer. "U-boats" would have sounded smart. But despite the giveaway subtitle, long story short, a better answer to her challenge question might have been "Suez Canal."

In the latter part of the nineteenth century, what became known as the Berlin-to-Baghdad Railway as an ambitious plan to connect the ports of Hamburg in Germany to Basra at the southern tip of Mesopotamia. This passage, entirely overland, would be a direct shipping route from the North Sea to the Persian Gulf and from there to the major sea lanes extending to India and the Far East.

As early as 1830, the major European powers were all interested in any direct route that would save the time,

# Jonathan's Journal

expense, and peril of having to sail around the southern tip of Africa. A canal through Suez (to connect the Mediterranean with the Red Sea) and the railroad were competing alternatives.

The French, their failing project salvaged by a partnership with the British, completed the canal in 1869. Although both governments were considering the train project as well, they chose to abandon after the canal opened, assuming the scale of the railroad project was so massive it would never succeed without their financing.

But the Germans teamed up with the Turks to try for it. Industrial giant Krupp had started manufacturing the steel rails in the 1890s.

Even though Elena might assume I'd delve into the railway story, without prompting she emailed me her own summary.

# The Russian Geopolitical Threat

## Elena's Notes

Jon,

I know you are fully capable of digesting the railway book, but I want to stress the Russian geopolitical threat. Bear this in mind:

*Wars are about resources and the logistics involved in stealing them.*

Inherent in the Eastern Question was the worry that the Russians, as much as the Germans, Austrians, Hungarians, and Turks, lusted after the power and resources of the British Empire.

Yes, as you remembered from your studies, the assassination of Archduke Ferdinand of Austria-Hungary was an inciting event, but it was hardly the cause. Ferdinand wasn't a diplomat. He was royalty, potentially as influential as Kaiser Wilhelm II. He was shot by a student who wanted independence for Serbia.

The root causes very much involved controlling the overland route from Berlin to Baghdad. To get from Germany to Constantinople (Istanbul), the railway would have to pass through Bulgaria and Serbia. So the Central Powers had to hold on to Serbia and control the Balkans. The fellow who shot the archduke wanted independence for Serbia. The country's independence could well have impeded the right-of-way.

The railroad would then traverse Turkey and dip down into Palestine and thence through Mesopotamia. And the goal wasn't Baghdad. The ideal terminus would be farther south, at Basra. To this day, the city is a major port, but it is not on the seacoast. From there, goods carried by train from Europe must be loaded onto riverboats, passing downriver to the northern tip of the Persian Gulf.

At first, the British and the French thought the railroad was a good idea. They offered financing so they could expect to participate in the traffic. But then they realized that the route of the train would take it out of range of the British gunboats patrolling the coast of the Mediterranean. And it took them a while to realize Baghdad wouldn't be the last stop. Germany's goal was to bypass the canal entirely. At the same time, they were building a fleet of U-boats, which they could use to threaten commercial shipping in the Mediterranean. Again, it was all about controlling access to the canal, thence to the Far East.

The last stop on that railroad might be the beginning of the end of the British Empire.

To this day, Basra remains a crucial strategic location and an international airport. The US Air Force maintained its Contingency Operating Base there during conflicts, then turned it over to the Iraqis in 2011.

E.

# Disraeli and Suez

## Jonathan's Journal

As I read through Elena's notes, I could understand why she kept insisting on the strategic importance of the Suez Canal as the fateful answer to the Eastern Question. Then I remembered, in the last year of her life, my mother and I had watched an old movie about how Benjamin Disraeli had manipulated the reluctant manager of the Bank of England to float the massive loan that bought rights to the canal.

I looked it up online and learned that we must have seen the 1929 version of *Disraeli,* adapted from the 1911 play by British playwright Louis N. Parker. That version was one of the first talking pictures, starring George Arliss as the prime minister. Arliss had created the role onstage. A silent film starring Dennis Eadie was released in 1916. I could now appreciate why the picture would have been so popular. Audiences at the time would have understood better than I did yesterday how the wars they were fighting had sprung from Britain's success at snatching the Suez prize from Russia.

My search turned up the play script. As he spoke vehemently in the play and onscreen, Arliss as Disraeli warns the young Viscount Delford, "While England stands alone, while France is crippled, and before Germany is recovered, now is Russia's chance to snatch at India. With India lost, the whole fabric crumbles, and England sinks into insignificance, a Belgium at sea."

And although Russia's tsar indeed coveted the canal, a subsequent twist of fate would have forfeited the deal to England anyway. After the Revolution of 1917 and the assassination of the Romanovs, the new Bolshevik government for a time gave up its international ambitions and summoned its troops home.

# Historical Context

## Jonathan's Journal

After a long night of poring over all this historical context, my mind was racing with questions. And, I admit, Elena's willingness to assist made her that much more attractive. I had an excuse to go back to the library. I resolved to be bolder. I would take her teasing as encouragement.

Odd that our email exchanges seemed so intimate. So far, I'd shared only scant details about myself. I knew almost nothing about her. I wanted to see her. I was captivated by her mind, yes, but by now I wanted to know her as more than a colleague.

Granted, I hadn't rushed back to the library. It had been several days since our first meeting. I was shy about my face, but I didn't think of it as a disability. As I considered going back there to see her, I remembered Fred's reference to his "injury." If, say, his arm had appeared misshapen, and if he offered no explanations, people he encountered might assume he'd been wounded at the Front.

I recalled a trip to New York when I gave a talk to art students at Barnard. My own classes at UCLA were used to seeing me, but as a guest lecturer I was nervous about my appearance. I wasn't used to riding the subway, and when I hastened on just before the doors slid closed, I dove into the first available seat. Now, this was easily ten years ago, and I didn't look particularly old, not that I do now! I hadn't noticed that I was in a seat reserved for disabled passengers. Several furtive glances came my way as I rode. As I started to pull myself up by the grab bar at my stop, two people lunged forward to ask me if I needed help.

War hero? Burn victim? No, a young punk who hated crowds.

---

From her regal seat at the reference desk, Elena rebuked me softly, "You might have said you were coming. I don't get my midmorning break for another hour."

I admired her for being so discreet. I searched in vain for the sparkle in her eyes.

I teased, "Can't I be just as interested in you professionally?"

She didn't appreciate my sarcasm. "This is not a job that inspires interest, despite the reputation of librarians as white-haired, obsessive Agatha Christies. I could be serving you a sandwich, and it would do you more good."

Her gaze dropped to focus on the open book on her desk. I'd been rebuffed. I was out of line.

She calmly put a call slip into the book and closed it. She lifted the cover so I could see.

"Do you know this? It's in your subject area."

"More about the railway?"

"No. Art history. When I picked it up, I thought it was a novel. But you might be surprised how much it has to do with the railway and the canal, although neither is mentioned in it."

The book was *Paris in Ruins: Love, War, and the Birth of Impressionism* by Sebastian Smee, recently published.

I said, "I saw a review. I know the author by his reputation as an art critic. I haven't bothered to read it though, figuring it might be a distraction from our project."

*Our project?* Perhaps I'd overstepped. My hint should have brought a smile, but instead she reopened the book and bowed her head over it. If she was hiding a smile or a smirk, I couldn't see. I took her indifference as discouragement.

As I began to walk away, she said, still focused on the pages, "If you have errands to run or if you'll be wandering in the stacks, I can meet you in the courtyard on my break."

I didn't dare speak and break the spell. She glanced up just in time to see me nod and give her my crooked smile.

Mixed messages from Elena. Surely it was only my topic that interested her. How many people actually seek her out, besides asking for the way to the restroom or the children's books?

Do we have a thing, or don't we?

This day was sunny, cool, and crisp. The library is seven blocks east of the ocean, and the temperatures here are typically ten degrees cooler than downtown. I didn't mind waiting. I had on my windbreaker, and in the courtyard I found a bench in the sun.

By now, I had the transcript of Fred's diary, copied diligently by Bettina Reinders, my research intern at school. I'd printed it out in comfortably readable fourteen-point type and bound the pages in a ring binder.

I began to reread, picking up Fred's narrative midway in his troop train journey through France.

# Leaving the Italian Alps

## Jonathan Comments on Fred's Diary

Leaving the Italian Alps, we entered the plains of north Italy where the principal crops were vineyards and maize. We reached our third rest camp at Faenza, which was well laid out. An abundance of fruit was available, especially peaches, and I was impressed with the fine taste of first berries.

We left Faenza on Sunday morning and reached Rimini on the Adriatic Coast in the evening. The following morning, we arrived at Castella Marc Adriatico, where we had four hours stay and bathed in the warm deep-blue waters of the Adriatic. Continuing along the coastline to Brindisi, we made for Taranto, which we reached at 1 p.m. on Tuesday the 21st of August.

## Leaving the Italian Alps

I KNOW some Ancient Roman history from my introductory-level coursework. Brindisi and Taranto were both deep-water ports for the immense slave galleys of Julius Caesar's army. Brindisi is on the east coast of Italy, located in the heel of the boot-shaped country. Taranto is directly across the heel to the west where it joins the sole. From here, Caesar sailed with his troops to his campaigns in Asia Minor. Even then, domination of the Black Sea and its surrounding regions was a strategic goal of the expanding empire.

Arriving at the port of Brindisi, Fred and his unit were at the jumping-off point for a voyage across the Mediterranean.

> This ended a very interesting ten-day train journey of 1,446 miles. We were fortunate to escape being shelled by Austrian monitors whilst moving along the Adriatic Coast as previous troop trains had been.

This was the war in the Balkans extending south into the Italian region around Trieste.

> The country along the latter part of our journey was flat and principally cultivated with olive groves and fruit farms. Quantities of peaches and figs were being sun-dried on mats.
>
> The camp at Taranto was very hot and deep in dust. But our stay here was short, as at 7 p.m. that evening we embarked on the troop ship *Saxon* (Union Castle Line), which was lying in the harbour.

The War Office had contracted with commercial liners and tramp steamers to serve as troop carriers and supply ships. Before and after the war, Union Castle ships carried passengers and cargo, especially the Royal Mail, between Southern Europe and Africa.

> The second-class salon was allotted for the sergeants' mess, and I had a comfortable second-class berth.

Here's the first clue of his rank at this point in his career. He may have been at the section-leader level in the cavalry back home, but whatever his duties at Ragland, it would seem sergeant was a promotion he'd attained before he was shipped out.

> We laid here for two days, weighing anchor at 6 p.m. on Thursday the 23rd of August. As we made way, all troops were summoned on deck at their respective posts and greetings were exchanged with the Italian Grand Fleet, which was an impressive sight. The populace of Taranto also gave us a hearty farewell from the Promenade on the sea front as we made for the open sea.

They'd loosed their moorings from Europe. Did he understand how momentous this would be? Had he even been briefed where they were going? And why? It was all about the Eastern Question, wasn't it?

> We entered the Adriatic escorted by three Japanese and four Italian destroyers, an airship, and a hydroplane. It was a lovely evening. The rich red sunset made a striking effect on the deep-blue waters.

I didn't know Italy had a navy, nor that the Japanese sided with the Allies, or even were involved, in the conflict! Decades later, of course, both countries switched sides, then Italy and eventually Japan switched back. Kind of destroys the notion of having perpetual enemies.

> We then commenced a race across the Mediterranean, which was infested with enemy submarines. Our good ship carrying 2,353 passengers (including 160 nurses) was quite a substantial target for a U-boat.

This was the first time in his account he seemed aware he was in mortal danger. He had not expressed concerns about threats until now. Moreover, to this point in his narrative, he has not expressed terror. I found this hard to believe.

I was thinking about submarines when Elena crept up quietly behind me.

# In the Library Courtyard

## Jonathan's Journal

I looked up as she set down two overstuffed canvas shopping bags, the reusable kind they once told us were all but mandatory but then during the pandemic discouraged because bringing in bags from the outside might contaminate a recently disinfected checkout counter.

"I don't know whether you'll want these," she panted. The bags were full of books.

Apparently, she wasn't winded from carrying these things. As she sat, I saw she was upset.

In anticipation of our meeting, I'd stepped into the library coffee bar and bought her an iced green tea. The ice hadn't melted yet.

"Aren't you the gentleman?" she said as she took a long sip.

"Seems you need to relax."

Ignoring my weak attempt at gallantry, she informed me, "After today, this building is closed to the public. Some of the staff are still in there, tidying up before they lock the doors. It's remodeling, fiber-optic wiring, electrical and lighting upgrades, building code conformance — I don't know what all. There will be more hours at the branches, but even then we'll be overstaffed. I'll probably be laid off." She gulped fully half of her drink then fumed, "No notice! You'd think this would have come up before the planning commission. But not a word!"

"I'm sorry. What will you do?"

"I could write my memoir. Or if I want to go commercial, some bodice-ripper romance." She added in a lower voice, "But I thought I'd start by helping you."

Aha! Research interns might get minimum wage. I'll bet her salary is at least double that, probably more if she has a master's. Not wishing to appear ungrateful, I decided I wouldn't ask whether she were expecting a favor in return for her gift.

I thought I stayed cool, asking, "So, which books? Did you steal them for me? And is Smee's new book in there?"

"Oh, yes. But, as you say, don't get preoccupied with it. The story is background, earlier history. But I've realized it's a puzzle piece that fits rather neatly."

"I don't mind spoilers. Go ahead." I wanted her to skip to the surprising part, and the lecturer in me hastened to add, "I got the gist from the review. It's about the love affair between Eduard Manet and Berthe Morisot. They were both from wealthy families. Manet was married, she wasn't, would never be. She modeled for him, studied with him. Some would say her paintings are more accomplished than his, but he had the reputation of being among the first Impressionists, and critics only began to appreciate her work years after they were both gone." Surely that was enough to help her get to the point. "So you say it fits with the railway, but Smee doesn't mention it?"

She explained, "What struck me, and I confess this period of history was something of a blank for me, were the consequences of the Franco-Prussian war. It was brief but vicious and devastating, particularly to the citizens of Paris, and it set the stage for everything that happened since.

"The timeframe here is from 1870 to '71. The Prussians had invaded. They laid siege to Paris, encircled the city, and bombarded it continually with artillery shells. Rather like what's going on these days in Ukraine and Gaza. Cut off from supply lines, the Parisians were starving, and disease was rampant. They were eating rats, when they could get them. A restaurant that served aristocrats was rumored to have butchered a pair of beloved elephants, Castor and Pollux, from the city zoo.

"The French economy was wrecked, the national government was in disarray as politicians fought among themselves, and a populist faction known as the Commune began a civil war inside the capital to take power and restore order. Eventually, the German troops simply withdrew. Kaiser Wilhelm had worries closer to home and may have thought he'd weakened France enough."

"I'm still waiting for the surprise," I said. Most of this was indeed news to me, but I hoped she'd hear me teasing.

She laughed, "Just this. The canal wasn't finished yet. The French ran out of money. If British investors hadn't come in, the passage through Suez might not have been completed for decades, or the Turks or the Russians might have swooped down to finish the job."

"Or," I eagerly interjected, "the Berlin-Baghdad railway might have been completed in peacetime!"

"France didn't stay beaten. Investment capital poured

in, a lot of it from Americans. The ensuing years were the Gilded Age in New York, the Belle Epoque in Paris. The French hosted a world's fair in 1889, by which time they'd built a new symbol of prosperity, the Eiffel Tower."

"So maybe the kaiser realized he'd taken his eye off the ball?"

"The British had troops in Egypt and Palestine, and they'd been in India for centuries. They would have no doubt finished the canal themselves. But, partnering with the French, they made an ally and helped them rebuild. The Americans, the British, and the French were now much more deeply invested in each other."

"Thank you," I said. "You're right. The piece fits the puzzle. Maybe I can skip that book."

She frowned. "Oh, you'd be missing the love story!"

"I don't remember enough about them. Were they ever… a couple?"

Here was another moment. She said, "I'm not quite finished. We'll both find out."

"Keep it then."

"No, you first. I'll have an excuse to ask for it back."

This should have been my cue to ask, "When will I see you again?" But begging the obvious might have implied "our project" was a ploy rather than a serious mutual interest. After an awkward moment, I simply muttered, "What's in the bag?"

We'd reset the stage. She was the librarian, I was the scholar. No uneasy hints. Here we were, comfortable professionals.

"The best sources I could find," she said, pleased with her effort and the gesture. "Not checked out to you, understand. There will be no more lending until they reopen. The system thinks they're still on the shelf.

Remember, we were reclassifying a lot of them, so that jumble will stay piled up on tables in the workroom until somebody bothers to care about them. You see, no one will know these are gone for however long it takes." I nodded in an attempt to seem grateful. She announced frankly, "I have a question."

I was prepared for something about the Impressionists. "Of course."

"Did you deliberately stand me up at the wine bar?"

Oh my. Did I blush?

"I didn't know we had a date. Like I said, I wouldn't be ashamed to drink *tea* alone."

"You went straight to the tearoom? You didn't even stop by the other place to see if I was there?"

I didn't want to admit my level of confidence was so low I never considered the possibility she'd even pretend to stop by.

Instead, I had an all-purpose excuse for the situation that I thought was rather amusing. "Can I tell you a story?"

"Captive audience. Please."

"You probably know the novelist Graham Greene wrestled with his Catholic faith all his life. In his later years, he felt the need to get closer to God. On a trip to Italy, he managed to get an appointment with Padre Pio, the renowned mystic and miracle worker who was later sainted by John Paul the Second. The story goes, Greene was in an outer room, waiting for his audience with the priest, then he abruptly got up and left. When he was asked later why he didn't go through with it, his explanation was, 'I wasn't ready for how that man would change my life.'"

Elena laughed, "Change your *life?* That's giving me a

lot of credit. What was it you were afraid I was going to do to you?"

"I think it scared me enough that I didn't know." True enough.

She shrugged. "I'm not one to make demands, even if we knew each other much better. What could be so terrible?"

"I've had some serious relationships. We didn't break up, more like the feeling faded out. I have a hunch it's because I'm not easy to live with." I touched my sagging cheek and muttered, "People think I'm scowling most of the time."

She laughed out loud and not ashamedly. When she caught her breath, she said, "Did you *live* with any of them? I mean, besides your troublesome mother? As for me, I keep to myself now. My personality type is a job skill."

"Will you be in a challenging situation because you've lost your job?"

"I don't need a place to live, not yet, if that's what you're asking."

"Is that where I was going? Now I'm embarrassed." She wasn't offended and wasn't teasing. She'd softened, which was an unexpected change from her usual feigned indifference. I leaned closer to say, "I suppose I've been fantasizing about a relationship we don't have."

"You're right, we don't. It's not that you're cold or preoccupied or self-conscious. I get that you're all wrapped up in yourself. It's not a character flaw so much as acquired discipline, the mindset you need for your work. As I say, I see it in myself. I use it to my advantage. I've told you absolutely nothing about me, and even casual friends would know more. I have my reasons." She stood up, straightening her shoulders as if preparing to step outside on a cold day. "This isn't goodbye."

And she walked away.

I could have called after her, at least to thank her for the books, but the suddenness of her exit startled and stalled me. Just when I thought she was about to open up, she'd cut us off.

Had I overstepped again? It wouldn't have been her habit to go stealing books for patrons.

I'd taken a long shower with sandalwood soap. I'd brushed my teeth and finished with minty mouthwash. I'd applied deodorant meticulously and even splashed on a dash of fresh-lime cologne.

Did I reek of trying too hard?

# What Did I Do?
# What Shall I Do?

### Jonathan's Journal

Until now, I'd given Elena research assignments as abbreviated lists of Fred's campaigns and postings. Now that I had a readable transcript as a computer file, I reconsidered my resolve not to share the full text with her. I didn't want her opinions about the story, but she needed context. And I worried her interest would flag. The money I had promised could hardly be a motivation in itself. We'd agreed she would send me invoices at her hourly rate, but so far she hadn't bothered. I assumed she was pleased to be asked intriguing questions, her role at the library being almost boring by definition.

At the base of my expectations, I hoped she wanted a friend. Her personality wasn't any more outgoing than mine. My permanent scowl might have put her off in the beginning, but by now perhaps she knows me well enough to be able to decode the expressions I've developed to signal appreciation and affection. It might be the twitch of an eyebrow or a wink, but to anyone who cares, those quirks should be telling, if not endearing.

I finally resolved not to share the full text of Fred's journal to Elena. I had been guarding it selfishly. Now I needed a stronger lure for her attention, and I changed my mind. I took some time marking up the manuscript before I emailed the file to her. I highlighted place names where I wanted background, local color, the sights and sounds Fred kept mostly to himself. He'd pasted in some postcards and photos he'd clipped from newspapers, which was one reason I judged the copy I had was unique. I didn't copy these illustrations for her. I don't know why I guarded them so jealously. It seemed enough I was letting Elena in on Fred's secrets, however terse and guarded he'd been.

I sent her the full text of the diary with a brief transmittal:

Elena,

Here's what I've been obsessing about. As you can appreciate, I understand so little of it. Your help means a lot.

JFW

Dry. Guarded.

She didn't acknowledge right away. There was no reply until her next report, which felt a long time coming.

I pored over some of the references Elena had given me. Even with her help, it was an effort to fill in the gaps in Fred's narrative.

Before his unit ever reached Basra, the British navy had sailed around Arabia to establish a base. Even when late in the war they realized they'd be successful holding off the Turks, they wanted a permanent presence there. Elena had told me Basra was strategic. It would give access by sea to India and China, and it was a buffer to protect their interests in the Persian oil fields to the east. Oddly to a modern reader, oil was hardly a strategic resource back then. Jolly old England relied on its coal mines in Wales, and most of the steamships still burned coal. Oil was a commodity that far-sighted investors and some politicians thought they *might* need someday.

The railroad was under construction all during the war, and the part between Istanbul and Northern Iraq was completed. But by war's end, it had stopped short of Baghdad by a few hundred miles. There was never much chance of it reaching Basra because the British controlled the southern part of the country all through the war. The Ottomans had the north, including Mosul and Baghdad, which was mostly Sunni Muslim. But the British had a commanding presence among the tribes in the south, which were predominantly Shia. Making alliances with tribal factions and pitting them against each other were strategies used by both sides during the conflict and afterward.

# The Past Responds

## Jonathan Comments on Fred's Diary

Back in my comfortable human terrarium, I fretted about whether I'd see Elena again, or at least correspond with her.

I resumed my review of Fred's exploits. I was beginning to feel I was with him in his moment rather than hovering over him in the remote future. I'd been thinking about submarines when Elena had bestowed that bag of books and then disappeared.

Once Fred was on that troop ship, he was surely in harm's way. The presence of U-boats in the Med was the most serious threat to him so far.

> We were soon left with the two Japanese destroyers as our escort, and when darkness came, the only lights visible were the sma ll signaling lanterns at the stern of our escorts.

## The Past Responds

> At 12:30, whilst I was in a dead sleep, our ship received a crushing blow. An alarm was immediately sounded, and everyone took up his position on deck without any sign of panic. The S.O.S. was signaled, which gave our position and rendered us subject to attack by any enemy submarine lurking in the vicinity.
>
> The searchlight of one of our escorts also played around us. It transpired that the other escort, mistaking the signal to change course, accidentally rammed us in the bow, piercing the plates above the waterline. The damage was not serious, and we were soon dismissed to our posts, and we proceeded full steam ahead. We afterwards heard that the destroyer, although badly damaged, returned safely to Taranto.

Still, it was a scare. No doubt he'd been warned of the enemy threats. But I suspect that at this point the peril was only beginning to sink in.

> The morning brought us off the Island of Corfu. We anchored close to the shore in a delightful bay. The ships, boats, and rafts were lowered, and we bathed most of the day. I swam around the ship's bows and saw the damage done during the night. The inhabitants of the island flocked around us in small boats. Their chief mission appeared to be collecting the empty boxes and tins which were thrown overboard. The island looked mountainous and barren.

I've been to Corfu. A vacation spot for Europeans, as New Yorkers might go during the hottest or coldest months to the Keys or Jamaica. A short hop for them. What I remember most vividly is nude beaches. European women exposing their naked, succulent breasts to the sun. And wondering who might be watching, who might be impressed. Probably not their mates, who reclined in canvas chairs reading *The Financial Times* or *Le Figaro*.

> The following day, heavy gunfire was heard at sea. There was a compulsory bathing for all the troops. Those who could not swim had to wear life belts. It was a sight to see two thousand men in the water around the ship's sides. It was difficult to get out of one another's way.
>
> On Saturday evening at 6:30, we sighted the approach of our fresh escort of two other Japanese destroyers. At 7 p.m. we started the next leg of our voyage. After an uneventful night, we entered the Bay of Navarinou. A church parade was held on deck. Gangways and boats were lowered for bathing. On our right, the tower of Navarinou nestled under the mountains of Greece.
>
> We moved off again that evening. It was a moonlit night. Our escorts riding out on our flanks in the moon-speckled water were a pretty sight.

Gunfire at sea may have been the first real threat from the enemy on this voyage. I've heard it said that war is long periods of boredom punctuated by brief experiences of sheer terror.

So this expenses-paid tourist was allowed moments of pure reflection. It was an adventure, the kind he'd looked forward to. The High Command had recognized that sending them by train through the theater of ground warfare might have exposed them to more violence than this sea voyage, which proved to be uneventful except for the damage to the ship just mentioned. They might be cannon-fodder where they were going, but at least they should enjoy the trip.

Perhaps it was because I felt abandoned by Elena and fearful of being left alone with my thoughts. I wasn't delusional, but I was so deep into it that at times I didn't know past from present.

# Boring? Hardly!

## Fred Speaks and Jonathan Comments on the Diary

*Uneventful, mostly yes, but not without worry. The big guns on battleships produce a thundering sound that shakes the soul, even from a distance. The notion that we were sailing in its direction was sobering. Despite such fears, my mates showed no reluctance to jump in the water whenever the opportunity was presented. Before taking the plunge, some asked out loud whether there might be sharks about, and a fellow who claimed he knew said those predators stay mostly off the Atlantic coast of Spain and are rarely encountered east of Gibraltar.*

I KNOW WHAT IT WAS, this voice of his, hardly a hallucination or the ravings of an academic starved of affection. As I had resolved, I was beginning to read between the lines.

> Monday found us running through some of the Greek Island waters, then Crete appeared on our port side, where we expected another halt. But then we found we were making a dash for Port Said. A call was made for volunteers for the stoke hole, for which there was a ready response, and during the night we travelled full steam ahead.

Crete would have been a luxurious resting place, the ancient home of bullfighting and other manly exploits. The notion that stokers for the coal-burning power plant of the boat would be voluntary is striking. These were soldiers after all. Again, I'm seeing how the High Command exerted a light touch. Better not to let the recruits know they will be chewed up like so much hamburger if the necessity presented itself.

*Jon, no one thought this a pleasure cruise! At best, it was calm before the storm.*

> The next day we ran through dangerous waters. A fire broke out in the coal bunkers with which the crew fought all day. At 10 p.m. we were safely piloted into Port Said. This brought us through the only dangerous part of our voyage.

Remarkable that acts of God and failures of technology should be the most threatening events so far in Fred's war. But to be at the mercy of gears and pistons and steam and smoke? At least on horseback he had known what to expect. But here? Adrift in the Mediterranean? An attack by a U-boat would be devastating and sudden, ending in choking death in the depths of the sea. Everyone onboard must have understood that possibility. But equipment failure on the boat? Was that an honorable reason to die for his country?

One of the books Elena had given me was *The Daughters of Mars* by Thomas Keneally. I wasn't familiar with this novel, but I remembered he'd written *Schindler's List,* which became the major motion picture. I thought it odd that she'd recommended another fiction work, but I learned a lot from it that bore directly on Fred's story.

From Elena's notes, she seemed preoccupied with the Black Sea and access to the Med. Strategically, this route was related to access to the Persian Gulf and the Indian Ocean via Suez. All caught up in the Eastern Question.

Keneally tells of two Australian sisters who enlisted as nurses and were dispatched along with troops from their home country to serve on a hospital ship in the Mediterranean. They ministered to the wounded and dying during the carnage of the battle of Gallipoli in 1915. This peninsula lies at the narrow choke point of the sea lane between the Med, the Aegean Sea, the Sea of Marmara, thence through the Bosporus to the Black Sea.

Her favorite topic.

I was dimly aware that some Australian soldiers had fought there, and I knew the name of the place. I didn't appreciate its strategic location. The waterway between the peninsula and the Turkish mainland is the Dardanelles, one of the narrowest navigation straits in the world, known in ancient times as the Hellespont.

Now I understood that Gallipoli was at the epicenter of the Eastern Question. The Allies marshalled British, French, Australians, and New Zealanders for that battle. Its objective was to press on toward Constantinople and attack the Turkish capital. The battle proved disastrous for the Allies, but it was early in the war. The heroism of those troops became legendary, and the survivors went to fight the same campaigns in the Middle East, which Fred's unit joined later.

Perhaps ironically from a modern viewpoint, at the time Russia was allied with Britain and France in a pact known as the Triple Entente. As Gallipoli was underway, Russian troops were engaged in losing battles with the Turks in the Caucasus.

*We all knew of Gallipoli and the devastating losses. As we sailed through the Aegean, the threat hovered like a cloak, reminding us that the Turks were to be feared. And the red crosses painted on the sides of the passing hospital ships might as well be targets.*

*Placing oneself in mortal danger is itself an act of bravery.*

*However, I find it matters not at all how one achieves that state, which may differ from one engagement to the next. As you charge, think of pink elephants or naked women. Press on, propelled by rage, pride, honor, or fear of shame. Blindly do. Do your thinking when you train, not in the act.*

> At Port Said the nurses and a number of troops disembarked for the Palestine front. Our boat took in coal, water, and provisions. The following day at noon, we continued our journey through the canal. In the morning, we anchored for six hours in the Bitter Lakes, and on Friday, the 31st of August at 2 p.m. we reached Suez.

> We then entered the Red Sea. The heat became intense, but we were able to have the port holes and watertight doors open day and night. This was not permitted during our trip through the submarine-infested Mediterranean.

*We knew if there were U-boats lurking that they would have been guarding the passage from the Black Sea through the Dardanelles, or lying off Port Said at the mouth of the canal.*

*Now that the war had dragged on, the Germans had improved the performance of their undersea fleet. None of us had to be told that a torpedo hit would wreak havoc and probably kill many if not all souls aboard.*

He'd passed through the Suez Canal. Apparently, he didn't think that transition remarkable. En route through that passage, they were taking some troops and resources to Palestine. It was a warfare front. But how had the conflict in Europe oozed over to engulf the Near East? Fred was being sent to the far reaches of that conflict, but the only reason given to him so far was that Kaiser Bill *might* be thinking of moving on Baghdad.

The war in the northern regions of Mespot had been raging from the beginning. No doubt the Germans hoped the Turks would do the job. At the time, it was not as well publicized in the press as the horrors in France, and later all but the more insightful history books ignored it.

> Sergeant Clift of the Warwickshire Regiment died as a result of the heat. He was delivered up to the sea after an impressive burial service, our boat being followed by sharks.

The sergeant who died onboard was the first fatality Fred mentions. No one shot this soldier. He didn't step on a land mine. He wasn't eviscerated by cannon fire. He just expired because he couldn't withstand the change in climate. Did any of them think that simply traveling to lower latitudes would incur this risk?

*This God, who presumably decides which side will prevail in battle, must be sleeping through this episode. There are few atheists on the battlefield. In moments of desperation, one prays in blind faith, if not in considered belief.*

> Off Aden we changed our course eastwards. We were then about ten degrees off the equator, and well we knew it. We dined in the sergeant's mess attired in only a pair of nicks and a towel around our necks to mop the perspiration.

This harsh, hot climate was different from what any of them had known in chilly England. Formalities among gentlemen were gone. Attending the officers' mess in one's underwear was not an embarrassment but a privilege. At least, the chow was substantial.

*Hah! Do you get a mental image of this? Perhaps humorous to contemplate, but at the time the oppressive heat made stomachs queasy and sapped the spirit. Comrades, yes — comrade sufferers.*

> The weather in the Indian Ocean afterwards freshened up, and the sea became rough, which was an acceptable change. We entered the Persian Gulf on Saturday evening, the 8th of September. The sea

became very calm, and the heat again made its appearance.

The Brits complained continually about the heat. Ask any of them who had served in Africa or India.

*Since then, I never complained of the dense, chilly fog at the seacoast.*

Monday evening, we reached Kuwait, where we transferred our sick to a hospital ship, which was lit up like a fireworks display.

As our good ship *Garcon* was unable to proceed any farther up the Gulf, we were met at 9 p.m. by a smaller boat, the *Caliph of Sparton.* Orders were given to pack kit in readiness to reembark. After a long wait in the stifling heat and carrying full kit, our turn came at 1:30 a.m. to transfer to our new quarters. We were packed in this small riverboat like tinned sardines.

Many of us collapsed with the heat. The sick quarters aboard soon became full. After seeing to the comfort of the men in my draft, I managed to find a bunk. I turned in at 2:30 a.m. in the company of numbers of cockroaches and crickets, which crawled over me, but I was too tired to let these distract me. I immediately drifted off to sleep.

By the time the ship reached the northern tip of the Persian Gulf, it had sailed around Saudi Arabia, Yemen, and Oman. Their destination of Basra is a principal port of present-day Iraq. But the port is inland, requiring them to sail north from the gulf into the estuary of Khawr Adb

Allah, probably transferring boats in the deep-water port of Umm Qasr. The transfer was necessary because the passage up the Arvant Rood waterway and into the Shatt al-Arab River, a route that traces the border between Iraq and Iran, can only be navigated with the shallow draft of a riverboat.

> I rose at 5 a.m. next morning and found we were running up the Delta. We passed numerous picturesque Arab dhows. The country each side was flat with date palms fringing the water's edge. The sailors aboard our boat were a daily crew who ate their food like animals sitting around a tray heaped with curry and rice. We passed the Anglo-Persian oil fields. The large chimney stacks looked out of place in this country. Farther on, the waterway considerably narrowed, and we saw the funnel and masts of a Turkish boat which was sunk in the early days of the campaign.

The oil fields of Persia would have been visible to the east on the starboard side of the boat in Persia.

*The heat was still our most obvious enemy. No hostilities on this leg. The nasty insects became a concern.*

> In Mesopotamia, we arrived at Basra at noon on Tuesday, the 11th of September, where we disembarked. I was glad to get my feet on *terra firma* again. We marched about a mile and a half to Magil Camp, and our kit was carried in bullock carts. We were accommodated in huts built of reed and mud. We stayed here for two days, drawing the necessary

kit to combat the intense heat. A canvas water bag, containing about two gallons, was issued to everyone. We were advised to drink as much water as we could, and it was no difficulty to dispose of a full water bag a day. The water was chlorinated, and it percolated through the pores of one's skin after a drink.

Here they are, having transported through the network of German U-boats in the Mediterranean, past the threats that most certainly would have been concentrated in Suez and the offloading of some troops in Palestine. They've traversed the Red Sea, sailed entirely around the Arabian Peninsula, and up through the Persian Gulf.

On Tuesday, the 13th September, we received orders to proceed to Shaiba (about fifteen miles out of Basra) to join the 6th Devons, which formed part of a mobile column. We reached Shaiba after a very hot and dusty walk across the desert. Shaiba was an oasis, with an old mud-built Turkish fort. This mobile column comprised the 6th Devons, the 108th Native Infantry, a squadron of Lancers and the Mountain Battery, with a long string of camels and mules for transport purposes.

When the column arrived at Shaiba, the 6th Devons commenced the building of bombproof dugouts, as this place was intended to be the base of operations for the winter. I was especially surprised to find such quarters. I left England expecting similar conditions to my experiences on our Western Front.

We made Shaiba our headquarters until March 1918, doing our first duties and expeditions protecting the railway line against attacks from the low-class and cutthroat Arab tribesmen. The hostile Sheik Ajaimi and his large bands armed with stolen British rifles and a field gun drawn by camels and was always present in the nearby desert oases.

Although we were out in the desert, it was a new country to me, and I found many things of interest. I had the opportunity of seeing Basra again and the old Bazaar of Ashar.

*Now it would begin. We would see action ... because we would go looking for it!*

# Basra, at Last

## Jonathan's Journal

Despite what she'd said that day she told me the library was closing, I feared it might be goodbye. Fault me for not reaching out right away to ask. Perhaps I was afraid of the answer. From a professional standpoint, I was sure she'd been engaged in our project. She found it interesting and didn't mind the extra income.

When she'd gifted me the bag of books, at first I hoped it was because she wanted to be more involved with me. A gesture not only of support but of friendship. But then the thought occurred that she might have intended the opposite. She'd dumped the books, dumped me. Having lost her job, she might be taking off in other directions.

I didn't even have her phone number. Unlike my students, who are permanently wired to their devices, she didn't text, at least not with me. Two days after our abortive meeting, I emailed her simply:

Please let me know how you're doing.

No reply. My email sig shows my office address and phone as well as my mobile. Her previous emails bore the sig panel of the library. No personal phone. I wasn't being secretive, but she'd implied she preferred to be.

I was surprised after three more days to see her pop into my in-box. It was one of her diligent research summaries. She was keeping pace with the project. Her transmittal read:

Basra attached. Also, my invoice to date. R/E.

That last, "Regards, Elena." Obnoxiously terse. This message had contact information in its footer. So now we had one and only one method of communication.

I paid her modest charges promptly via bank transfer, as I had done previously.

My message was needlessly formal. I resisted confessing my fascination. "My dear" was new but hardly revealing. Was I suggesting she'd have trouble finding work? I was paying grocery money, which is not nothing. More than a hobby, less than a job. Fascinating for me, possibly not uninteresting to her.

I may have overestimated her enthusiasm, whether in my project or with me. Now I was sure, the more I thought about it, I saw her gift of the books as a polite dismissal. She may have generated all these reports in a single afternoon then doled them out as I needed them. If she's lost interest, she may soon put full stop to the end of our conversation.

I was tempted to put all these complaints, in kinder

words, in my message. I was upset enough, but I couldn't find the courage.

Keep it businesslike. I replied:

What are your plans, my dear? Do you wish to continue? Perhaps we should raise your rate now. I value your help!

I was hoping she'd answer right away, but she didn't.

She might regard repeated queries from me as pestering, and seeming too eager had always been my worry with her.

Now I wondered whether sending her the diary was a mistake after all. Because I'd taken care to mark it up with my questions, there was now no need for me to dole out research assignments.

I'd blown my excuses for reaching out, and my shy vanity prevented me from pleading. I was sure that unwanted persistence could get me cut off.

But maybe that's where we were already.

---

Other than her personal email address, I had no way to reach out to her. I set data drilling for her private self as an assignment. I searched for her on all the social media sites I could think of, especially the business-focused ones where presumably the bars to entry and proofs of credibility are higher.

But she must not do those. Or if she does, under a different name.

And only now came the thought she was married. Even so, I don't see why she couldn't have colleagues, even close friends. She had been so guarded with me. If I'd known her even slightly better, I might have learned the reason why.

From time to time, my own interest in the project flagged. Often it was because I had too little information, insufficient understanding of what was happening to Fred or why. Other times, it was in frustration, which I chalked up to annoyance at having to find another research assistant.

---

It was simply because I hadn't heard from her and feared I wouldn't again ever.

Despite the panoramic view of the Pacific Ocean at home, it felt like the walls were closing in on me.

I've been self-absorbed. Story of my life. Disappointed in my inept attempt to recruit a new friend.

Time to venture forth.

# Figurativo Gallery

## Jonathan's Journal

The library has an underground garage, and proof of a visit or borrowing privileges are not required to park there. Most of the meters on the streets have ridiculously short time limits, and the gated lots charge exorbitant rates. If you want to stroll around downtown with the option of hanging out at some posh watering hole, that place is a good option. Tourists don't know it's there. Even though the building was closed to the public, the useless suspicion may have lingered that I'd see her coming or going.

I left my car tucked under the library, and I walked three blocks west to the Promenade. The retail lease space there is more expensive per square foot than anywhere on the Westside, and even high-end brands are struggling to break even. It's an international destination, up there with Venice Beach, Disneyland, and the Queen Mary. What's the use of traveling at all when you can tour the same shops in Montparnasse or Mumbai or Montevideo or

## Figurativo Gallery

Mazatlán? Buy your wife a jumper from Zara here, and if she finds it too snug, return it as you stroll Las Ramblas in Barcelona or roll down the steep Taksim hill in Istanbul.

I happened into a new boutique art gallery. I'd venture into any such establishment, but the name Figurativo had a particular attraction for me. My field is Neo-Romantic painting. Pretty faces and partially clad bodies were its stock in trade. In the late-nineteenth century, rich, old white men were fans of such soft porn, especially if placed in a classical Greek or Roman setting, clothing the fleshy subjects in culture as well as cloth.

I'd heard that figurative art was becoming a retro thing with some of the new painters, who must be attracted to layering in oils much as some audiophiles won't buy anything but vinyl.

The gallery had two adjoining rooms, one at the entry and dazzlingly bright because of the full-length storefront windows. The other was in back with subdued overhead lighting and dramatic spotlights on featured works. The exhibits in the front were contemporary and moderately priced, on the order of a sports car. The spot-lit canvases in back were vintage oils, museum quality with no sale prices less than six figures.

In the center of the back wall with nothing nearby to upstage her was the star of the show. I had to catch a breath. Here was perhaps my favorite painting in all the world by the artist I've come to know best — *An Enthralling Novel,* dated 1885, by the American-born Parisian realist painter Julius LeBlanc Stewart. A dark-haired beauty, primly dressed in a frilly bodice, sits casually and demurely gazing down at the open book in her lap on a blissful afternoon.

It hadn't occurred to me until this moment how much she looks like Elena!

My next thought on a more practical level was that this must be a reproduction. In all the catalogs, this work is listed as being in an unspecified private collection. It's probably worth half a million, and if it ever came onto the market, it would almost certainly be up for auction at Christie's or Sotheby's. To find it tucked away in a shopping mall, however upscale, was unheard of. Finding it here was so outrageous that, if I trumpeted the news to any of my colleagues, they simply wouldn't believe me. Or they'd assume it's a forgery and would be urging me to quietly inform the authorities.

That is what I was thinking of doing when the pretty young salesperson sidled up, accosting me with the time-honored line, "Please let me know if you have any questions."

She was not much older than my students. I could see why whoever owned this place had put her out front.

There was no one else in the store, but I instinctively answered, "I am very familiar with this painting. It hasn't been on the market. I can't believe you have it here."

She sniffed, "It's not for sale, actually."

"I don't understand."

"It hasn't been sold recently. It's been in our owner's family for two generations."

"Why have it here?"

She smiled. "To intrigue collectors such as yourself, of course. We'll be building an event around it."

"And who is the owner?" If she were to blurt it out, I'd have a news release for the art world.

But she wouldn't take the bait. "Our lead investor, a

prominent family in Mexico. That's really all I'm permitted to say."

Despite the plausibility of her story, the likelihood that this was, in fact, a forgery — although obviously masterful from what I could see without close inspection — was still great.

Off my skeptical look, she added, "We're waiting on a shipment of paintings by Shang Ding. Perhaps you know of him? Fans of Stewart will be delighted to discover Shang."

I knew Shang Ding to be contemporary American. Born in China where he studied and gained a reputation. A craftsman as accomplished as Stewart perhaps. I could appreciate why they'd want to exhibit the artists together. With good publicity and a buzz, Shang might well add a zero or two to his asking prices.

I couldn't stay there. I was unnerved, upset that this model of Stewart's, who was in several of his paintings, looked so much like Elena. And yet I hadn't made the connection when I'd met her.

Was I more captivated by this image of a now-dead lady than the flesh-and-blood Elena? You can't be rebuked by a character in a picture, after all.

It confounded me that I'd missed the resemblance until now. Could it be that my memory of the painting was altered by the reality of seeing her in the flesh? If I'd noted the coincidence right off, I'd have been smitten to helplessness.

I had a new way of thinking about *love at first sight.* Matching these images had come too late. For me in this moment, the mysterious librarian was as inaccessible to me as the one in the painting.

# Back to Basra

## Jonathan Comments and Fred Speaks

So here I was, back home with Fred my only companion.

*Would Jon have been a chum had I known him in life? I judge he has the meek character of a callow shop owner. I know because I was no less shy when I risked my modest comfort to undertake my adventure. I didn't count myself among the timid at the outset, but the realities of war were quickly sobering. I had chatted with such fellows in my daily dealings, but I had never lifted a pint in their company. Like me, he professes to be a storyteller and therefore would have been welcome in any public house. There is one thing we have in common. His fascination with this woman, I can understand.*

On another occasion two other sergeants and I visited the old mud-built City of Zobeir. On our way,

> we fell in with an Arab and his donkey: we commandeered the latter and took it in turns riding. When we arrived at the gates of the city, we rewarded the Arab, who was up to then naturally very unpleasant.

Perhaps more than anything in his account so far, this snippet gives me a glimpse of Fred's character and of the attitude in general of the British expeditionary forces. Note the sequence of this transaction. They "commandeered" the beast *then* tipped the "naturally very unpleasant" Arab afterward. If the Arab spoke no English, negotiation at the outset might have been difficult. But you'd think waving some money under his nose and pointing to the donkey would surely have conveyed their intentions. Or did they fear he'd assume they were trying to buy it? In that case, the price would be far too dear. Did they brandish their sidearms? I doubt threats would have been necessary.

I've had some experience in my travels with Arab tradesmen while on a vacation in Spain, including the ubiquitous sellers of rugs and ceramics. Had those Brits paid up before jumping on the poor animal, the Arab probably would not only have been pleased to make the deal but, as tradition requires, would have bestowed some small gift as a gesture of goodwill. Instead, these fellows demonstrated their arrogance by rudely taking control of the donkey, and I wonder whether the Arab feared it wouldn't be returned to him. "When we arrived at the gates of the city" suggests they rode it for some distance. The Arab must have followed them closely, whether he still hoped for a monetary accommodation or simply needed to keep an eye on his property.

## Jonathan's Journal

*I will freely admit that our treatment of the locals was not enlightened. An unquestioned assumption in all our campaigns was that we were there ultimately to colonize. Who wouldn't prefer to be British? Nevertheless, the owner of this beast was rude. I can proudly say we treated our beasts of burden much better. As well, consider that daily life for us was, when not facing threat or enduring hardships, a crushing bore. Having exhausted our fun, I rewarded the fellow with a few coins, but as I was not familiar with the currency, I cannot say whether he considered the tip handsome.*

> We called on the sheik, who happened to be out falconing. We were, however, received by his sons. The sheik had come under British protection, and his sons were being taught the English language under an American tutor. The palace was full of interest: in the courtyard were falcons on the stands, and the sheik had recently adopted the European custom of carving off a table. We were given black coffee and then shown around the city by one of the sons. Camel flesh, covered with flies, appeared to be the principal meat sold in the bazaar. It was a pitiful sight to see many Arab children with their diseased faces also covered with flies. A gun shop full of antique Arab weapons interested me.

All through the war, it was British policy to befriend and ally with tribal factions. The army would offer protection, use bribery, and if the tribesmen seemed loyal, they'd sell them guns. They'd used the same strategy in India, where they conscripted locals into the Royal Army. But they were never so successful with the unruly Arabs. The Turkish tradition was to rule rather than just occupy, and the Ottomans and Germans focused their attention on political leadership in the north.

Fred mentions starving children and guns almost in the same breath. It's a good guess he'd rather spend his money on buying an antique pistol as a souvenir than helping feed those kids.

It's pretty clear he didn't think he was sent there to help. I suppose it's a postmodern interpretation that he should have cared and been more involved with the locals.

To the British, the Arabs were part of the scenery, like animals in a zoo. Their plan was to civilize and Christianize their colonies. And in a generation or two, those foreigners would learn to behave themselves. And all while the gentlemen occupiers were exploiting resources and creating wealth that would flow back to London.

*The civilizing influence of the British Empire became more obvious in India, despite decades of conflict and struggle there. All said and done, we left a parliament and a body of laws. In Mespot, it was to be the same design, much less success. We subjects of the king understood and appreciated our rights and privileges. We felt honor and duty-bound to bring them. After all, our Parliament had abolished slavery decades before the Americans had to fight a war among themselves to decide the issue — and not even then!*

---

I dove back into the research, which was a good way to avoid fretting about whether I'd be seeing any more of Elena. I'd be more inclined to think we weren't over if only we'd begun. A lot might depend on whether she felt she needed a friend. Or employment. At least, in me, she would find a like mind.

Is that enough? Perhaps for her, it's all she can manage. For me, I'd crave more.

Her personality impressed me as fearless. She kept her secrets, not because she feared exposure or embarrassment but by choice for reasons I could only guess.

As a lifelong student by profession, I've developed the attention span of a marathon runner. Our healthcare providers these days caution about the adverse effects of sitting for long periods. After a recent scolding by my doctor, whom I saw too rarely, he said, I resolved to set a timer on my phone to mark intervals after which I'd stand and stretch. But I abandoned the practice after less than a week. Being coached by machine is not something I can tolerate. Besides the annoyance of taking direction from a device, the arbitrary, measured intervals and then the alarm would inevitably occur when I was in the fast current of the flow, so absorbed I resented the interruption. Then at other times my focus would be broken as my mind flitted to minor tasks, as if avoiding some daunting aspect of the work — shopping lists, missed personal care tasks, laundry cycles, kitchen cleanup.

Often, a daydream of Elena, a pang of longing, would sidetrack me. I didn't regard those interruptions as annoying, more like a muscle cramp to be endured until it passed.

During those times of missing her and wondering what she would be doing at that moment, I'd once again try to find her, or evidence of her, online. I searched for her name on social media platforms, academic and professional society lists, and personal information search engines. I found many matches on the name, but the profile information, and especially the photo, if there was one, would be obviously wrong.

Most probably, I concluded, she'd changed her name or reverted to the real one. She might be using a married surname now or had gone back to her birth name. The change might have something to do with her immigration status.

Weeks went by as I continued to live in the past — then began to thrive there.

# Boring? Hardly!

## Elena's Notes

Almost a month later, Elena broke her silence by sending a backgrounder on significant events of the war leading up to Fred's arrival in Basra.

Her accompanying note was terse as ever:

Jon,

I feel I must apologize again for my delays. It's so rare that I have an opportunity to work with a diligent scholar on such an intriguing and original project. Worthy as your effort is, I have had more pressing concerns.

E.

Cryptic as ever! Maddeningly so!
Her report was rich in detail and no doubt would be

valuable to me, but its length and thoroughness made me wonder whether this report would be her last.

I'd ask her, as a friend, about the seriousness of her concerns.

But first I would study her summary lest she receive my hasty reply as a complaint. Then when I asked if she were in some kind of trouble, she wouldn't think I was digging for private information.

I wanted to ask whether she needed money, but she might take it as an insult. A student might take a job as a librarian to scrape by. But a woman of her age and education? Her clothes were tasteful and not cheap. I wouldn't know designer fashions, but her look was classy. She had her hair done up in back, as might have been considered prudish in years gone by, but there were chestnut highlights in its Mediterranean raven black. Clearly, she spent money on it, and regularly. She might have money from a trust. Or a portfolio of investments from a high-toned position that she'd left. Was she taking a career breather here in the quiet of the stacks?

To her email, she appended a concise report on the southern regions of Iraq where Fred describes his first postings in the region, significantly occurring after Gen. Maude had taken Baghdad and thus representing more of a military occupation than open conflict with the defeated Turks. Nevertheless, his unit must have confronted occasional raids by and skirmishes with rebellious Arab tribes.

Thus far, Elena's report was objective and scholarly, written in the third person. She then shifted to a personal tone, as if she were sitting back and reflecting on what she'd learned. Here, salted among facts, she permitted herself interpretations and opinions.

## Jonathan's Journal

Jon,

The British Imperial War Museum has a collection of military diaries. Fred's is not among them.

Modern scholars apparently assume the strategic targets at Basra were the nearby oil fields in the Shatt al-Arab River region. Persian oilfields were also close by. However, you and I know how much the railroad and the larger geopolitical Eastern Question figured in. Oil was not the strategic global resource it is today. Certainly, no one gave a thought it would ever run out. English homes were heated with wood or coal, and steamships burned coal. More than at home, petrol was needed now to fuel army tanks and transport vehicles.

Soon after the outbreak of the war in 1914, the British defeated Ottoman Turkish troops to take control of Basra. The British navy had sailed up the Persian Gulf and landed at Fao, the southernmost tip, on the Persian side of the river. Then, tracing the river's route overland, the army marched north, where they defeated Ottoman forces in the six-day Battle of Basra.

Five months later, the Ottomans regrouped. The Battle of Shaiba lasted just three days and again resulted in their defeat, then again at Qurna, and again at Nasiriyah a year later, in July 1915.

As in France, except for skirmishes with Arab tribal factions, the order of battle was often trench warfare between infantries, at times involving cavalry and strafing by German Fokker aircraft. Trenching was particularly difficult because much of the Iraqi landscape is either sandy or swampy. Also like the conflict on the Western Front, slogging through mud slowed the soldiers' advances. Gaining several hundred yards in a day was a triumph.

But the British weren't content simply to block Ottoman access to the gulf by holding Basra. Beginning in early 1915, under Maj. Gen. Charles Townshend, they began to fight their way towards Baghdad. Because the land route this time of year was swampy (the wet season is roughly from November to April), Townshend chose to make a frontal attack on Amara by sailing upriver on the Tigris using anything that would float, ranging in size from a warship to a flotilla of small native boats. Whether foolish or brave, the effort was reported in the press as "Townshend's Regatta."

In their push toward Baghdad, British and Indian forces suffered a sobering defeat near the ancient city of Ctesiphon in November 1915, made all the more challenging because the weather there was freezing. They fell back to Kut, a town they already held but where they nevertheless had to dig new trenches under fire from Turk rifles, machine guns, and artillery.

Beginning in December, General Townshend's 6th Division was held under siege there as they waited for reinforcements, which failed to arrive before his troops had exhausted their rations, then scrounged for food, including from rare air drops, then began to eat their horses and mules. From January to April, British and Indian forces under General Aylmer fought their way north toward Kut but couldn't break through.

After holding their own for months during the

Siege of Kut-al-Amara, Townshend and his 13,000 soldiers surrendered to the Turks on April 29, 1916. The Turks held the Brits as prisoners of war, including Townshend himself, who spent the rest of the war in relatively comfortable exile in Egypt, far from the field of battle, while his imprisoned troops were tortured and starved. Having survived all those months during the siege of Kut, many men died in detention, some of them poisoned.

Despite Townshend's humiliating defeat — or perhaps enraged by it — British forces under Gen. Maude achieved their objective in the Fall of Baghdad on March 11, 1917, then moved on to win the Battle of Ramadi in September 1917, one of a series of later victories.

In the same month, Fred set foot in Mesopotamia for the first time.

Most of the conflict there was already over.

Your faithful researcher,

Elena

# Reply to Elena

## Jonathan's Journal

She'd given me a lot to think about. Understanding that Fred had arrived in Mesopotamia after the British controlled most of the south lent some credence his expectation that his deployment would be more touristic than aggressive, occasionally adventuresome and even dangerous, but not so much from shot and shell.

I gave myself a few days to reflect on Elena's findings, then I replied:

Elena, my dear,

Thank you so much for your recent report. Please send your next invoice with your reply, and I will remit promptly, cheerfully, and gratefully.

I already knew something of the battles in the south from reading *Desert Hell,* the first book I'd borrowed from the library. I'd assumed it was a memoir, the author's name, Charles Townshend, being the same as the general's. Amazingly, he is careful to point out in his preface that he bears no relation whatever to the soldier, who would have been in his great grandfather's generation. (You knew this?)

The reader is left to assume that the scholar became interested in the subject matter because of this coincidence. I was struck by the oddity of my own initials and possibly my full name being the same as Fred's. You never said whether you'd searched for my name in the military records. I suppose you would have turned it up anyway in the results of whatever other search terms you used (Devons, etc.).

I appreciate that the essential truth was this. By the spring of 1917, the Brits had lost Kut but gained Baghdad.

I stand by for whatever riches you so generously share.

J.

# Fully Engaged

## Jonathan Comments on Fred's Diary

The taking of Baghdad stopped the train. The crucial railway line wasn't completed until several years after the war had ended, the construction undertaken by the occupation forces. Fred wouldn't set foot in Basra until six months later in September. He'd missed the decisive fighting.

> On our return journey from Zobeir, we visited the ruins of old Basra. In an old fort was an Arab rest house, which we found full of travellers. We had some black coffee, the water of which was boiled with dried camel dung. Our route back to Shaiba was a rough one. I found some pieces of blue and green lapis-lazuli, and we disturbed several jackals from their lairs. We came across the remains of many dead Turks partly buried, who fell in Townshend's advance.

Those remains of Ottoman soldiers would not have been fresh. In the fetid climate where decomposition of flesh would have been rapid, Fred may have seen skeletal torsos stuck in the ground with scraps of their uniforms still clinging to them.

What fascinates me about this passage of the diary is what little is said of Townshend. Son of a marquess and married to the daughter of a French aristocrat, he was reputed to be not only a brilliant military strategist but also an egomaniac who thought himself equal to Napoleon.

Fred remarks on the slain Turks as though Townshend had mowed them down in a wide swath, when in fact the general's progress had been halting and erratic. He apparently feared and even respected the German command, but his low opinion and underestimation of the Turks may have led to his downfall. The unspoken opinion in London was that the general's vanity had brought on his humiliation.

Townshend's defeat was later judged to be one of the worst the Allies suffered during the war. I have to assume Fred and his unit had heard of it. Fred's omission was appallingly respectful. A loyal soldier would not dishonor his superiors, regardless of their failings.

*I confess, at times I regarded my role in Basra as a tourist with military privileges. In the months leading into the Christmas season, I recorded no significant military maneuvers, noting only times passed pleasantly, despite hardship conditions.*

> On another occasion I visited a race meeting at Basra, which was promoted by British Army officers.

> Arabs came from all parts of the desert, and the most interesting event of the day was the Arab Derby. There was a large entry, and the race had to be run off in heats. The Arab mounts were fast at the start, but they did not have the staying powers of the British Army horses.

Jolly times! Although some Arabs did have horses, it's amusing to picture them astride their camels as the British soldiers flogged their quarter horses. In sprints, the camels would prevail because of their long strides, but the horses could go the distance at speed.

> We made the best of Xmas 1917 and dined off Arab chicken and Xmas pudding from India.

At Christmas, still in southern Mespot, Fred was in a waiting game, able to celebrate the holiday with special rations. He still seems to have no idea why he was sent there or what his expeditionary force was expected to achieve.

*Whether patrolling the sands of our domestic coast or pitching tents in the desert, every soldier understood the importance of maintaining a presence. Keeping the peace might be wishful thinking, but deterring attack was a vital mission.*

During this respite would have been a good time for him to reflect on his dear ones back home. Officers encouraged their men to write letters, as long as they didn't give specifics about their location.

If Fred had attachments, whether emotional or dutiful, he mentioned them not at all.

*True enough. When on shipboard, our outgoing mail was offloaded at ports of call. Since Basra was to be our posting, we expected to receive correspondence there. I addressed one brief letter to Henry, which was posted at Port Said, but his unit in the Balkans also had no fixed destination. I felt estranged from Sarah even before I left, but the fault was as much mine for enlisting in this second tour. Frankly, if I survived the conflict, I was not at all sure she'd be waiting for me. I didn't want to live in hope for a reconciliation.*

When Fred described Basra, he focused mainly on his unit's encampment at the military base in nearby Shaiba, which to this day is a strategic position with an airfield. Again, among the blessings he enjoyed during the holidays was his friendship with members of the logistics corps.

> I made many friends at Shaiba. The Supply and Transport Corps, which was attached to our column, had comfortable quarters in the old fort. They were Anglo-Indians, and I spent many pleasant times with them. Being in charge of supplies, they were able to get some of the delicacies available in the country, and they were blessed with good local servants. On Boxing Day, we had a sumptuous dinner off sand grouse, which I shot in the morning. Flocks of these pin-tailed sand grouse were to be found in the neighborhood at that time of the year, and they were a nice change from bully beef and biscuits.

Good old Fred! He used his rifle and precious ammo to shoot grouse rather than Turks. He might as well have been back home, hunting game for a festive dinner on a country estate, except in his modest social class he wouldn't have been among the invited guests of the landed gentry.

*Throughout both tours, expertise as a rifleman has been my foremost skill. What else is one to do? Granted, conserving ammunition was a serious consideration. Whether engaged in sport or in battle, we were trained to pick up our spent shells. The type and caliber of our weaponry would be valuable information for our adversaries.*

Occurring right after the holiday, this next passage hints at a genuine military mission for Fred's unit.

> Whilst at Shaiba, we made many expeditions into the desert, lasting several days.

The objective was likely two-fold. First, survey and locate the Arab tribal factions surrounding Basra. Co-opting those groups one-by-one was a major goal in British policy to maintain control of the region after the war. Second, although by this time Ottoman presence stopped far short of Baghdad, the British commanders no doubt wanted to make sure that no bands of Turkish marauders were grouping here in the south.

> Everything had to be carried by mule and camel transport. Our water ration was usually one water bottle full a day, which one was tempted to drink during the first half hour's march. The thirst was terrible, but how we looked forward to our mess of tea at the end of our day's march. The lancers carried out our flank van and rear guards. It was an eye-sore to me as an ex-cavalry man to see these natives

mounted on fine Australian Walers, whilst I tramped along the burning desert with my rifle and pack on my back. When the column halted for the night, these native cavalry men slept in tents, which they were able to carry on their horses, whilst we British infantry had to sleep in the open.

On occasions, my platoon was detailed as escort to the camel transport. These were principally animals captured from the Turks. These animals were lazy, continuously wanting to lie down and perpetually shaking off their luggage. It was hard work keeping them up with the column.

The veterinary at Shaiba ordered several camels, which were suffering from mange, to be destroyed. This was carried out the following day. The Arabs got news of it, and they came in large numbers, dismembering the carcasses like a pack of jackals and carried off the meat for to eat.

Although this time of year it was rainy around Basra, in the nearby desert was perpetually dry.

We had some blinding sandstorms. It was necessary to take cover until they were over. They were very penetrating, and everything became covered with dust and sand.

A weird mirage was often present, which looked like water and gave distant objects an inverted appearance.

Fred was next dispatched upriver with an assignment that comes closer to revealing the purpose of his unit's presence in the region.

> Leaving Shaiba on the 5th of March 1918, we made our camp among the date palms on the banks of the Euphrates at Nasiriyah.

Nasiriyah is about as far north of Basra as Amara is but farther to the west. As Fred noted, the city is on the Euphrates River, and Amara, the first objective of Townshend's campaign, is on the Tigris. Both Nasiriyah and Amara are much closer to Basra than to Baghdad and thus are in the southernmost sphere of influence were Shia tribes predominated, and the British military held control after Gen, Maude's troops prevailed there in 1915.

> This was a pleasant change after spending several months in the desert. The date palms were then throwing out their massive trusses of yellow blossom. The river was full of fish, which the Arabs caught with a purse net thrown with great dexterity. The net opened as it touched the water and closed when drawn in. Numbers of tortoises were also seen with their heads above water. The best species of fish was the Euphrates Salmon, which resembled a bass and often weighed up to forty lbs. We had fish rations once a week.
>
> Our camp was on the riverbank opposite Nasiriyah, with which we were connected by a pontoon bridge.

With the region mostly if not entirely pacified by now, Fred's assignment amounted to displaying the Union Jack to make the intimidating presence of the Allied forces obvious, especially to tribal leaders.

> Our work at Nasiriyah was similar to that at Shaiba. On occasions, it was necessary for the column to march through the city with fixed bayonets to show the flag to the sons of the desert, who were a treacherous low-class crew. We also made expeditions out into the desert and lying out at night on outpost duty being continuously bitten by sand flies was not pleasant.

With no more Turks left to shoot, the soldiers amused themselves by chasing and firing at wildlife.

> The 6th Devons was commanded by Lt. Col. R. L. Soames, C.M.G. C.B.E. He was a Canadian who had served in France with the first contingent of Canadian cavalry. He occasionally delighted to give vent to his cavalry instinct. A jackal would often be disturbed from its lair whilst we were on the line of march: the colonel would draw his sword, apply his spurs, his knowing old charger would pick up his ears, and away they would go pell-mell to bag the jackal. The horse would do his share in the combat by using its fore feet. On other occasions, the colonel would stop the column and bring the big guns into action at a flock of passing flamingos. These incidents amused the troops.

Another role for the soldiers was to scout for ancient artifacts, presumably on behalf of the British Museum.

> On the 5th April 1918, the battalion marched out to the partly buried historic ruins of the Chaldeans, being an ancient Temple of the Moon mentioned in

the Book of Genesis. The tower is about 150 feet high and forms a prominent landmark in the desert. An excavating party of Arabs under the control of a British officer was opening up the buried ruins, and large quantities of earthenware believed to be 2,000 years old were unearthed. I kept a small piece as a souvenir. The uncovered brickwork showed good workmanship of the ancients.

I infer that Fred had done no fighting whatever so far. His unit departed Nasiriyah in March 1918. The war in Europe would officially end later that year in November, which was supposed to bring about the cessation of hostilities everywhere else.

After the peace treaty, you'd think the British army would give their soldiers the option of returning home, especially those with families who were heads of households. But if Fred had been tempted to quit, he didn't say so.

Now I'm furious with him! I can't believe he had no one back home, no attachments, no longings. If his diary were personal and intimate, if he were capable of writing about his feelings, here is the point in his story where I'd imagine he'd think twice. But these pages don't hint at decisions or doubts. His descriptions are so dry you'd think he wrote this journal as some kind of report to his superiors. But then why paste in all those pictures as if it's some tourist scrapbook?

No, I'm beginning to suspect Fred's fretting was all about his legacy. And if he didn't have a wife or children when he was documenting his adventures, perhaps he expected that someday he would. Here would be his proof he'd done something honorable and worthwhile with his life. But his narrative goes nowhere near expressing anything so ambitious or profound.

So far, he'd recorded generalized threats, but he hadn't noted any visceral fear that his young life would be cut short. And especially now that the armistice was signed, perhaps he expected, should he choose to extend his tour, that now he'd rarely if ever be at terrifying risk, much less in combat. Like his assignment in Basra when his troop's assignment was mainly to dress up and march around to impress the locals, perhaps Fred thought his ongoing mission would be to display the "Colours," as his own enlistment had been inspired by a parade.

# Transitions

## Jonathan's Journal

So far in my reading, Fred was about to leave Basra for a new deployment. Ceremonially, the war was already over. Fred had said at the outset he wanted to see India, and that's where his new orders sent him. Having won the war, the British were anxious to protect their colonial interests by preventing the next one, which could well have been a confrontation with the Russians. Reasons for dispatching Fred to India must have had more to do with ensuring the longevity of the empire after the armistice.

It's significant that supply lines from India were crucial to the British effort in Mesopotamia. The German navy had a presence in the Persian Gulf but did not engage. Based on Elena's hypothesis about the Eastern Question and claims on trade routes to the Far East, one might think the war would be over when the German railroad was thwarted. In practical terms, it was. But Britain in its ascendency wasn't content to simply hold the fort. There was a world empire to expand, maintain, and dominate.

JONATHAN'S JOURNAL

I am furious with Fred for not returning home when he had the chance. His decision smelled of cowardice, not of war but of some unnamed threat or bitterness back home, a resentment that kept him running away, perhaps the real reason he enlisted in the military to begin with.

*I believe I had been clear enough about having little desire to return home. I had seen enough of danger to appreciate the risks. For the army, and especially for our Indian troops, we expected times of trial and conflict were far from over. Oh yes, I longed to see India, which I imagined to be more exotic and intriguing than the deserts of our Mespot campaign. As well, having endured and at times thrived in new experiences, I was intrigued by what I had yet to become.*

*I have stated my desire to see the Far East, and in my mind at the time this motivation was paramount. I also hinted at unhappiness back home, and I have avoided details. I kept the diary to highlight the experiences I wanted to remember. It was hardly the confessional of a lovelorn female, although I'm embarrassed to say in some episodes it might have become so.*

My birthday falls on February 29, once every four years. This isn't a leap year, so I'm just as happy not to have a birthday to celebrate. During the self-isolation of the pandemic, which seems to have carried over into my life of today, I had an excuse not to invite a friend out for a festive meal on Valentine's Day. After the infectious period had peaked, people were out and about, donning their masks on entering a restaurant, keeping them on as they gave their orders to waitstaff, then taking them off as soon as the drinks came. To many, these precautions seemed a pointless ritual, especially since more than ninety percent of residents in this town claimed to be vaccinated.

And then with the encouragement that we shed our masks and pretend the world was somehow normal, suddenly I was eligible and potentially kissable. But for me the feelings of self-isolation persist, even though it's already been several years since healthcare experts predicted we may live with a low-grade strain of the virus indefinitely, much as we do with other corona strains such as the common cold and seasonal flu. More relevant to Fred's era, the recurring H1N1 flu virus is essentially the same bug that caused the Spanish Flu back then, and although not as virulent, it's still occasionally fatal.

Looking back, the end of the pandemic was more stressful for me than the duration. The lockdown had given me a sense of self-satisfaction. Everyone was hiding from the public. Now we're free to move about, even to shake hands!

Even now, years after the pandemic has been declared over for the mainstream, I maintain a lockdown mentality. Before, I had an excuse to stay inside. I had formal permission not to mix with people. Now, my freedom is scary. Cultivating a friendship with Elena was nudging me out of my shell, but now that she was gone, like a coward I'd snapped back inside.

When feelings of loneliness well up, I should be angry with myself. But instead I focus my discontentment on Fred. I think on news of the armistice he should have decided to return home as soon as his command offered him a discharge. I can't believe there was no one in his life he held dear. Except for the incident when he was sent home from the front in France to recover from the unexplained wound to his elbow, he'd been absent for years.

## Jonathan's Journal

And he hadn't mentioned sending so much as a postcard home. He preferred to paste those in his journal, as if someday he'd be able to find someone who would take interest in them.

Both during and since our war against the virus, I have read that mental illness, suicide, and divorce were — and still are — on the increase due to the stresses of living in isolation. Having loved ones close at hand obviously tests the limits of affection. Troublesome as she could be, I have to admit I miss arguing with Mum.

# My Role as Caregiver

## Jonathan's Journal

For most of my life, I have been a mild-mannered fellow. From early childhood, when I began to stumble my way through Golden Books, I have been a bookworm. In class, I rarely said much. I hardly ever asked questions. I didn't sleep, didn't gossip, didn't pass notes. Teachers didn't fret about me after in the first days of whatever year they called on me for an answer. Some accused me of reading from the dictionary, but on seeing not a scrap of paper on my desk, they were sure I'd memorized something. Eventually, I became the last-resort responder to prevent the conversation from getting stalled. "All right, Jonathan, give us the answer."

These were typically moments of frustration for the teacher, who, when facing blank stares from the others, was often too tired to explain. The sarcasm sometimes came through. "Jonathan, please reach into that warehouse mind of yours and share its fascinating riches with us."

Before I became afflicted with Bell's, Mr. Evans took

me aside after class. "You know, I have recommended you skip a year."

I protested, "We haven't gotten to long division yet."

"We'd get you a tutor for about a week, maybe not even that long. Or give you a book. You would do fine."

"I won't know anybody."

He stifled a chuckle. "My boy, can you name your best friend?"

When I hesitated, before I could answer, he said, "This will sound nasty, but you don't have one, do you?"

I muttered, "Guess not."

He sighed deeply. "Sorry to cause you concern, Jon, but they won't let me do it."

I wasn't disappointed. I didn't feel anything at all, except curious. "Why?"

"They said you'd build a wall around yourself."

"What does that mean?" I was confused, not understanding why he would bring it up at all if it wasn't something I'd have to worry about.

"It means you'd have trouble making new friends."

"You said I don't have any."

"You don't, but they don't know that. I suppose they see you're not unhappy, so they assume you are getting along. They call it *benign neglect*. It's neglect, all right."

"I'm not sad."

"You're never sad. I know that." He might have said more, probably something like, "You don't seem all that happy, either." But he just gave my arm a gentle shove. "Go play." As he turned away, I believe he said, "Or whatever it is you do."

I'd been surprised by this news that I'd earned some favored status then been promoted and demoted without my knowing. I thought it odd, but she'd made it clear I hadn't been involved in the decision.

Perhaps remarkably, I had been so bewildered by the come-and-go of it that I hadn't thought to ask who *they* were. At the time, I must have assumed these were her higher-ups, some nameless education administrators. Among them, certainly, the headmaster, whom I'd never met. At that age, I had a sense there were advisory sorts, but I hadn't yet learned the existence of social workers and psychologists.

I didn't learn the truth until two years later when I was finally summoned to the headmaster's office. Leopold Czerny. I remember the name. Goatee and reeking of Balkan Sobranje tobacco. Perhaps also Slivovitz plum brandy, but I wouldn't have yet known the customs of his country.

I'd been called in because I'd retaliated against a bully. He'd called me an ugly name and then smashed the bridge of my nose with his knuckles. When he tried to put his hand over my mouth, I chomped down on his finger and drew blood.

"You're a good student, I understand," the old fellow said, avoiding my gaze. "You should know better."

"Good student? Yes, I believe they were going to promote me. Sir, may I ask, was it you who put a stop to it?"

"Goodness, no. I was aware, of course. It was your mother, dear boy."

---

Mum had been widowed for ten years, living by herself in a seven-room Victorian flat in Kensington. During those years in London, among their neighbors were Will and Ariel Durant, who could be seen of mornings shuffling arm-in-arm down the footpath in the park. Richard Harris lived in a modest-sized castle on the next block.

The lease was held by his employer, a Canadian engineering firm that managed mining operations in various foreign lands.

When Mum joined me, I'd turned thirty-four, and she was about to pass her sixty-fifth birthday. Her health was failing with COPD due to her persistent two-pack-a-day habit, but nevertheless she insisted she wanted to stay in her place and hire a caregiver.

The real reason, I am sure, was she refused to leave her antiques.

Despite my lack of enthusiasm for having her as a housemate, my begrudging loyalty and dogged insistence prevailed. By now, it was clear from the news of the Covid outbreak that the pandemic posed an intolerable risk, especially since her respiratory vulnerability would be a major factor should she contract the disease. Our last-round of telephonic negotiations concluded when I reluctantly agreed she could surround herself with a few pieces of her favorite furniture. The fine china and crystal were never in question.

Having me had been childbirth at advanced maternal age, occurring after rare but diligent efforts on the part of my rapidly aging father to finally inseminate her. He was sixty at the time, she twenty-eight. She, a trophy wife whose fame peaked in a teenage swimsuit competition at the Kansas State Fair. He, the CEO of a Canadian mining operation with its head office in Regency Park.

Dad refused to retire and expired nineteen years later from a sudden and devastating heart attack at his desk.

## My Role as Caregiver

There at the end, he no longer had operational responsibilities but still served on the company's board and reported almost daily to the office, where arguing heatedly with the new leadership was part of his daily routine, or so I was told years later by Mum, who resented being abandoned just as she reluctantly shouldered her new role, abjuring breastfeeding but unable to retain any of a succession of nannies for very long. The spike in blood pressure that felled my illustrious father was a surprise to no one but him. My only memory of him is as a grinning face, tanned and wrinkled from a lifetime in the sun on golf courses and boats, yellow-stained teeth, and a body odor I used to think was cologne but may well have been the VSOP brandy on his hot breath.

The experts say infants and even toddlers can't remember much, but I have that frozen image of him. Since she never acknowledged any of her own birthdays, presumably I'd caught up with her in my teens, and by the time she moved in, I was many years her senior.

My memory of the headmaster's telling me she'd held me behind was triggered for me one morning as I delivered her breakfast tray.

As she sat up, she pulled the tube from her nose that extended to the green oxygen tank and reached over to fetch a stamped envelope from the bedcover and handed it to me, wheezing, "Mail this. I've paid off your car loan."

"You needn't have. I use the tax deduction."

"Interest is a malicious invention."

Generosity and resentment. Never one without the other. "Thank you," I muttered gently. Mailing the check involved little more than putting it in the mail drop beside the elevator, literally steps away.

I didn't really mind being her caregiver. She didn't

need medical attention as a matter of routine. In the beginning, I'd intended to hire someone, then after she'd been here a week or two, I'd realized she would drive anyone away. At least, I'd learned though long transatlantic harangues to know how to joke with her. I never got a laugh. A sarcastic wrinkling of the lips would suffice.

I used the moment to tease her, "Just curious, why didn't you let me skip a grade?"

She was quick and amused. It might have been yesterday. "You're what? In therapy now?"

"It's early for life review, I hope. But I was unpacking some of your things, and you saved that yearbook. It made me think."

She sipped her tea as though it were bracing whiskey and barked, "You were an arrogant child. Why make things worse?"

I indicated our panoramic ocean view. "The cloud layer has burned off. It will be a bright, sunny day. Why don't we walk along the beach, drink in the fresh air?"

She huffed, "You're too brisk. Never heard of *stroll?*"

"I'll slow down. We'll go at whatever pace is comfortable for you."

She looked in the direction of the window, squinting as if the light hurt her eyes. "You have work, don't you? I'll be calling Dr. Mortinson. There's a throbbing in my right temple. I can feel my pulse. No headache, oddly. You may have to run me over there."

"If it's worrying you so much, we'll go to urgent care."

"And wait in that room with all of them coughing and hacking? I should say not!"

Her phone was on the nightstand. I handed it over and left her alone.

Throughout her stay with me, she was technically

ambulatory, but her bed was her throne. From there, she insisted on managing not just her own investments but also all our household accounts. She guarded her laptop computer as though it were a designer handbag, and within it a string of rare pearls. Keeping the accounts seemed an innocent enough chore to let her handle, and given how much she was prone to fretting, it kept her occupied.

Yet, competent as she was tracking balances online, she made all payments by check, written out meticulously in her elegant longhand with her prized Graf von Faber-Castell Guilloche Rose Blush fountain pen, using turquoise ink she special-ordered from Iguana. I worried the banks might only accept blue or black, but the only time one of her checks bounced was the next check after she'd paid off the loan for the mini-Beemer hybrid I rarely drove, especially during the lockdown.

# Fred Departs for India

## Jonathan Comments on Fred's Diary

IN FRED's departure for India, I sense not one but several significant turning points in his life.

> The Indian Army Council issued an order that one NCO from each battalion in Mespot should proceed to India to go through a musketry course on the then new methods in force. A short time previously, my platoon won a Battalion Field Firing Competition, and as a result I was the fortunate one selected from my battalion. This was a pleasant surprise to me, as I had a great ambition to see India.

In this passage I get the first inkling of ambition in Fred. He'd excelled as a sharpshooter, although of innocent critters rather than aggressive Turks. The prospect of the musketry course must have brought opportunities for promotion.

There is also a hint here he'd made new friends. Now that he was leaving the assignment in Basra, he'd be able to salt his stories with it, referring casually to Mespot to imply his hard-won familiarity with that theater of the war.

> I left Nasiriyah on the 4th April 1918 and embarked at Basra on the S.S. *Aronda* on the 13th. The accommodations aboard were crowded with leave parties for India, but I met several old acquaintances, and making the best of the circumstances, the trip became very enjoyable.

Old acquaintances? Who might those be? All through his previous campaigns, Fred had mentioned no one, not even a friendly nurse during his recuperation. Here was a new Fred, chatting up his mates, perhaps boasting of his riflery skills, and looking forward not only to venturing into the mysteries of India but perhaps also sharing those experiences with companions, all of it underwritten by King George V. This next passage strongly suggests that Fred was beginning to think himself as much tourist as soldier:

> After three days bon voyage, we put in at Muscat in the Gulf of Oman on the Arabian Coast for coal. The harbour was small and sheltered by precipitous cliffs. Our boat was soon surrounded by natives in small canoes. They were the best divers I had ever seen.

He's pulled out his army-issue binoculars and marveled at the habits of the locals. How could he judge the skills of these divers? Had one of his mates with

JONATHAN'S JOURNAL

aquatic experience told him? When he referred to "we" and "our boat," who were his comrades?

> Leaving Mespot we made a beeline for India through the Indian Ocean. We ran into several schools of flying fish, which travel like swallows a considerable distance above the water, and occasionally we overlook small, heavily laden Arab boats en route to India.

Here was more of the tourist viewpoint and observation. Fred was ready to impress his future readers with the exoticism of India. He might have known that Arab sailing boats had traversed the Indian Ocean for centuries, propelled by prevailing trade winds that blow southeasterly between June and September and then reverse direction for the rest of the year. In ancient times and until the advent of steamships, many sailors would shack up in port until the winds shifted, maintaining two households, one in India and the other in Arabia or East Africa.

> We sighted the shore of India on the 19th April and ran into Bombay [Mumbai] docks at 1 p.m. after six days' good voyage, and my ambition to see India was realised.
>
> On disembarking in the afternoon, every man was presented with a useful gift bag containing toothbrushes and toiletries presented by the ladies of Bombay.

I expect these ladies of Bombay were the ivory-skinned wives of British army officers and diplomats, perhaps also including those of Indian nationals, especially men who

## FRED DEPARTS FOR INDIA

had served in Force D in Mesopotamia. Fred was being welcomed as a war hero, and these patriotic women were celebrating not only the return of their husbands and brothers but also the assurance of their continued Britishness. Fears of Russian designs on the region percolated in local gossip, especially among expats and the officer corps.

> We took up our quarters at a Colaba, which was situated in pleasant surroundings. In the evening, Sergeants Clive, Evers, and myself took the opportunity of seeing what we could of Bombay. Our first thought was a substantial meal, and we dined to the accompaniment of an orchestra at The Graces Hotel on the seafront. It was a nice feeling to be again among civilization after several weeks in the wastes of Mespot. We then visited the native quarters and bazaars which were densely crowded. These travels were a striking contrast to the beautiful buildings of the European portion of the city, which were brilliantly lit at night. On our way back to Colaba, the wide pavements were strewn with sleeping natives.

Aha! Here some of Fred's previously anonymous mates have come forward in his narrative. What's more, they are chums now, embarking as his posse to visit local attractions as well as go off to shooting school. Fred was quick to point out that he was no longer suffering in the desert heat with primitive amenities. He would eat sumptuous meals in luxurious surroundings in fine *European* style. But he also acknowledges the mean existence of the lower classes, whom he saw as conquered menials rather than potentially rebellious brigands. These slaves were British subjects after all.

Jonathan's Journal

> The following morning, a small party of us received orders to proceed to a School of Musketry at Satara, which was a station at the foot of the Western Shoals. We left Bombay that evening. The station was a fine building with marble pillars and mosaic floors.

Satara city is east of the western coastal mountain range, and records of a British musketry school there date from its first class in 1907. The school trained British and Indian infantry in the use of small arms and machine guns.

In general, Fred expresses himself well, but in a few instances his meaning isn't clear, such as:

> The station was a fine building with marble pillars and mosaic floors.

From context, I think here he is describing the railway depot in Bombay. But in the very next sentence, he uses "station" to mean "military base."

> We arrived at Satara Road Station at 2 p.m. on the 31st April, after a twelve-hour railway journey, and we travelled the remaining few weeks to Satara by road in bullock carts. The going was slow, hot, and hilly.

Bombay might have been temperate, but the climate in Satara was hot — perhaps not so hot as the Mespot desert, which by now Fred no doubt wished to be a distant memory.

## Fred Departs for India

> We found very comfortable quarters in large, well-built, and airy stone bungalows lying outside the city of Satara.

I'm guessing he's still in the company of chums, possibly soldiers of his rank, who would have the same privileges. What's remarkable is that Fred was beginning to think of himself as more of a leader. Perhaps this wasn't his own gang, but he continued to suggest that certain of their destinations were his idea.

> This place provided me with many interesting experiences. We commenced work on our musketry instruction at 6 a.m. and finished at noon. The climate was intensely hot, and it was the custom in the afternoon to take a siesta or study. After tea, I usually made excursions into the adjoining jungle or visited other places of interest.

Here he seems to be suggesting he would venture out on his own, but later it's clear he was still with his mates. Fred wanted his readers to think he was independent of mind, but until now his personality had been more follower than instigator. Perhaps his opinion of himself was changing.

> On the top of the Shoals overlooking the city is an old fort I was eager to explore. I found a small family, and after a continuous climb for over an hour up a winding track, we reached the massive gates of the entrance. An old Sepoy pensioner was in charge, and he showed us around. The fort, which was built in the twelfth

> century, is now disused and in a state of decay, but the officers' quarters, with elaborately carved ceilings and panels and the shrine, were intact. The fort overlooked the city of Satara and commanded an extensive view.
>
> On our return journey, we entered some caves in the mountain side, which we afterwards discovered was a dangerous venture, as they were the home of panther and bear.

Here is further evidence Satara is the place. The city is in the Maharashtra state of India, near the confluence of Krishna River and its tributary, the Venna. Ruins of the fort he describes are still there.

*"I* found a family," but *"we* reached the massive gates." He's still in a tour group, even if he wasn't being led around.

> On a neighboring hill stands a Parsee Tower of Silence. The tower is round with a grading on top, where the Parsees place their dead and leave to the mercy of vultures, the bones falling through the grating into the temple, there to remain.

Someone guided Fred to the tower. How else would he know these religious practices? The Parsees (Parsis) are a sect of ancient Persian origin that follows the spiritual teachings of Zoroaster (Zarathustra) and worships the sky deity Ahura Mazda *(Lord of Wisdom)*. Legend has it that Zoroastrians practiced powerful *mazda,* from which our word *magic* derives.

> About three miles out of Satara is the sacred village of Mahuli. The Hindu temple, with its weird carved

## Fred Departs for India

> images and terraces running down to the holy river, was very interesting. Here the neighboring Hindus burn their dead and throw the ashes into the river. A corpse was burning during my visit, and the smell was very obnoxious. Thousands of flying fox hung head downwards like large pears on the trees around the temple.

Like a storyteller boasting over a pint in a pub, if there was a grim aspect, Fred would never fail to mention it. Again, he seems to be quoting his tour guide on the local customs. Generations after he lived, cremation would become a common practice in Europe, mostly for lack of real estate for burials. Burning the bodies openly would have shocked him. But rather than remarking on Hindu beliefs or mortality in general, our practical Fred simply noted the creepy presence of flying fox (I'm guessing *bats*), which would be the size and shape of pears as they hung in the trees with their wings folded around them.

> On Sunday the 30th of May, 1918, I was isolated in a large stone bungalow, having contracted a diphtheria throat. For two days I was unable to swallow. Three phials of antitoxin serum were injected into me at different times, which gave me much relief. It was a monotonous time, as I was not allowed to receive any visitors for a fortnight.

In Fred's day, the treatment for diphtheria, a highly contagious airborne virus, involved the injection of antitoxin, a serum made from the blood of infected horses. The presence of foreign troops greatly contributed to the spread of diphtheria among the locals, just as the troops

## Jonathan's Journal

fighting in Europe had probably brought the Spanish Flu across the Atlantic. Diphtheria was usually fatal in children, but adults who were treated often survived.

> The only human beings I saw were the medical officer and a native servant who attended me. I slept on the veranda outside. The nights were weird and presented curious spectacles. In India, the animal and insect life seem to sleep in the daytime and become active at night. The lamp burning by my bedside attracted awaking toads and numerous insects through the open doors. On several occasions, the floor of my bungalow was strewn with exhausted swallows, which had been disturbed by some night marauders.

The nocturnal predators of swallows would have likely been owls and kites, a type of raptor resembling hawks, their often-abortive aerial attacks knocking the birds out of the trees. Snakes would also prey on small birds, but if serpents were anywhere near his living space, I'd think Fred would have mentioned it. He does note later that snakes are commonplace in Satara.

He would have had time to reflect in that clinic, but he shares his preoccupations and imaginings not at all.

# My Illness
# and My Mira

## Fred Speaks

Jonathan is correct in detecting the objective tone of my journal. He judges it was not a confessional, nor was it at all reflective or emotional in the ways some women keep their diaries. I've not read any, except for snippets of early Victorian romance novels, which seem written along those lines.

I have said I expected my readership to be houseguests in my comfortable retirement, possibly my heirs. It was to be a report from the field, citing mainly the events and my impressions, superficial as those might seem to more insightful readers such as this Worthington fellow.

Of course, if in later years I would prove to be the only one to pick it up or to bother with it at all. A straightforward recounting of the journey would be sure to excite more subjective memories in me.

Apparently, someone sold it to Jonathan's mother, which should tell you how little they may have valued it.

Now I must come clean, as the accused must eventually confess — set the record straight, as they say. Not to justify myself, although I wouldn't mind being thought of in a better light, but to at least fill out my story. Histories are necessarily interpretations but should not, when evidence exists, mislead.

Jonathan is also right in concluding that my departure for India was a major turning point, not only in the trajectory of the war but also in my personal development. Although the situation in the Far East might be worrisome for heads of state, for those of us who were charged to fight, it was a sigh of relief. True, we were still in dangerous circumstances, but we were to be an occupying force. To say we would be peacekeepers might be a stretch though. Just as when we were in southern Mespot, we were there to maintain a presence, this time almost assuredly with less possibility of conflict. Granted, another full-scale war might break out. Presumably, such was what we were there to prevent or forestall or mitigate.

I had not meant this aside from my story to be a history lesson. Considering Jonathan's academic interests, he probably thinks his curiosity is motivated by his studies. Scholars obsess about context. However, this chap — and I'm the one surmising now — seems to be after something more like understanding of me as an individual and, I venture to say, himself and his own soul's journey through history.

At this point where I interrupt my narrative, Dick Clive and Morris Evers had indeed become my mates and regular companions in off-duty hours. These were the first close friends I'd made in some time. I had palled with a chap named Mike during my deployment to France. My injury prevented me from assignment to the trenches, but during my convalescence at home, I got word he wouldn't be making it back. I'd never been a comradely sort, downing pints at the pub, as it were. After the news of Mike's demise and then my volunteering for another tour, I resolved that making close friends in the military was not a wise plan. All through the long voyage to the Near East and then in the reconnaissance missions out of Basra, I kept mainly to myself. Nevertheless, I was cheerful enough in my dealings with subordinates as I trained them in musketry. My accomplishments in those postings, largely due to my demonstrated competence in riflery, gained me the promotion to staff sergeant.

In transit from Basra to Bombay, we were all less anxious, and it was because of acceding to invitations to card games on shipboard that I chummed with Clive and Evers. Casual conversation was made easier as we all held the same rank. In the chatter over cards and talk of distant loves, I mentioned I had a wife back home who might not be thrilled to see me again. I was relieved my friends could see it was a sore subject with me. They didn't urge me to say more.

My initial treatment for diphtheria was at Satara Station under the care of the medics, as I wrote in my diary. I confess I omitted the next phase of my recovery. After those three injections, my cough subsided, but I was still considered unwell and not fit for duty. I was then admitted to a clinic in town, where I had a decent bed in a ward set apart for the British and Indian soldiers from the musketry school.

My reasons for not describing this episode in my memoir will become apparent.

My nurses were Mira and Priya. Mira was the senior on day shift, probably the more trained because she administered injections by syringe. Priya attended me at night, and hers was the unenviable task of tending to my bedpan. Mira was slender and pretty, possibly younger than myself, but I was no judge of age in persons of her complexion. Priya was younger, perhaps not yet twenty, with a round face and chubby cheeks, full-figured, and even at her tender age tending toward matronly. I saw Mira daily on her rounds and whenever I had an urgent need. It was useless to ask for a cigarette, but a hard candy could be soothing.

Although the infection was in my throat, it made me feverish and weak, thus bedrest, though not a strict protocol, was thought to be salutary. I would see Priya less often. During her visitations, if I was lucky, I'd be snoring blissfully. When the heat was most oppressive and sweats drenched my pajamas, I'd greet her smile on my sleepless nights.

My attending physician at the clinic was an Australian, Dr. Aleister McGraw. What little hair he had left was snowy white. He had almost none on top, but tufts stuck out from behind his ears. His odd demeanor was all the more curious because he wore a patch over his left eye and managed a crooked squint to hold a monocle in the other. I had read that Aussies had fought valiantly at Gallipoli, but this fellow's campaigns must have been decades earlier. He ambled about with an aged stoop.

The first indication I was feeling better occurred when I became impatient if Mira were late on her rounds. Her appearance was the highlight of my day. Granted, missing a meal would have been a disaster, but the food tray came with regularity by way of a callow, young male attendant, whose demeanor was so taciturn and his eyes so evasive that I wondered whether he was mentally challenged in some way. I didn't dare speak with him. I don't know why.

My developing fondness for Mira was against my better judgment. It amuses me to think I could summon anything like wisdom in those days.

Mira. So much like *miracle*.

# My English Patient

## Mira Speaks

HE WAS NOT TROUBLESOME, but he did complain a lot. I had been on leave for the weekend. I'd have preferred to picnic with sandwiches by the river with friendly colleagues, but I wanted simply to rest. My day shifts often stretched to ten hours, sometimes twelve or more if Priya was late or had difficulties. My junior was not yet out of her teens and applied herself to her studies in late afternoons after awaking and before reporting for night duty. Priya also admitted to having a boyfriend — or at least a persistent admirer — about whom she provided no information, and I suspected it wasn't simply the girl's studies that made her almost habitually tardy.

The diphtheria ward was located at the far west end of the facility to provide a modicum of isolation because the disease was so contagious. A tented area just outside held new admissions, along with cases that resisted treatment. Eighteen men with persistent coughs were laid out there on army cots spaced six feet apart. Most of them were soldiers, a few British and the rest of them Indian from Force D.

Although administered by us Eastern Christian nuns of the Malabar Independent Syrian Church, this hospital's patients included no women or children, who were housed in a separate ward. Mothers who survived the disease were there to supplement professional care because the little ones needed constant attention. Children were not only the most vulnerable to it, but also it was fatal to most of them who caught it. The disease caused a membrane to form in the throat, eventually resulting in suffocation by blocking the airway to the lungs.

Our facility was in a rural area a day's walk distant from town. The grounds were verdant and flowering. Stands of plane trees were clustered in attractive groves. I assumed, as many did, that the soldiers were better cared for because the church received a generous stipend from the military. The infirm in the east wing were mostly the injured from gunshot wounds and amputees. The High Command must have concluded that these expenses were considerably less than operating their own military hospital.

At six in the morning, most of the men were already awake and grumbling. No bugle reveille here, only the discreet tinkle of a brass hand bell, yet hardly necessary. Especially among soldiers who live by their routine whether sick or on the march, the stomach is a reliable alarm clock. I made my rounds to the others before approaching the English because, even though I was supposed to make sure all were roused before breakfast, I didn't want to wake him.

For the patients like him who had already been through the course of injections, bed rest was the cure, supplemented by whatever food they could manage to swallow.

This English was snoring loudly, having pulled the mask off his face during the night. I wore a mask routinely along with rubber gloves. I was instructed not to approach until the patient was awake and sitting up with his mouth covered.

As I approached his bed, I halted a short distance away. I wasn't to bend over him. I spoke through my mask clearly, but I was never one to raise my voice except in emergencies.

"Good morning, Sergeant!"

His eyes opened narrowly, which I saw as a cue to lower my mask. I flashed him a sincere smile, followed by a mock-stern look as I raised my own mask back up. It was my polite signal for him to do the same.

The sight of my smiling face captured his attention and jolted him awake. To a man who had always prided himself on acting properly, he could not hide his delight at seeing a pretty woman.

His amazement was quickly followed by embarrassment. He pulled his mask hastily over his mouth and nose as if he were a green recruit caught with his pants down.

"Wh-what time is it?"

"Moments after six," I replied softly. "You slept through the bell. Did you not sleep well?"

"Trouble nodding off," he said. "The heat, you know. Bedclothes soaked with sweat, then a chill when the breeze kicks up. Not so different me, but some of these gents are sawing wood a minute after lights out."

"It may help you to remember you are sweating out toxins as well. It goes with the healing. We must be diligent about keeping you hydrated. Here, have some water."

I offered him a glass and said, "Perhaps your throat is not so raw. Your voice sounds better."

He sat up to take it and replied, "Yes, better. Will there be tea?"

I took the empty glass from him. "An orderly will be bringing your tray shortly. I must make my rounds now." My mask still on, I believe my smile showed in my eyes, and I told him, "For you, perhaps no more jab. We shall see what the doctor says."

"I am so grateful to have a bed inside."

"Yes, and fresh sheets! You are indeed fortunate."

He managed a chuckle. "Promise me, no more jabs!"

With a slight bow, I assured him, "Sir, I will endeavor to make it so."

---

Breakfast was tea — strong and black — with lemon (or whatever citrus could be found) and sugar. There was no milk to produce catarrh and mucous. Also soothing on the throat was salty bouillon, or on occasion more substantial meat broth. Those who could swallow it would get soft bread, spread with margarine, ghee, or oil. Porridge was the more substantial meal for those who could take it, but without milk. The men kept asking for sausages, but there were none to be had.

The orderly who brought trays in the morning was Max, a Scotsman who had previously fought with the regulars. He claimed he'd been mustered out because of a hernia. It seemed odd that most of the orderlies were British and white rather than Indian boys too young to join Force D. The rumor among the patients was that men might sniff cordite, which would bring on irregular heartbeat. Cardiac problems could cause them to be deemed unfit. Rather than being discharged, they'd be assigned to noncombatant service in clinics, supply depots, and maintenance yards. Even if they didn't get their wishes granted to get shipped back home, posting in India, even with the heat and the bugs, was no doubt far more pleasant than slogging through the desert sands or muddy swamps of Mespot.

My rounds included ministering to the newer or more persistent cases who slept on cots outside under the tent.

Before I'd give each injection, I'd apply a blood-pressure cuff, insert a thermometer (in the mouth, thankfully for both of us), and inspect throat, eyes, and ears for telltale redness of inflammation. After injections, I'd cleanse and dress wounds, check sutures and splints, and replace bandages. Among the soldiers in the clinic, few had gunshot wounds. There were eye injuries, fractures, and bites from insects, rats, and snakes.

I noticed the sergeant studied my waltzing movements as I cooly performed my routine. He had reason to be joyful he'd been transferred inside to less intensive care. Not only did he have a bed with a mattress and clean linens, but avoiding the jab would be a huge relief. A vaccine to prevent or mitigate diphtheria would not be available for years yet.

The means of injection was no pin prick. Antitoxin fluid had to be shoved into the patient through a glass tube resembling a bicycle pump, terminating in a wide-bore needle. The men would get it in their buttocks, which at least had the advantage of making them face away from the injection site. Although these were hardened soldiers, many complained, not necessarily in jest, that they'd sooner take a bullet. If any were squeamish and stubborn, two orderlies would be summoned to help me and hold them down.

This morning, as I was making my rounds, one of the patients judged to be in serious condition began to wheeze and couldn't catch a breath. I responded to this emergency before I could administer jabs to the others. This fellow was older, which was worrisome in itself. The protocol was that if any presented difficulty breathing, I was to fetch a wheelchair, help him into it while making sure his mask was in place, and take him to the procedure room. The attending would be summoned, thence to intubate the patient. However, Dr. McGraw's hands shook with palsy these days, and he would supervise while an army medic did the job. Without administering anesthesia, the medic would make an incision just below the larynx with a scalpel, then insert a rubber tube, bypassing the inflamed, engorged throat to permit free flow of air to the lungs.

All patients on the floor had been advised in advance that this extreme measure was a possibility. Although they dreaded the routine jabs and greatly feared intubation, they knew enough not to resist. They were soldiers, after all. Many of them had seen and no doubt endured much worse.

# Her Eyes and Her Smile

## Fred Speaks

I HAD no business lusting after this nurse. My feelings were natural enough. There had been nurses onboard as we were crossing the Med, but they were segregated in a dormitory on another deck and weren't even allowed to join us for mess. More than a thousand men ogled them from a distance, and I was surprised not to hear rude jokes and catcalls. The sobriety of war had apparently descended on the ship. Once in theatre, of course, as we faced shot and shell daily, we would all be rowdier, but the battlefield medics were men, and needless to say you wouldn't catch sight of a nurse then unless you had a dreadful reason to be in some surgical tent. It was not a fate to be wished.

One morning, Mira was no longer on call for emergency intubations, a duty she would have sooner avoided. She explained a new nursing intern had been assigned to night duty, and Priya was promoted to the day job, where she would assist in emergencies. As for me, Mira kept her promise, and I received no more jabs.

And after a few days more days in this comfortable setting, old Dr. McGraw judged me ambulatory. I could now take walks around the grounds in the afternoons, as long as the heat was bearable. He didn't announce this to me. She did.

"Would you walk with me?" I immediately requested.

Masks were no longer mandatory whenever she came to see me. Now I could revel in the sight of her sweet smile.

She sighed and flashed those pearly whites. "Oh my, such would be quite irregular. I might be needed."

"What if I fell? Tripped on a cobble?"

She seemed amused I didn't take her no for an answer. "If you ask, an orderly could accompany you. Such would be normal."

I grunted, "They're all ugly blokes! Is there no way?"

She thought for a moment, her lips cocked in a coy smirk. Then she confided, even more softly to avoid being overheard, "I am permitted an interval at four for tea. At half three, summon an orderly. Tell him you wish to venture outside, but you're feeling a bit weak. Request a wheelchair. Do you have enough strength to wheel yourself?"

"Oh, yes!"

"Then, once outside, dismiss him to go about his business. Wheel yourself past the grove of jacarandas, and I'll meet you there."

Thus began a courtship of sorts. I sincerely believe my intentions were honorable, and at one point I informed her I had a wife back home. I wore no wedding band as a matter of safety, but I kept it in my kit. She asked me if we'd been happy, and I answered honestly that we had not. I did not tell her I'd been betrayed, because again in honesty I had only suspicions, and appealing to her as a victim not only seemed unfair but unmanly as well.

I finally asked her about the caste mark she wore on her forehead, centered between her dark eyebrows. I thought the nuns were Christian.

"Oh, my *bindi!*" she exclaimed, as if I'd asked about her intimate apparel. "The red dot over my third eye, my portal of insight, may be worn by a woman as a sign of marriage."

"Oh, I see." It probably came out as though I'd been told my disease were terminal.

She chuckled, "It is also acceptable as a fashionable touch. I am not married, but in the hospital it serves my purpose for these men to assume I am."

"Are you *pretending* to be Hindu?"

She was embarrassed and giggled, "Promise you won't tell? As I say, it is a cosmetic thing only. Perhaps a sin to have it, but I wouldn't know. Keeping you fellows at arm's length without incident, that's the trick of it."

"May I kiss you?"

Again, the sweet smile. "I could wish it. But, no, you may not."

Each day, I counted the hours until I could see her. I called for the wheelchair habitually, this time letting my mates assume I might have shrapnel lodged in my thigh. My behavior went unquestioned, and as far as I knew Mira received no reprimand. If there were rumors of assignations in a broom cupboard, I was not aware.

Neither of us was comfortable sharing personal details nor life experiences. What we had was something bright and new, not colored by anything that had gone before. One way we passed the time pleasantly, she schooled me on the local flora we saw on the grounds. There was the greenery of teak, sal, and bamboo, as well as flowering trees like the jacaranda and its lavender blooms, the red and yellow gulmohar, and the fragrant, night-blooming harshringar.

Our blissful strolls lasted barely a week, exactly four outings. Much to my disappointment, but I hadn't dared, there was no kissing, and a gentle hand on my shoulder at times was the barest caress.

Mira had waited until the conclusion of our last lovely stroll to inform me, "Doctor is aware of our walks. He has asked after your welfare, although I suspect he knows you are not disabled. As to your recuperation, he says you may now be permitted leave from the facility until such time as your commanding officer approves your release and issues your orders." She took a breath and gave me a lingering look. "And I suspect you'd enjoy being off on your own at times. A few of your colleagues will also be given permission to go about, so you have all earned some fun."

I asked, "No question of your coming along?"

It was a sad look, the stiff upper lip. "I've told you all this now also because I must once again assume duties in respiratory care, including the intubations. Priya's boyfriend has been granted permission to marry her, and I must take her post."

"We won't be seeing each other much, will we?"

"Sadly, not."

I had not planned to speak so soon, but now was obviously the time. "My marriage is at an end. When I'm home, I will send for you. Or if you wish, I will return, and we will sail home together."

I resolved not to speak until she said something. While I waited, I had time to worry someone would come to fetch us before she could answer. Finally, she told me gently, "I have no wish to see England. If I ran away, if that were even possible, I would have to abandon my family, my faith, my calling. I would never be regarded as a British lady, even if I knew the customs and learned to speak so others could understand me." She giggled, "You know, they even treat each other so shamefully! It's not only poverty that makes one an outcast. I see it here. It may be worse there."

"I can live here with you. Can't a man buy a farm?"

"You mustn't raise cattle for slaughter, you know. Sheep and goats. You might buy a place, but you won't make a go of it. The British will shun you because of me, and the locals may refuse to buy from you as well."

There had to be a way! "Australia! Isn't everyone an outsider there?"

She was a strong-willed woman, and I had no doubt she'd follow me if she were so resolved. I had assumed it was love we were beginning to share, but perhaps it was merely affection, precious as hers had been to me.

She was silent all while she wheeled me back inside. Before we reached my bedside and out of earshot, she confided, in the tone her profession uses for imparting the worst news, "My family will not permit it. Our marriages are arranged. I'm not yet promised, but I must honor their choice."

# My Recovery

## Fred Speaks

After a fortnight in bed and isolation, I had recovered sufficiently to be allowed some sightseeing, but I was not yet healthy enough to return to active duty.

There was no question of Mira accompanying me on these outings. I wasn't alone, however. My mates Clive and Evers had also recovered by this time. Morris joked that it was oddly coincidental the three of us had shipped over together, had contracted the disease and recovered at the same time as we endured the nasty stinks of each other, and yet remained friends. Dick suggested, also in jest, that simultaneous onset of sore throat could be explained had we all been sharing the same girl. It got a laugh from Morris. I barked back I thought the remark tasteless then worried my taking it seriously might betray my intimacy with Mira.

I then worried the joke was aimed at me, perhaps taunting a confession to some rumor they'd heard. I said no more about it during our time together, and neither

## Jonathan's Journal

did they. I was fairly certain these two chaps had not hired female attention during our tour, although at times there were certainly opportunities. Neither spoke of wives or lovers back home, but crude observation of local lovelies was a commonplace.

Visions of Mira's loving smile haunted my days, as well as the dreams I could remember. I was glad to have the company of these two fellows as we sought diverting experiences.

# Satara Walkabout

## Fred's Diary with Jonathan's Comments

During my convalescence I visited the city of Satara, which is very old and historical. It was the seat of the last King of Marulis and played a prominent part in the Indian monarchy. The population of the city was about 25,000. A long bazaar ran through the city and the marketplace in front of the old palace, which was crowded with natives.

It was a picturesque oriental sight. A fakir was lying on his back continuously beating his stomach. The fellow was doing a religious penance, and the natives gave him shoes and food. The principal industry was extracting oil from monkey nuts by means of a bullock pound, making cakes of soap from the pulp.

Jonathan's Journal

Who explained to Fred what the fakir was doing? I doubt he'd know without being told. Notable that he doesn't remark on religious practice. As in so much of his narrative, he simply observes and reports. Because of the tropical locale, at first I assumed monkey nuts were palm kernels, which also grow on our palm trees here in Southern California. But a quick search tells me monkey nuts are peanuts. The Indians here were using cattle to stomp the nuts, mashing them into something like peanut butter, then using the extracted oil as a fatty emollient in their soap.

> During my few remaining days of convalescence, I wandered among the banana and sugar plantations. The bananas are picked green and allowed to ripen in mixed herbs. I bought a large bunch for 1/3 rupee (4 pence). The natives used a crude method of rolling out the sugar from the canes and bashing it down into a brown pulp.

Fred seems awfully energetic for a recovering invalid. He was taking long hikes, not mere walkabouts in the city. And he was a close observer of events. I'll give him that. But he gave no hint he was sensitive to feelings, whether in himself or in others.

> Since my arrival in India, everything was dried up and parched with the heat, and in places there were large fissures in the ground. An early monsoon season then arrived, and the country immediately assumed a mantle of verdure. The fissures closed up, bringing with them snakes and monsoon frogs, which had laid

down deep into the cracks for moisture. These frogs are as large as dinner plates and are continuously orating.

# Thankful and Worried

## Jonathan's Journal and Elena's Message

By now, a wiser person would have at least gradually given up fretting about Elena. Granted, it would be perfectly normal to worry about the welfare of a distant friend. Healthy and reasonable concern would inevitably focus on the state of their health and whether lack of communication was due to some unfortunate circumstance. But I continued to despair that I'd done something to ward her off. My habitual scowl would be an obvious reason, but too easy to assume, relieving me of responsibility for my attitude and actions. I have enough self-awareness to know I can be perceived as aloof, and often enough I have used my deformity (I hate the word, but it comes up unbidden here) as an excuse for indifference, rude behavior, and worse.

On this portentous morning, I hadn't slept well. I'd left off my analysis of the diary just as Fred reported his recovery. I imagined he'd regained the ability to speak in a clear, confident voice without rasping or choking, which would have irritated him and possibly made him sound irritable to his caregivers and mates.

I continued to blame him for not choosing to go back home. He'd hinted at having the wife, and no matter what the betrayal on either side, he should have been emotionally invested in her.

Did they have bitter words before he left? If she cared at all about him, wouldn't seeing him sail off into war zones be a wrenching, perhaps resentful, moment?

I'd left my laptop on the nightstand, having closed the lid in the wee hours. I'd taken to making my notes as annotations in the transcript file. I have learned, since the oppressive routines of Covid, which seemed like minimal-security imprisonment, not to check my phone first thing upon waking up. It's nowhere on the nightstand, and not because I have heeded warnings of radio-frequency emissions somehow disturbing my sleep.

I sat up in the bed, kicking my legs over first then pushing up. Mum's caregivers had coached her to do it that way to minimize strain on her back. Reaching out to the nightstand, I took two drops of sodium carboxymethylcellulose in each eye, swabbed with a tissue. These days, I lack nothing for self-care.

I'd programmed the coffeemaker. The brew's aroma is as effective and much more pleasant than an alarm. During this sabbatical, there is no reason whatever for regular wake-up times. Again, it's caregiver advice to maintain a consistent sleep routine. Only the obligatory bathroom trip keeps me from the coffee and the blessing of caffeine.

But this morning I felt the urge to lift the display screen before the toilet lid. No password required from the machine's sleep mode, the email client still open. In the dim light of the bedroom, the bright light before I was fully awake struck me like the glare of a flashlight in the face.

The effect of what I saw was just as startling.

There it was. I gasped as my heart skipped a beat, and I read it twice.

My dear Jonathan,

Please accept my profound apologies for being out of touch for so long. I know in your isolation you feel that everything that happens to you is because of you. Not so. I will explain.

However, first in your reply let me know where you are in the diary. When I finally could attend to less urgent matters, I realized I'd failed to send the concluding portion of my research. I attach it here. I didn't dig deeply into Fred's journey home. His time in Constantinople dealing with those dispirited Turks would have been a consequential episode, and perhaps you'd like to know more about that phase in the city. I just haven't been able.

I've returned home to Kiev. My sister Tanya's husband Stefan went off to join the forces at the front. They have two young daughters, Larissa and Anna. Tanya is ill but, I believe, now recovering with my help. I admired your dedication as a caregiver. Now I too must do what I can.

I'll spare you the details of this war. If you are

seeing the news reports, you know what is happening. You see the threats and the suffering. You may imagine the fear, but on a daily basis the prevailing emotion is resolve. We have a routine now. Food and shelter and warmth. Medicine for Tanya. And of course attack warnings and hurry to designated refuge. The resolve gives way to terror then, but we can't afford to dwell on it any longer than the huddle in the basement. Usually hours, not days. Not yet days!

I've read through Fred's diary several times by now. It's a welcome distraction, also a reminder of how human history repeats itself, albeit with variations that interest scholars like ourselves. I'm attaching the rest of the diary with my notes. I've tried to keep those comments to factual summaries rather than inserting my personal opinions of Fred's actions or inaction. You are on your own adventure, and you don't need spoilers from me. Perhaps you've already pored over all of it, and my contributions are coming to you after you've lost interest in the project. Again, my apologies for not keeping up with this.

I trust you are well. I hope to see your reply soon. I may need to gather my thoughts and find the moment to share more than postcard trivia. Ukraine still has excellent infrastructure, but we do have outages these days, sometimes protracted.

Your friend and colleague,

Elena Svenskya Bogomolova

In my excitement, I'd ignored the urgency in my bladder and wet my pajamas. I remembered Mum's humiliation at soiling herself, which always amplified her fury.

Besides craving relief and coffee, I decided not to reply right away. I needed time to collect my thoughts.

# My Fretting About Elena

## Jonathan's Journal

I WAS angry with her because she'd not told me. And I feared she was risking her life when, having made a life here, she should have been content to stay. Caregiver is a reluctant role, no matter how virtuous and necessary taking it on might seem at first. I expect it's as rewarding as swabbing a baby's bottom — no more, no less, not that I have any experience. Despite the truism of motherly love, I can't imagine Mum wearing an affectionate smile as she wiped my dimpled little ass. She'd hold her nose and get it done. When the roles were reversed, I'd take out the garbage, make sure she saw the doctor, count out her pills, always suspicious she had spit them out. I admit there were times I ignored her when I was preoccupied or upset with her. One way or the other, her lunacy seemed unaffected. I was keeping her alive. I could have read her stories or played checkers with her, but she'd rather watch old movies, which we often did together. We shared a few chuckles as we watched, and sometimes she wanted to talk about it, but I'd be annoyed when she repeated a comment she'd already made.

It was a totally selfish thought. *Why would Elena do this to me?*

I had little reason to think I was in any way special to her. She'd been kind to me, and she had been generous in her help. But perhaps she was kind to anyone who paid any attention to her. She had been reciprocating my appreciation. A close professional colleague might do as much.

In my frustration, I searched repeatedly on all the social media platforms I'd tried before for the new name she'd used in her sig. I found no presence whatever. She was more anonymous than before. I did find the origin of her surname, which might be her father's or her husband's, dating back at least as far as the Bogomils in Bulgaria. The root word means "pray to God" and became the name of a medieval, heretical Christian sect that despised the materialism of the Church and lived as impoverished separatists. The most devout among them retreated to cloistered communities. Many who weren't sheltered behind stone walls were hunted down, tried and tortured, and burned at the stake.

So much for another topic of curiosity and online search.

Defiance was in her heritage!

I wanted to express my support, perhaps offer to send her money. I'd check the urge to be angry with her. I had no right to expect my feelings outweighed her love of family or her sense of duty. They needed help, and she went. My thinking her selflessness was foolish was selfishly foolish for me, and yet I'd have to overcome my resentment of her to write a reply that didn't read like an insane rant.

Now, at least I understood the time difference. By now it was late morning for me, so probably after bedtime for her. I had an excuse for not composing my reply right away.

"Sleep on it" was the time-honored advice of wise counselors, although at the time I had none. I told myself, *Your thoughts will be clearer and kinder in the morning. Who do I think I am, and what to her?* I've invented this relationship because, even though the pandemic is long past in the minds of many, I'm in self-imposed lockdown. I'm poring over a dead fellow's diary, himself an unemotional dullard who seems to have even less imagination than I do about what to do with his precious life.

# Exchanged Messages

## Jonathan's Journal

Elena,

Your news was a shock. It seems only yesterday I was seeing TV news reports from Kiev, the American correspondent describing the explosions of missile attacks in real time. Then footage of apartment buildings reduced to rubble, sometimes showing fatalities, those segments prefaced by warnings of "graphic content." But more recently, the scenes of devastated neighborhoods have shifted to Gaza, as if the conflict in your valiant country longer commands urgent attention.

Watching those clips reminded me of video reports from Syria and the bombings there. I didn't pay much attention at the time, hardly suspecting there would be so much more of the same to come.

I remember particularly the scare about the

Russian attacks and then occupation of the Zaporizhzhia nuclear power generation station. There has been no recent news of it at all here. The US viewing public had to be reminded that Chernobyl lies within your borders, and it was mismanagement from Moscow that brought on the tragedy, dating from the days before Ukrainian independence.

The reports we get now are briefs on Russian attacks, almost like scores of sporting events, which must surely be serious, but mostly of abortive peace negotiation attempts, so aligned with Putin's war aims that the proposals seem more like dictated surrender terms for Ukraine.

Realizing I knew so little of your situation, I dug into current reports online, and I read now, belatedly, that much of the struggle in the Donbas has been trench warfare — still going on — and I was reminded of my imaginings about Fred on the Western Front, as well as my recent understanding that trench warfare had been the order of the day against the Ottoman Turks in the push north of Basra just prior to Fred's arrival in country.

What a cruel and wasteful way to resolve anything!

My heart goes out. "Thoughts and prayers" has become such a cliché, but please know that you and yours are on my mind continually now. Since your layoff from the library job, I have been reluctant to ask if you need funds, but please let me know how best to send support.

I will press on with my studies, mainly because I must fill my head and the days. Frankly, I'd been ignoring the news, scanning only headlines on my email feeds from the major outlets. Now I will pay closer attention!

Don't fret about me, but do send brief notes as you can to let me know you and yours are staying safe.

Jon

I HAD her reply the next morning, which would have been early evening her time.

Jonathan,

Rest assured our circumstances are not dire. Our neighborhood has not been hit. The apartment building is of recent construction, and the amenities are comfortable. In the last year, supply chains have improved, and there is food in the markets. Desired items are not always in stock, but there is almost always something to fill our plates. We retreat into the local subway station on hearing the alert sirens, and I imagine what it must have been like in London in the second great war during those V-2 rocket attacks.

It's the old story of long periods of boredom punctuated by brief bouts of terror. The boredom is more tense and difficult to endure in wartime because at any moment the terror may come.

It has surprised me how resilient the children are. They know joy, hurt, and fear vividly. They experience eagerness, but they don't have expectations because they have not learned to plan. So they are more capable of joy in the moment, even when we're hunkered down in the shelter. Worry and persistent anxiety afflict us old planners who are burdened with thinking through all the possibilities.

Our people endure as the English did back then. Putin can't break our spirit.

The reactor scare was indeed chilling. It was before I returned here, but people still talk about it. I can believe Putin would threaten to damage or destroy it, but I never thought he would be foolish enough to actually do it. I worried at the time about the much more likely scenario of a mishap, especially amid the chaos of war. And of course Chernobyl is a deep and lasting wound.

We have enough money for groceries, rent, and utilities. Really, the infrastructure here is still quite good. We've been high tech for a while. Our telephone and Internet run on fiber-optic and microwave.

Your donations to Doctors Without Borders and Save the Children will help the cause of peace and recovery both here and in Gaza, hopefully when access is permitted.

Like you, I need things to fret about besides current events. I append my report on Satara. I was happy to have an interesting assignment!

I too have become engrossed in Fred's diary. Thank you for sharing it. I will have more to give you.

Fondly,

Elena

# Musketry School

## Jonathan Comments on Fred's Diary

As I said at the outset, the task I'd set for myself in studying Fred's diary was reading between the lines. As a historian, that's much of what we do. Yes, we gather what facts we can find in the existing documentation. If the events are recent, having occurred within a generation or two, oral histories and even interviews can help give subjective points of view to the stories. Fred's diary is an oral history, a first-person account, which he bothered to write down. But I think it would be a mistake to assume he's simply reciting facts.

Now that I'd had hopeful news of Elena, I redoubled my efforts to delve deeper into Fred's story. I felt some personal attachment to it, although other than the book being one of Mum's treasured collectibles, I still assumed it had no place in our family's history. You might say my renewed attention began to draw more heavily on my professional skills and analytical methods. Historians fret a lot about relying on primary sources, remaining skeptical about subsequent writers who offer their interpretations of those sources. But if you go back far enough into the past, even the earliest documents are likely to be copies, summaries, or even revised editions. For example, not a single word of the Holy Bible can be regarded as original, unless you subscribe to the notion that Almighty God dictated it or at least permitted only the corrections to survive.

Throughout my career, some scholars in my own field of art history have built the whole of their reputations on their carefully considered opinions. There's really no other way to get at the truth. We're rather like Talmudic scholars who take sides to argue heatedly until they decide they've exhausted the topic.

But I've always been uneasy about theses from historical analysis that, in the absence of undisputed fact, are based on plausibility. And many scholarly opinions are based on only that. Their premise seems to be that if humans usually act rationally and in the best interests of themselves or at least of their tribes, filling gaps with the most logical motivations and realistic outcomes must be the closest we can come to anything called *truth*.

History is written by the victors, or at least by the survivors. But survivors, as a rule, may not have lessons to learn or to impart. The dead won't have the opportunity to recover from their fatal mistakes. Having made fewer errors, or perhaps none at all, survivors are the least qualified to tell what happened. They may have no understanding whatever of why they prevailed! Righteousness might be cited in their legends, but as practical advice it's worse than useless.

As I dove back in, I understood I'd be making inferences — plausible guesses, at best — about Fred's character and his decisions. A surmise might make for good storytelling, but I'd be wrong to suppose I'd fleshed out this man's life from a century ago. The risk was, the better I thought I knew Fred, the more speculative I'd allow myself to be. Imagining what could go in those white spaces, unrestrained by academic cautions, was amusing. And even if horribly wrong, I had the luxury of never having to apologize to him.

> After my discharge from hospital, I started on a free musketry course on the 5th of June.

I've theorized he was already a riflery instructor, and I believe that's why he was eventually promoted to sergeant. I'll hazard some further guesses here. Yes, he'd been discharged from the clinic, but he might not yet be considered fully fit for routine service. Or he was simply awaiting the orders for his next posting. His mentioning the course was "free" might be telling. If this program were mandatory military training, there wouldn't be a cost, so it would seem a voluntary option.

> The country around Satara was full of large and small game and I had several interesting hunting experiences.

As well, if the musketry course were free, he would not only have access to weapons but also to ammunition. He might otherwise have had to pay for any ammo he used in his off-duty hours.

Here is his first reference to hunting as sport. He did

say he'd hunted when he was stationed in Basra, but there is the strong suggestion any supplement to his rations there would have been a welcome alternative to eating horses and camels when there was little else. It's difficult today in the post-industrial age, when meat is so plentiful that its wastes are threatening the health of the planet, to appreciate and excuse Fred's eagerness to hunt. Blood sports were after all an unquestioned privilege of the landed English aristocracy. I recall reading that Prince Philip complained he had to eat so much venison every time the family stayed at Balmoral.

I seriously doubt, from the tone of his screed, that Fred's social standing at home was among the idle rich. He's too grasping, for one. But there being no stigma to hunting in his background, it's understandable he'd consider it a pleasurable pastime. As well, whether then or now, let's not forget that the ethic of hunters everywhere is to eat what you kill, trophy hunters excepted, often to the scorn of their peers.

> I made friends of two fox terriers belonging to the musketry school, which accompanied me on my evening rambles through the jungle at the foot of the Ghats. Although they are plucky in other directions, they always shouted fear and warned me when in the vicinity of a snake. I saw several specimens. One was over twelve feet, which glided very rapidly through the trees.

Ah, the terrier, the tenacious small dog that will stop at nothing! Named *fox* for the quarry it was bred to fetch. Once again, we're talking about the sporting pastimes of the landed gentry. Somewhat larger dogs, the hounds, lead the hunt for the wily little fox, which will outrun the mounts of the hunters at full gallop until it begins to tire. At that point, the fox dives into a hole in the ground, or in a hollow fallen tree, for cover. That hole might be its den or burrow, the exhausted thing thinking it has made it safely home. The fox terrier has been riding happily in the saddlebag of a hunter's mount, thence to leap out and "go to ground," after the shivering fox.

Traditionally, it was common practice to crop the tails of those dogs to serve as a handy way of pulling them out of the hole as they clutched the prey in their clenched jaws. The Jack Russell terrier is a popular breed, slightly smaller than its progenitor the wire fox terrier, a finely crafted mix of crafty genes pioneered in the early 1800s by the Reverend John Russell, specifically to optimize its size and abilities for fox hunting.

Mum had a male Jack as a constant companion before she came to live with me. The little critter would nip at the heels of any man who came within two yards of her. A German shepherd could not have been a better protector!

> On one occasion, I came across a pig shooting party. Some of the pigs broke cover, and suddenly I discovered a large herd charging down the hillside on my path. I hastened out of their way and counted twenty-four, which passed me within a few yards. There were several large-tusked boars among them.

For a fellow who brags about his hunting experience, his terminology here is not precise. A boar is a wild male swine that has not been castrated. The pigs he refers to, if they were not simply sows and young swine of these boars, were likely pygmy hogs, the smallest wild pigs in the world, which are indigenous to India and today endangered. Having noted the distinction in my brief search, I see that the two types do run together and might even interbreed. Domesticated pigs would not be among the animals the shooting party was stalking. A wild boar, which might weigh as much as 300 pounds, would be nasty and dangerous when threatened.

> A few miles out of Satara, there were numerous peafowl and on fair Sunday mornings, staff sergeant started off about 2:30 a.m. on cycles in quest of these birds for the job. We were armed with a rifle shot guns. It was a lovely piece of country with a river running through a refreshing valley, and early in the morning several pea fowl were to be seen feeding in the monkey nut fields. The peacock is a wily bird. It required some maneuvering to get within range.
>
> One morning, I was stalking some birds and whilst going through a deep end I encountered several large monkeys in the wild fruit trees overhead. They made uncomfortable threatening grimaces at me. On each occasion we went out, we brought back two birds. They were good eating, but we had to prepare them for the pot ourselves. The native cooks would not cook them, as they were sacred birds, and one morning a Sepoy guard doing duty at our station discovered we were plucking our bag, and they came outside our bungalow and paid their reverence to the dead birds.

As I began to read this, I assumed Fred's terminology was once again inaccurate. I was expecting him to be hunting banties, or jungle fowl, a type of small, wild chicken common to that part of the world. But when he mentions peacock, he got my ire up, and I realize his reference to peafowl is to the colorful male with the glorious, multicolored tail-feather display and the dull-colored peahen. Yes, a peacock, like its relative the wild tom turkey, is indeed a wily bird. To this day, hunters learn to imitate their mating gobble by blowing on birdcalls, but no matter how skillful they become as turkey musicians, they complain they may pass an entire day in the forest and get a rare, fleeting look at only one bird. It's no surprise at all that the locals would strongly disapprove, even be horrified, at Fred's willingness to kill such a gorgeous creature. Of course, given the shooting habits of his countrymen, he'd regard the brightly regaled male pheasant as game for the pot.

> A party of staff sergeants went out to this peafowl country one Wednesday afternoon following our success and had a very uncomfortable time. Over two hundred natives from an adjoining village molested them, and they were unable to shoot.

Two facts are evident here. Fred now considered staff sergeants his peers. Even if he didn't yet hold that rank, having passed through the musketry course, his was an instructor now. And news of their killing peacocks gave the locals who were not serving in the British Indian forces another reason to resent the occupiers.

> On our journey out one morning soon after dawn, we met a party of natives who had just killed a large boar pig, which had been raiding their village plantations. It was a gory spectacle. The whole of the men belonging to a small village armed with spears turned out for the hunt at 3 a.m. with all the village dogs. The dogs were so gored by the boars' tusks that several had their rib bones exposed, and the boar was covered with spear marks.

In this encounter, the locals were not hunting the boars for food but to prevent further decimation of their crops. And if those hunters were Muslim, they might not eat their kill in any case.

> Although I had difficulty obtaining ammunition, I occasionally got sufficient cartridges to carry a shotgun on my evening rambles. I shot a few hares, which were small compared with their English cousins, and I also shot a four-foot two-inch rat snake, the skin of which I preserved and sent home.

How Fred would have gained access to a shotgun is an open question. The weapon would not be among the standard issue firearms in musketry school. And the rarity of the ammo suggests he would have to purchase the shells. For British expats, it's possible the shotgun would be household weapon for personal defense.

Until now, Fred hasn't mentioned taking souvenirs, nor anyone he'd want to buy for. Like the handsome leather-bound diary itself, he might have intended the snakeskin as a prize he'd show after-dinner guests in his retirement. Unlikely that his wife would be at all impressed with it or that this would be the kind of gift he'd send as a first offering.

He'd mentioned that his brother Henry had seen duty in the Balkans. Plausible here, Henry had either been wounded or discharged and returned to Exeter, and Fred wanted to impress or cheer him.

> Satara is a noted place for snakes. I saw several cobras and killed one with a stick near our quarters. The next morning, the whole of the carcass was devoured by kite hawks, which are the scavengers of India.

Happening on several of those aggressive, venomous snakes would be a sobering moment. Killing one with a stick would be either brave or rash. Natives who have experience with the creatures may have learned to snatch them skillfully by the neck, just behind the head, and then throw them into a bucket they keep in the home for just such occurrences. The kite hawk is as big as an eagle, dusky brown and robust, and might be mistaken for one. Like ravens and other scavengers, they are often seen in pairs.

> I witnessed an exciting battle between a mongoose and a cobra, which were caught and brought into our quarters by a native. It was a fierce fight. The cobra entwining the mongoose, and the two rolled over in a ball, but the mongoose eventually finished off the cobra.

Aha! This native fellow must have known how to grab that snake. How he managed to chase or entice a mongoose into the bunkhouse is anybody's guess. The Indian equivalent of a cock fight ensued, and Fred's penchant for wagering would have been teased. Hopefully the native remained sober and attentive in the unlikely event the snake prevailed.

Bored soldiers. How else to pass the time?

# Secunderabad

## Elena's Notes and Jonathan's Reply

I RECEIVED this note from Elena, who had become more closely drawn into the collaboration, likewise fascinated now that she possessed her own copy of the text.

She sent a surprising personal note.

Esteemed Professor,

We haven't shared much with each other on a personal level. You've told me a bit about your dear Mum, and although tending to her must have been a chore at times, that you did it and undertook it without complaint suggest you were closer to her than you've said. As for me, I've held back the most relevant information about my Ukrainian background and the career I followed until recently.

My ancestors farmed in Eastern Ukraine and spoke Russian. My father was a schoolteacher, won scholarships for his advanced studies, and retired from Cherkasky State Technical University as a professor of mathematics. I went there as an undergraduate, then on to the Military Institute of the State University of Telecommunications. My concentrations were in languages — bilingual Ukrainian-Russian, some Polish and Italian — as well as in military history. I chose Italian not only because I longed to travel there but also because my subject area drew me to the ruthlessness of Machiavelli and the Medicis.

My military expertise is in naval warfare.

After graduation, my skills were particularly attractive to the US diplomatic corps, and I was employed as a translator, interpreter, and analyst at the American embassy in Kiev. I worked there for ten years under Ambassador Marie Yovanovitch, although at my level I didn't report to her directly.

You mention Syria. The conflict raged there during my diplomatic service, the uprising against Assad having begun in March 2011. The Obama and Biden administrations supported a series of peace negotiations begun around 2017. The US, particularly Secretary of State Clinton, wanted Assad gone but US forces held back from fighting alongside rebels who in turn were allied with ISIS. Indeed, US fighter jets conducted targeted bombing runs on jihadist camps and weapons supplies. Some historians are already claiming that US lack of military commitment created a vacuum the Russians were only too eager to fill. Now, with the benefit of hindsight and the context you and I have been discussing, Russians' lust for access to the Med should have been seen as a rehearsal for their incursion into Crimea. You may not remember that some analysts insisted that the Soviet designs on Afghanistan had everything to do with building a pipeline between Caspian Sea oilfields and the Persian Gulf.

I also endured and advised during the nonsense that preceded the fall of pro-Russian President Yanukovych, the financial crisis of 2008, and then Poroshenko. For a time there, optimism ran high that we'd soon be joining the EU and NATO. Free-world investment capital would gush in, and the Western investment bankers would help us restructure our national assets and manage our huge debt.

It was not to be. During the first Trump administration, the ambassador was recalled abruptly, and shortly thereafter, I resigned. I applied for employment at RAND in Santa Monica, and after a promising round of interviews I moved there. But I must have missed a step somewhere, because the offer never came through. I took it harder than I should have, and I decided my next position would not be in service of government policy. I thought a job as interpreter for the Getty Foreign Scholars program would be ideal. I'd be serving visiting scholars like yourself who came seeking rare books on art history!

That one didn't work out either, and I landed at the desk where you found me. It wasn't highly paid, and it was certainly boring at times, but the occasional intriguing inquiry made it fun. (Yes, yours!) I never regarded that job as anything but temporary, but then the situation back home went from interesting to dire.

So I too am a caregiver, and I will serve as long as I am needed.

Your colleague, admirer, and friend,

Elena.

I replied eagerly:

Elena,

Your brief, confessional bio fascinates me, not least of all your secret love of art history and Renaissance Italy. Although I also resolved to visit there someday, my stay-at-home inclinations and responsibilities have prevented me.

Naval warfare!? Oh my. Perhaps you can tell me more about the buildup of the German sub fleet and its stunning impact on both world wars. Does your expertise extend to present-day strategic thinking? Perhaps I shouldn't ask.

Now that you are, as I am, dug into Fred's narrative, I look forward to your insights!

Please stay safe. Hugs and kisses to you and yours. I will certainly donate to those assistance programs, but I trust you will not hesitate to let me know whenever you need more direct support.

You are likewise in my heart, I assure you,

Jon

## Jonathan's Journal

It seemed doubly ironic Fred was sent to Secunderabad. Having recovered from diphtheria, here he was being sent across the country to another hotbed of the disease. He would have some acquired immunity for a time, but had his caregivers so advised him? Surely the rumor mill among the soldiers would have alerted him to the situation where he was going.

As well, his posting on arrival proved to be a second paid vacation. Even though his stint at the musketry school may have been an official assignment, from his description of those shooting expeditions, he had a lot of enjoyable free time. But no sooner did he get to his new posting after the long train ride than he had to wait for new orders. The army hadn't yet decided where he would be needed next. He was off, presumably with his usual chums, on further adventures.

> Having been at Satara for over two months, the musketry course ended, and I left for Secunderabad on the 16th July. The thirty-six-hour train journey was comfortable, four to a compartment with a sleeping berth for each. We travelled via Puna and Wadi. Large numbers of natives appear to travel. Every train station was packed.
>
> The country had a similarity most of the way down, long cultivated plains running away from the Western Shoals, but on entering the state of Hyderabad, the scenery became more varied. Here were large lakes and enormous boulders balancing one on top of another looking as though they had been placed in position by human force. The Nizam of Hyderabad's palace with its white walls and gilded

towers standing against the blue Indian sky was an oriental picture.

On our arrival at Secunderabad we reported to the officer commanding the Leave Depot Trimulgherry [Tirumalagiri], who turned out to be Maj. Robert Clarke of the 4th Devons. We then handed over our rifles and equipment to lead a pleasurable time, free of duties, pending instructions to proceed on leave.

Secunderabad was a large military station lying outside the city of Hyderabad. The permanent military quarters were pleasantly situated, and every possible comfort appeared to be provided to make soldiering in India tolerable. We expeditionary troops were, however, quartered in temporary bungalows outside the station.

The history of Hyderabad in this era, and the development of the rail service there, was nothing like I'd expected. I had assumed the British were responsible for construction of tracks throughout India, the main purpose to transport troops and military supplies, also for carrying products of agriculture and mining to commercial centers and ports. Indeed, before the 1870s, the Trimulgherry depot was little more than a military siding. The Hyderabad region had not yet been connected to the emerging Great Indian Peninsula Railway (GIPR).

But the reasons for this apparent disconnection had nothing to do with the region's unimportance. For centuries, Hyderabad had been governed autonomously, almost a country within a country. It was a wealthy and proud principality, ruled by Arab royalty of Turkish descent.

*Nizam* in Arabic means "organizer." The populace was predominantly Muslim. The region was not consolidated with the Indian Union until after the country's independence from the British in 1948, and even then only after armed conflict with the forces of the national government.

Although Hyderabad persisted in asserting its unique identity, the Nizam and the aristocracy preferred instead to pledge their loyalty to the British Crown. In 1870, the Nizam helped underwrite the construction of railway connections between Trimulgherry at Secunderabad with the GIPR network, including extensive passenger and freight lines, along with a grand railway station. To this day, Secunderabad Station is about three city blocks in length, as immense as any in a European capital.

When inaugurated in 1874, the new line was named the Nizam's Guaranteed State Railway. Its three-day grand opening was celebrated by British and Indian color guard parades, fireworks, and rocket displays, attended by both local and colonial authorities in dress uniform.

In short, the railway was intended not only as a crucial military asset for colonial forces but also a gift of ready and regular passenger transportation from the Nizam to his people. Rather than all in uniform, the crowds on those trains were locals, tradesmen, and families bustling about on their daily business.

> I met many acquaintances here, and we made the best of our time, but the heat was intense with mosquitos and sand fleas very troublesome. It was impossible to rest without the protection of a mosquito net.

Fred was more gregarious these days. This quiet fellow

was coming out of his shell. His recent promotions may have helped his self-esteem.

Mosquito nets were mandatory not just to prevent the annoyance of disturbed sleep. Malaria has been a common affliction throughout the world, even in locations with moderate temperatures. The tiny insects breed prolifically wherever there is standing water. And especially in tropical climates, they carry other parasitic diseases, including dengue, zika, chikungunya, and yellow fevers, as well as various forms of viral encephalitis.

Mosquitos have killed more humans than all the wars in history.

> One did very little for themselves, each sergeant had a native servant, and when you woke in the morning, you found you were being shaved by a native barber standing over you, razor in hand. This was generally followed by Bombay oysters (raw eggs and vinegar).
>
> Whilst at Secunderabad I saw the 4th and 8th Native Calvary Races, which were held about four miles out. The going was very hard over a 2-1/2-mile course, and the betting was done by totalisator.

Fred's fondness for horses certainly went back as far as his days in the cavalry units assigned to the southern seacoast of England. But it's odd he never refers to a horse by name. He'd have had a regular mount on his daily patrols.

Back in England, horse racing was as popular among the middle and upper classes as was hunting as a pastime. From context, I figured the totalizator that so impressed Fred was little more than an adding machine in those days, a rudimentary mechanical computer.

The totalizator, I learned, was an electromechanical scoreboard used to display betting odds and results in horse racing in real time. In former days, bets recorded by bookies were posted on a big chalkboard, or tote board. The odds of winning for each numbered horse are shown on the board, updated in the moments before the race until betting is closed, then after the race as results. The odds determine what shares (as a ratio $x:y$) of the betting pool each of the three winning horses (and their wagerers) will earn.

Fred's fascination with the device made me wonder whether he was an accountant by profession.

*Like so many of my countrymen, I'd caught the bug of betting on horse races. As a cavalryman, I thought myself a keen judge of horseflesh. A glance at the withers on a tour through the stable and I could tell which steed would prevail.*

*In England, having a flutter on the races and shooting pheasant on the wing each have their seasons. Beside the Bible in the most respectable homes, bedside reading was either handicap tables in the* Turf Guide *or adverts for tweeds and shotguns in* Country Life. *Either pastime might be canceled in the event of drenching rain or socked-in fog, the benefit being perpetual greenery everywhere. It was likewise verdant in India but accompanied by stifling heat and all manner of vermin, some annoying, others poisonous.*

*As to hazarding a wager on the horses, to a chap in my circumstances, the risk was negligible. Even during these rather peaceful postings, we'd endure far graver risks from unexploded ordnance or knife-wielding saboteurs. And whether deployed in theatre or on leave as we were now, we received duty pay fairly regularly, and there were dashed few things to spend it on that cost more than a pittance. So putting one's whole purse on the nose — even losing it all — was cause for little worry. Come the very least or worst, we were sure to receive our rations next mealtime. Or if on leave, one could always cadge a few shillings from a mate.*

> I made many rambles into the neighboring country and visited the adjoining villages and bazaars. One large village, which contained some fine oriental buildings, was void of inhabitants. I afterwards discovered that it had been plague-ridden. It was interesting to see the natives tapping the tall palm trees for toddy (a native liquor).

Fred isn't referring to the Spanish Flu, which was devastating, but to the equally virulent Bubonic Plague, which had originated in China, spread by infected rats and transported by shipping, with an outbreak in Bombay in 1896, killing millions in India, especially in areas with poor sanitation. But by 1917, the angel of death from what became known as the Third Pandemic had finally passed over the subcontinent.

# Calcutta

## Jonathan Comments on Fred's Diary

After a fortnight at Trimulgherry Secunderabad, a small party of us left on the 31st July for a month's leave at Calcutta [Kolkata].

Calcutta, on the eastern border with the state of Burma (now Bangladesh and Myanmar), had been the capital of the British Indian Empire until 1911. When Fred was there, the capital had recently moved to Delhi.

I'd learned so little of India in my education. Calcutta was a name to me only because Mother Teresa had served impoverished children there. My visions of the place therefore pictured barefoot children shuffling though the dusty streets of lurid slums in perpetual days of sweltering heat.

In fact, the city is vibrant, populated by millions, and has been a crucial trade hub for centuries. The British East India Company began to trade here in 1640. It was a multicultural center of learning, today hosting fourteen universities, many of them judged among the best in the world.

> Leaving Secunderabad Station at 9 a.m., we travelled through the independent state of Hyderabad on the Nizam's State Railway. Crossing the British frontier, we arrived at the railway junction Bezwada [Vijayawada] at 4:30 p.m. Here we had an eight-hour wait. We dined that evening in the Indian Medical Service, hosted by its director, who had attended the Medical Conference at Exeter in 1911. He was very conversant with the Ever Faithful and its neighborhood. After a good meal, we laid on the open platform, the waiting room being too hot and vermin-ridden. Sleep was impossible owing to the multitude of natives and intermittent heavy showers. We left at 3:30 a.m. on the Calcutta rail.

Vijayawada is hundreds of miles to the southwest of Kolkata. Fred's train was heading southeast from Hyderabad (designated as the state of Telangana in 2014), toward the Eastern Shoals, before wending its way along the coast, northeast to Calcutta. By "British frontier" in this case, he must be referring to a past boundary between the independent state of Hyderabad and the region of Andhra Pradesh (statehood, 1956). His destination is more than six hundred miles distant at the eastern edge of the Bengal region.

Here is one of Fred's several fond references to his hometown. He's proud of his heritage. Recall the episode when he told of meeting a school chum on shipboard. "Ever Faithful" is synonymous with Exeter, as the Big

Apple is for New York, the Windy City for Chicago. The original motto in Latin is *Semper Fidelis,* more familiar to Yanks as the credo of the Marine Corps. Exeter won that honorific for the city's loyalty to the Crown during the English Civil War in 1660. And endearing it further to Fred and his mates, the Devonshire Regiment adopted it as its pledge for serving with enduring loyalty.

> Daybreak brought us into fertile valleys running through hills covered with tall, stately palm trees. The principal crops were rice, cotton and tea, all deriving full benefit from the recent monsoons. The fields were mostly edged with coconut and toddy trees, and the ponds along the railway were covered with beautiful water lilies. The rice fields were irrigated by natives continuously dipping water from canals into small channels running through the fields. Numbers of men and women were standing knee-deep in mud and water hand-planting the rice. The villages were picturesque, with their round homes thatched with large palm leaves.

Now that Fred is officially on leave, he can enjoy being a tourist, traveling as an emissary of king and country. Likely, Fred and his mates traveled in uniform, but for the time being they wouldn't be parading around on guard or supporting the locals with heavy-handed peacekeeping.

> We eventually crossed numerous waterways forming part of the delta of the Ganges and ran into Howrah Station, Calcutta, at noon on the 2nd August.

Fred's reference to the Ganges Delta is to the confluence of several rivers in the region. Kolkata is on the Hooghly, which flows from the Padma to the north, a major tributary of the Ganges, with its headwaters in the Himalayas, ultimately depositing its broad, fertile delta on the Bay of Bengal. The mouth of the Padma, now in Bangladesh, might be considered the eastern edge of the delta region formed by the confluence of the Ganges, Brahmaputra, and Meghna rivers.

> We reported to the garrison quartermaster, who allotted us accommodation at the Soldiers' Club Hastings which was situated about a mile out of Calcutta on the Circular Road facing the Maidan. The arrangements were excellent. Each bed had an electric fan, everything was scrupulously clean, and they gave us good food.
>
> The following morning we spent sightseeing. We visited the site of the Black Hole of Calcutta, adjoining the G.P.O., the old building having been demolished. A stone tablet denotes the spot. The European portion of the city is elegantly built, especially the government home and Chowringhee Road (the Oxford Street of Calcutta), which faces the exclusive and well-kept Maidan. Leaving this one, we immediately entered the native portion, which is a striking contrast with its narrow and insanitary bazaars and hovels and bullocks and goats lying about the streets.

Again with "we," the newly garrulous Fred hangs among his peers, typically in a group of three. His rank qualifies him for more courteous and commodious treatment by obsequious locals. He will remark repeatedly about more comfortable circumstances, now that he is effectively "on holiday."

Perhaps an Englishman's fascination with meticulously manicured gardens explains his admiration for Calcutta's Maidan Esplanade, an extensive central park that, then as now, provides multiple playing fields for concurrent matches of rugby football and cricket.

Reading this and imagining Fred tearing up as he felt blessed to be an ocean away from the Desert Hell, I flashed on my fond memories of Mum taking me on walks in Hyde Park. I was just old enough to read. I announced in the full voice I should have used for recitals of memorized sonnets the polite advisory on a cautionary sign:

**Any gentleman whose dog fouls the footway shall be liable for the sum of £5.**

Have they since updated the sexed reference to the canine's guardian? Did they increase the penalty amount to keep pace with inflation and the conversions from pounds to euros and back again?

The spring flowers were pretty, and the green carpet of closely cropped grass was moist from recent watering. Mum pulled me away when I tried to test whether the soggy soil would take lasting impressions of my Start-Rite shoes.

At a place I later learned to call Speakers' Corner, a man in a trench coat and dusty bowler was standing on a platform at eye level above a dozen variously listless and rapt onlookers. When I felt the tug of her hand as I lingered to listen, she pulled me away again.

"Why can't I…"

She grabbed my shoulder and turned me to face her as

she bent to whisper, "Because that man is a communist!" And she led me into the zebra crossing and over to Marks & Spencer, where she bought me a scratchy wool cardigan and didn't scold when I blackmailed her for a sweet.

Oxford Street is that same shopping district in London, famously home to High Street retailers. However, there is also an Oxford Street in Exeter. Since Fred's comments regarding Exeter seem both possessive and provincial, I'm wondering whether he's intending the audience for his journal to be locals back home, perhaps close family. Many of his jottings here read like postcards, intended to fascinate but mostly to impress.

As to the Black Hole of Calcutta, it was a name to me from early on but nothing more. A bad place no one would ever want to go. None worse, actually. Possibly more horrific than the lowest circle of Dante's Inferno, the dreaded privation of Devil's Island, or a dank, solitary cell at Alcatraz. Not surprising Fred made a point to visit the site and the plaque. He may have been disappointed to see that the despicable torture chamber no longer existed. My research disclosed its legend traces back to conquest of the city by Nawab Siraj-ud-Dowlah in 1756. On one night of terror, the victorious warrior-potentate threw 146 Europeans, including some survivors among the defeated troops led by Lord Clive, into a single cell just twenty-feet square. The next morning, only twenty-three were left alive.

Nevertheless, Clive and allied local forces defeated the vicious fellow the next year, beginning two hundred years of British rule in India, with Calcutta as the seat of the British Raj, and the continued control of trade routes by the East India Company.

The significance of the Black Hole becomes apparent,

not just as an ugly legend, but as a patriotic theme of the Royal Commonwealth.

I can imagine Fred's heart swelling at the thought that he wouldn't have been standing there reading the plaque's inscription were it not for the sacrifice of the Nawab's victims.

> In the afternoon, we visited the Monsoon Races. Calcutta racecourse is considered one of the best in the world. The large grandstand is filled with electric fans, and it is possible to see every inch of the course. The native populations were very enthusiastic gamblers, and all the betting was done by totalisator.

Again, with the totalizator! Fred delighted in the thrill of the odds changing in real time in the breathless seconds before bets were closed and the starting gates opened.

*I won quite a bit of money and the next day sent a bank draft to Mira care of the hospital. I refrained from making my accompanying letter intensely personal, simply conveying my thanks for her care and her kindness. I was, however, hoping she would read my affection between the lines.*

*I hadn't dared to overstep. More important, I didn't want to seem to be making promises I feared I would not be brave enough to keep. I'd asked her once, and she'd been clear enough. Even now, I can't guess her feelings. Perhaps she was being polite and cared little or nothing for me. She may have been intimidated by differences of race or status. She hinted she was pledged, or would be, but not yet. If she'd had someone in mind, she'd not mentioned him. Of course, likewise, I'd shared nothing of myself, only my vague aspirations.*

*Should I have been bolder? Expressed myself with embarrassing frankness?*

*Her vision haunts me. I fear it is a fantasy with no useful purpose or barely possible realization.*

> The city market was large and interesting. Japanese goods were in great prominence. I bought some silk very cheap and sent it home.

*Yes, I broke my silence after what had been more than a year. I sent the beautiful cloth to Sarah with a brief note. I can't recall the message word for word. It must have been, "I saw this and thought you might like it." No apology for my silence. No begging for forgiveness or for a future. I had no right to expect one,. Neither did she!*

*In point of fact, I was feeling guilty about having sent the money to Mira. Throughout my travels, I had resolved not to buy trinkets. Despite my occasional thoughts of home, I was adventuring rather than soldiering. Most of all, I didn't want Sarah to think I was having a jolly time of it. I hadn't been writing. The snakeskin had been for Henry, perhaps to amuse and impress him, my smarter, older brother. I was thankful he'd made it back safely from the fighting in the Balkans. He wouldn't have had much chance to spend his pocket money on snow-covered battlefields. Unaccountably for a native of the North Atlantic, I would much rather endure intense heat than intense cold.*

*Either could kill you just as dead, of course.*

> I spent an afternoon at the Zoological Gardens which contained a wonderful collection, especially the bird life. I also visited the Botanical Garden with its fine specimens of tropical trees.
>
> In the evening, the Maidan, which is about two miles long, becomes animated with sport. The wealthy play rugby football to keep fit, and the native plays with their bare feet. It is a spectacular site to sit on the Maidan and watch the better-class natives taking their evening drive in various elaborate oriental conveyances. The horses were exceptionally fine. A band played in the grounds of the Garden of Eden, which was brilliantly lit up at night.
>
> The Law Courts attracted me on two occasions. It was interesting listening to the native pleaders.

Unquestionably, regardless of other consequences of colonialism, the British Parliamentary legal system did become an enduring legacy for India. Although cultural differences and notions of justice have been enduring, especially between Hindu and Muslim, abiding by secular law has had its unifying, if not egalitarian, effects.

> I also visited the Bengali deaf school. The institution with eighty pupils was run on similar lines to ours. The school principal had visited England, and he gave me a good reception.

"Along similar lines to *ours.*" Hmm. Fred might simply mean that the school followed the English system of years and key stages. Or, much more intriguing, he was alluding to experience he'd had back home with special education for family members. But I still rather doubt he had had children before his first enlistment.

> Returning to the club one afternoon, I walked into a flock of about 200 vultures resting on the Maidan. As I approached, I expected them to rise, but they simply hopped out of my way.

*With selfish aforethought, I had marked my letter to Mira with the return address in care of my 4th Devons at Trimulgherry Station. She wrote back with thanks, but the tone of her letter suggested finality, with no prospect of reunion.*

*Her letter was as cold as mine had been. I suppose I deserved as much.*

# Guest of a Rajah

## Jonathan Comments on Fred's Diary

Since the posting at Trimulgherry, Fred's notes change in tone. He is beginning to get used to being treated as an officer, often in characteristic British luxury. I have to wonder whether these experiences made him think what life might be like here as an aristo expat.

> An evening that will always rest in my memory was one as a guest of Rajah Kumar Nogendro Mullick at his Marble Palace, Calcutta.
>
> A party of about twenty leave men was invited. We drove in a grace through the native quarters, when suddenly we opened out into a gorgeous, illuminated palace, lying back off the road. The grounds in front were studded with marble statues and illuminated fountains. Uniformed bodyguards met us at the gates. We entered the palace up wide marble steps, and in the vestibule stood an enormous statue

of the late Queen Victoria. The palace was built in a square block with a large courtyard in the center.

The whole place was full of marble imported from all parts of the world. Peacocks were roosting on the balconies looking down into the inlaid marble courtyard, in the center of which was an illuminated fountain, with live storks perched on the top. The rooms were spacious, with marble tables, statues, and vases. Most of the walls were inlaid with cultured glass, and from the ceilings of wonderful design, hung rows of massive chandeliers. There was a valuable collection of original paintings by Sumner, Van Dyke, Reynolds, and Rubens, etc. The rajah and his son received us with a few remarks expressing their loyalty and we then sat down to a sumptuous meal. Wines and champagne were ad lib. At that time, these were expensive, as it was difficult to import them into the country.

We were afterwards shown into a large thickly carpeted room well-furnished with comfortable lounges. Each guest was presented with a buttonhole, and a group of Bengali dancing girls entertained us with their weird dances and songs.

Fred was too modest to describe the dancing as *erotic* or even *exotic*. All he can manage was *weird*. I seriously doubt he was offended!

I had interesting chats with the rajah and his son, who were both educated at English universities.

Here is an implication that Fred himself was a college man. His reciting the famous names of oil painters is further evidence he knew the significance of the rajah's appreciation of and wherewithal to afford fine art.

> We departed at midnight after an enjoyable evening. A rickshaw was provided for each guest, and my boy ran the whole three miles to my quarters without a stop.

Treated as a lord of the Raj!

# Antique Valuation

## Jonathan's Journal

Fred was beginning to seek out curio shops and tourist stops rather than machine gun emplacements and land mines. Would that we lived in a world where soldiers thought of themselves as peacekeepers rather than warfighters and on their foreign postings fretted about where to find gifts that sparkled or smelled.

His obsessions on this phase of his journey made me think again about his diary as a memento, a collectible my mother had valued for reasons I could only guess. Its red-leather spine and gilt lettering did make an impression on the shelf. If that were how she valued it, perhaps she never opened it, much less attempted to read the calligrapher's tangled cursive. She could be forgiven for being an avid collector, regardless of monetary valuations. It focused her mind. In her sunset years when she lived with me here, her eyesight was failing, so even if this soldier's story had not engaged her, gazing at its clippings might have been all she could manage. I never saw her touch it though.

When I happened upon the book three months after her passing last year, I had been in the process of cataloging her things. She had not been one for recordkeeping, but then a binder I found labeled "Valuations," which had not been maintained. Dad must have made those neat, early entries years ago, before his wife had managed to fill their flat to overflowing with old white people's stuff. Here was an inventory of her collectibles. Photos, clippings, and printouts of ads and sales listings. I doubt he cared about any of those things individually. His concerns would have been more about how much insurance to carry. If there were a fire or theft, he wouldn't feel loss of the item. But he'd want to be sure he was compensated for the full amount he'd spent or even more because, if rare, those things would have appreciated in value.

Dad was the organized one, his discipline no doubt informing an orderly mind that mulled daily over momentous and monetarily sizable business decisions. The contents of the Valuation ring binder were segregated by colored tabs: Furniture, Silver, Cheese Trays, Scrimshaw, China, Curios, and Horse Buckles.

*Horse buckles?*

Cheese trays seemed odd as well, but I turned first to find out what could possibly have attracted Mum, who as far as knew was no horsewoman, to riding tackle.

Following the tab was a copy of a page from the catalog of *Horse Brass World.*

**Antique pendant-style English horse brass (1840-1914)** A horse-brass pendant is a cast or stamped circle of solid brass about the size of a jar lid. Its top is formed in a loop, which resembles an old bottle-cap opener (and used as such in more recent times).

> Dating from the late 1700s in England, these buckles were heavy-duty fasteners on the bridles of dray horses. The center of the circular part is ornamental, possibly dating back to tokens gypsies once affixed to their horses to ward off evil spirits.

Dad had made a photocopy of the brasses they'd collected. However, I never found any of them in the boxes of Mum's things.

These brasses must have once decorated the mounts of British cavalry officers.

All four of those pictured in Dad's inventory bore insignia of the Royal Devons.

Here was my first indication that one or both of my parents had some interest in the military history of Fred's regiment.

This coincidence triggered a memory. I remembered the day Mum bought those horse buckles, which at the time I guessed were fancy bottle-cap openers.

---

I was seven years old when they sent me off to boarding school in Torquay. This was before the onset of my palsy. I was hardly an outgoing child, but I was surely a curious one. I tended to blurt out questions as if thinking to myself out loud. Sometimes I'd get an answer if a respectful adult happened to be standing nearby. As I'd learned at school from studying boys who might intend to do me harm, I was a close observer.

I was home on a half-term summer break, one of the six intervals during the academic year, during which I'd be with my parents in their flat in Kensington.

I was Mum's constant companion during these times. I'd reluctantly tag along on shopping excursions, which were her favorite pastime. On those trips, she'd at least let me wander off to some department of the store that captured my interest, such as fishing and camping gear that I had no opportunity to use but stirred fantasies about "roughing it."

She taught me to play cards while warning me about the perils of gambling. She'd take me to watch tennis matches and cricket games but never football or rugby. I believe I mentioned joining the scouts more than once, but she was wary of "the types who lord over boys." I might have got the chance if I could convince a few chums to join up. Some of my schoolmates no doubt also lived in the environs of London, but there were none I counted as friends.

Dad was often away conducting transactions in distant lands. I recall mention of copper mines in Zaire and a fertilizer plant in India.

When he was home with Mum and me during one of my breaks, he'd organize outings on family weekends as though we did those all the time, a deliberate and well-intentioned effort to introduce normality into a family that was rarely, if ever, close.

This memorable outing on a Saturday morning was a shopping excursion to Portobello Road, the massive open-air flea market in North London. Mum liked going there, obscure curios and collectibles were the reason. For household furnishings, she frequented instead the lavishly adorned shops of exclusive antique dealers. And for dresses, handbags, or shoes — designer emporia.

But on this trip, she may have been scouting items for him.

Dad had no patience with any of her snobbish lady haunts. But the flea market held some intrigue for him, and some of those interests we shared. I coveted toy soldiers and miniature trains. The irony of those choices occurs to me now. Military history must have been one of his. He knew which wars the soldiers had fought in from their uniforms. I liked the ones in the red coats, and he let me know those were the chaps who fought the unruly Americans, losing half the world for King George III. Those brightly painted figures were cast from lead, things you can't buy for kids these days because of the toxicity of both the metal and the paint. Perhaps not aware of the risk back then, Dad bought a dozen riflemen for me, all the vendor had.

When we asked the fellow where we'd find model trains, we learned there were none to be had. The newer electric miniatures were to be found only among the High Street retailers. Preferring to emphasize the prizes in hand, Dad wanted to talk about the soldiers. He counseled, "Those chaps marched in straight lines, fought in formation. It was the old way. The other side would march up to them across a field within firing range. They all go down on their knees and shoot at each other. Had to reload each time. Took bravery and a steady hand. The better marksmen and the more numerous the troops, they'd win the day. Very formal. Ambush? Ungentlemanly! Ridiculous. Plucky Americans refused to fight that way, dressed like ruffians so you couldn't tell 'em from the locals." He sighed and added, "Nothing to be gained by any of it. You won't be having any guns, mind you." And I didn't. Ever.

An item that really held his fascination was a wooden box that opened on a tray of glass lantern slides. These were dim, grayed images captured by some early portable camera circa 1880. The seller informed us these were tourist snaps taken by a British physician on holiday in Switzerland. Dad bought the set. The slides were square, about half the size of a postcard. The slots in the tray were meticulously numbered, and under the lid a likewise numbered list gave the location of each. The slide that he studied most carefully featured a tall stone clock tower in a town center, a horse-drawn trolley pulling away from it, toward the photographer.

"That's the clock tower in Berne!" Dad exclaimed and paused for my reaction as if I'd be impressed. When I didn't react, he explained, "This is where Einstein got his idea. He was on the streetcar, pulling away from the big clock, and it occurred to him time might pass at a different rate for a traveler in motion. He had no experience of that, and it's not something he could have measured that way. But it was a thought experiment, do you see?"

"Sorry, Dad. I don't see at all. We'll have some science next year, I'm told."

He patted me on the shoulder and muttered with a gentle smile, "Time enough for all of that, Son. Get the poetry while you can." He winked. "Might serve you as well later."

He and I had been circulating among the vendors for more than an hour, and I could see he was getting tired. Mum was off by herself. He was happy to walk but had to support his weaker leg with an ebony cane. Tweed trousers and a cardigan with a starched white shirt and an ascot at the neck formed his habitually distinguished look. His full head of hair, worn in a kind of pompadour with brushed-back wings over the ears, was mostly white, flecked with gray.

Seeing he might need a rest, I looked around for Mum, who was nowhere to be seen among the hundreds of eager folks who were milling about.

"Where's Mum?" I asked him.

He chuckled, "You needn't worry. Over the years, I've learned to spot your mother in any crowd."

We didn't find her for another hour. By that time, he'd treated me to a lemon squash, and we'd pored over several displays of rare postage stamps. I didn't mind that we found no more trinkets for me because I had his attention. That was when he talked about Zaire and India, about which he could describe the flora and fauna, but he didn't share details of his purposes in going there.

It was Mum who finally spied us. She rushed up gleefully, carrying one of those shopping bags that look like fish nets. She'd found a silver serving tray, a rosewood box of steak knives (counting five, three short of the full set) with deer-horn handles, and a handful of those shiny brass things.

When he asked her to identify her purchases, she pulled the bag away, saying, "Oh my, I meant to have them wrapped. Your birthday, you see."

His smile wrinkled the crows' feet at the corners of his eyes. "Bless my soul!" he said as if it were news. "Another one already?" Then he turned to me, rested his free hand on my shoulder, and leaned over to confide, "Son, I'll tell you the secret of a long and happy life."

She heard and piped up, "Yes, marry a gorgeous lady who keeps you thinking young!"

He shrugged as if to agree but said to me, "You breathe in, you breathe out. You take one step, you take another. Then you repeat those actions as long as you're able!"

As he cackled, she smirked. She felt her advice was the better plan.

---

Returning to school brought me a special privilege. Dad's driver pulled up to their flat in a Rolls Royce Silver Cloud. Despite the airy suggestion of its model name, the car was as shiny black as the gleam on my father's wingtips. My kit was loaded into the boot, and Dad rode with me all the way. When I asked him why Mum wasn't coming with us, he said, "Just us boys this trip."

Apparently, the car was new. I hadn't been in it, nor was I acquainted with Cyril, our neatly uniformed driver.

"Is this your car, Dad?"

"Company car, mine to use. Day trips and the occasional short stay in Edinburgh, Liverpool, Cardiff."

The backseat was wide and comfy as a couch, the compartment padded and roomy.

I risked a joke. "It's almost as big as Mum's closet!"

My quip landed without offense and brought a mischievous grin. He said, "My chums call it the Roll-a-bed." His chest heaved with a chuckle that ended in a wheeze. He was decked out "to the nines," as he said, in his usual business attire, gray pin-striped suit with vest and gold watch chain, dazzling white shirt with a silk tie. Might have been regimental stripes, but I wouldn't have known.

I sighed with happiness and observed, "It's so nice in here. I suppose Cyril could take you all the way to Africa."

"Hardly, Son. Perhaps possible on a trek, but much too far when urgent matters press. Seas and mountains to cross, you see." He thought for a moment and must have decided I was finally old enough he need not guard the secrecy of his travels. "I fly, do that a lot actually. Company plane, mine to use. Also nicely turned out, like the Rolls. Turboprop, a retrofitted bomber from the war."

He was enjoying his own story now, leaned closer again to gesture with his hands. "Mind you, one doesn't climb stairs to board. When it's time to go, the bomb bay doors open, and a lift descends. Step on, takes you up into the belly of the beast, and there you are. You'd think you were in the dining car of a train or some plush cocktail lounge. And the liquor isn't for parties. Whenever possible, I'm joined by clients, colleagues, advisors. Fill my glass with tonic, no one's the wiser. Let them get pleasantly pissed, and the spirits loosen their tongues. Many a man has given full confession to me at twenty thousand feet."

He caught himself in the revery, which had more to do with his fond memories than any explanation directed at me. He cleared his throat. "Son, I must tell you how proud I am of your performance in your studies. As you say, science is not a preoccupation for you as yet, nor must it be ever. You're bright, and you will find your way, I am sure of it. I insist only that you go where your heart leads you. You are sensible enough not to waste a productive life on idleness and pleasure. Your mother is a woman of the world, enjoys finer things, and we can appreciate her love of beauty. We men though have missions to pursue. I only wish to emphasize there will always be ample funds to support your education until you begin to make your way in the world."

His cough brought up phlegm. He swallowed hard, took a deep breath, and added, "You have the talent. You will learn the discipline. You are sure to succeed at whatever vocation you choose."

It was an impressive speech. He made it sound so final.

"Thank you, Dad. You are so generous with Mum and me. I expect your job must be difficult, many worries for you."

He smiled and relaxed. "Oh, no, I have people who do that for me."

His afterthought was cryptic, but his speech had been more like instruction than sharing. I didn't inquire further when he added, "There's your Uncle Ted. Not a bad chap, but don't seek him out. Don't look to him for guidance. And if he asks for money, don't give it him."

Having delivered his benediction, he said little else for the rest of the trip. His head nodded back, and he began to snore. Sometime later, Cyril asked if we wanted to stop for a sandwich. Dad was still resting peacefully, so unaccustomed to giving orders I simply shook my head, and we motored on.

The greenery of the English countryside. It's ever lush. I miss it.

When we pulled in to the courtyard of the school, Headmaster Albright soon strode out to meet us, engaging Dad in a hearty, congenial handshake.

"So pleased to see you, sir," he said, ignoring me as I clambered out. "To what do we owe the pleasure?"

Dad's voice lowered into the register he used for serious discussion, glanced over at me, and evidently decided, as he'd done in the car, that I was mature enough to hear whatever he had to say. "I want to assure you, Albright, that Jonathan shall be provided for at all events. There's a trust fund. I will send you the details and my letter of authorization to draw upon it. His mother is not to be troubled. She is kind and charming, as you know, but has no head for business." He turned to me, rested a hand on my shoulder in another of his ceremonial gestures, and pronounced, "I'm proud of the boy, and he will make his way. His guidance is in your capable hands."

He shook the capable hands again as if recharging them with his vital energy.

Headmaster smiled sheepishly and could only ask, "May we give you lunch?"

Dad declined, saying, "See to the boy. Business in the city."

He was not one to kiss or hug. He'd imparted his blessing.

Cyril had left my kit on the stoop. As the Rolls sped away, Headmaster put a protective arm around my shoulders and led me inside to a hot lunch in the anteroom of his office.

I was left to my own company. He must have already had his lunch. Before he returned to his desk, he told me where to report to the proctor in the dormitory, and he asked me whether I was looking forward to the coming year.

"Yes, sir. Thank you, sir."

The day's events had been bewildering, but I'd been told everything would be all right for a long time to come.

Mutton stew. Hearty but not a meal I would be eager to have again.

---

Two of my young mates had seen me get out of the car and no doubt noted the deference the administrator had accorded my father.

It was afternoon break. As I tossed my kit onto the bunk to which I was assigned, Pickering, perched on his, spoke up eagerly, "Baggett-Smith's uncle has a car like that. He says they call it the 'black bedpan.'" He and Donaldson, who was leaning down like a hovering demon from the top bunk, didn't bother to stifle their giggles.

I offered, "He calls his the Roll-a-bed. I don't know why. It might be useful for camping trips, but he says it's a business vehicle."

Donaldson, who was two years older and thought himself wise, chimed in, "Not for sleeping. For shagging. Odds are he's got something on the side."

"I don't believe it has a running board," I said as I unzipped my bag and began to unpack.

Their giggles became hysterical. Top bunk jumped down, barely missing me, and they ran from the room.

---

I was fourteen. Weeks after I returned to year nine of senior boarding, Headmaster Albright told me my father had died at the desk in his office. Mum had informed the school I was not to return home. There was to be no service. I learned later she'd had him cremated and then set off on a cruise of the Aegean.

Headmaster inquired whether I wished for leave. I didn't know what to say. Bereavement was not a thing to me. My father was off on another trip, this time without promise of return. A phone call was duly made to Mum to confirm that I should stay. When the receiver was handed to me, I asked, "What about Uncle Ted?"

She replied tersely, "Who told you there's an Uncle Ted?"

I said, "Dad says he's a topping fellow but not to seek his advice."

"Did he say why?"

"He has commitments." It was a guess, but any man of business must've.

"Jonathan, his commitments do not include to you or to me. You're best off where you are. Work to be done, right? That's how you are to honor him. Be about your father's business."

I doubt she knew she was quoting Jesus. I'd have willingly obeyed, but I had no idea what my father's business was.

She may have informed Ted of Dad's passing. But she never told me of any contact with him, and his name was never mentioned during all the time she lived with me. There was no record of him among her things, and all I had was a name. Theodore Worthington? Might as easily be Edward. Too many of those to go searching.

I thought it unlikely I would ever hear from him.

An urn with my father's ashes was not among her things. I doubt she would have given it to Ted, who in her mind didn't exist. She probably scattered Dad somewhere at sea, perhaps on her way to Santorini.

---

I tried to picture the event. At his desk? Not his writing desk at home (the Davenport escritoire where I now sit), where I used to see him with a book propped open, but over a much larger, glass-topped, hand-carved table in a carpeted room where people bustled about, keeping step to the continual clatter of typewriters and ringing telephones.

Were they too busy to notice? He'd given them all something else to worry about.

Mum had taken me there once. I must have been five. We were meeting him at midday for lunch, and he'd be taking us to his club in Mayfair, a regal place where the waiters were all dressed for a church wedding.

His workplace by contrast didn't have much in the way of decoration. The guest chairs were butternut-colored leather. The pictures on the wall showed wooded landscapes verging on placid lakes. He sat in a room by himself with a lady who looked after him when she wasn't typing. Outside his door, a larger room housed lots of people who were seated at smaller desks.

"Mum, why doesn't Dad have anything on his desk?" That day, we'd been told he was in a meeting, and I'd be allowed to sit in his enormous swivel chair until he returned. The worried people in the office, the ones who had modest-sized desks instead of little tables only large enough to hold their typewriters, were shuffling through stacks of papers as they frowned and marked on them and shifted piles from one stack to another.

"Your dad is the boss," she said proudly, adding, "He keeps a clean desk."

"He's the boss because he keeps it clean?"

She was amused. "Yes, that's it. When someone brings him something, he doesn't put it aside. He deals with it straightaway. He reads it, makes a decision, and makes a call or dictates a letter. Or if he can't decide right then, he gives it to someone else, who will bring it back later and tell him what they did with it or what new thing he must decide."

"Which he does right away!"

"Bright boy."

But what was his job? He was a "businessman," and from her description, his job was to do as little as possible.

## Antique Valuation

I told myself that, in finally going through her belongings, valuation of my mother's acquisitions would not be my main concern. As anyone must when rummaging through keepsakes, the decision for each item was "keep, sell, or give away?" I didn't need the money, and selling was bothersome but often necessary. The possible regret from discarding presumptive junk will bring a sharp pain if later the thing is found to be a coveted prize to collectors who are eager to spend money to hoard such things for themselves. Having never raised the question with her, I'd wondered what had fascinated her so about any of it.

It wasn't prettiness. Some of the things were inarguably ugly, even distinctively so.

There was a time before television, I'm told, when stamp collectors focused not only on rarity but also on imagining travel to exotic locales. Fred wanted his readers to think those dreams had sent him off to war.

Mother was not a collector with imagination. She liked owning stuff, loved the idea of possessing stuff few others had.

Her inventory was not up to date. Unfamiliar as I was with her holdings, I knew she'd bought items and not recorded them. After Dad was gone, she'd employed a personal assistant for some years, Clare Penniman. The handwriting in the ring binder changed from Dad's meticulous printing to her tightly looped cursive. Then notations ended abruptly, the last entry date being seven years ago, when Mum had written Ms. Penniman a polite letter of reference and bid her goodbye.

Mum was not one for paperwork of any kind. Yes, she insisted on writing paper checks to pay her bills, but she'd complain about the chore every time she sat down at her escritoire to do it, which might not have been on time if I had not marked my day planner to remind her and sometimes failed to do, thus rousing her irritation and a scolding for me. Neither of our responsibilities were so complex as to require the time and expense of hiring a bookkeeper. But for years I'd employed a tax preparer each spring, and I was a regular client of Grace Gibbs, a woman of Mum's age, still of razor-sharp mind and so organized she might well have catalogued stamps as a hobby back in the day.

Mum had a life insurance policy for a modest amount she insisted would cover funeral expenses. However, she refused to have the premiums deducted automatically from her bank account. After she'd received two reminder letters in the mail for a missed payment, I'd endured my ritual tongue-lashing, and her check was in the mail accompanied by an excusatory note written in her own shaky hand, I phoned Grace and asked for her advice on keeping up with our limited challenges to cash flow. She wisely informed me I needn't study accounts for due dates or set a specific reminder for each. Rather, I should simply do what accounting departments the world over do, review accumulated bills and bank balances on the tenth and twentieth of every month. On the tenth, pay all the bills due by the first. On the twentieth, pay all the bills due by the fifteenth. Try to keep the minimum balance in the checking account to cover the totals you usually pay on each of those dates, plus about twenty percent extra when you can manage it to cover the unexpected. More significant overages would necessarily be drawn from a savings account or investment portfolio.

I set two endlessly repeating monthly reminders in my

phone's calendar. After that, my gentle reminders to Mum were so regular that, having no reason to fault me for missing them, she'd snap, "Can't be. You pestered me about that yesterday."

The days did not pass slowly for her, but I had no clue what she'd found to occupy her mind.

# Trip up the Ganges

## Jonathan Comments on Fred's Diary

After a week in Calcutta with its hot humid atmosphere, which was almost unbearable, I yearned to get out of it for a short time during my leave. I discussed the matter with my two comrades, Sergeants Tolkin and Swann, who fell in with my proposal.

Interesting that the names of his comrades have changed, yet there are still two of them and of the same rank. These friends are peer officers, and although Fred is becoming more outgoing, they would be his most convenient and accessible connections. Remarkable in this instance that Fred is the one who is proposing the plans. He has been a follower, and now he is beginning to act like a leader. The role may have been easier now. It will be an adventure, and they are in full tourist mode.

## Trip up the Ganges

Having heard of the possibilities of an interesting sporting trip up the Ganges, I endeavoured to hire a shot gun and rifle, but without success. The same evening we were having a meal at the Y.M.C.A. which was run by the Ladies of Calcutta for the benefit of leave parties, when a Mrs. Huddleston-Matthews soon came and sat at our table for a chat, and in the course of conversation we mentioned our proposed trip and referred to the difficulty of obtaining a shot gun and rifle.

The following morning, I received a letter of introduction to Mr. N Smyth of the Royal Exchange Buildings, who was a Calcutta jade magnate. He gave me a hearty welcome and said he had heard with much interest of our intended trip from Mrs. H-M and offered to obtain for us our requirements. The result was that he not only provided us with guns and ammunition but insisted on making the necessary arrangements with the shipping people and paying for our trip.

*Mrs. H-M gave the impression of being very much the Victorian lady in appearance and demeanor. Some WRENS were in attendance. This lady was not in uniform but dressed in a silk native sheath with gold jewelry that may have been handed down in her family. Raven hair, ivory complexion, sparkling eyes accented discreetly with kohl. She was more assertive than one might expect in her approach to our table, and she being the most striking presence in the room, I expected she would introduce herself as our hostess. She may well have been, but instead she announced without reservation her situation as a war widow, hence her devoted support of this Christian organization, so renowned for putting on much needed diversions for weary troops all over the globe.*

*I must admit her looks and manner were captivating. She was without a doubt the most alluring woman I'd met during my tours, except notably for Mira.*

*Afterward, the lady's image stayed with me in my reveries, and she was for me Her Ladyship, though she never hinted she was titled. However, her later invisible influence with Smyth was unmistakable. The letter he received may well have been from some government poohbah or a military gentleman at the command level. The fellow never dropped a name, so indeed the letter may have been from herself, and he was protecting her modesty. During our discussions that evening, her comfort with the topic of blood sports, and our need for weaponry further attested to her station as a member of the sporting elite.*

*I like to think she was taken with me. She was most attentive to my descriptions of our intended outing, more intent perhaps than her interest in the subject matter of our conversation. As we talked, I sensed her devotion to these events might be evidence of a strong desire to find a new husband. While I was no lord of the manor, I was university educated, Christian, and white. Once again, I entertained thoughts of returning after the war. I might not be a man of means, but if she were the beneficiary of inherited wealth or the legacy of a captain of industry, physical attractiveness might be the more decisive criterion. She was not young, no recent bride. She was perhaps my senior by some years but likely not many. It would not be an inconceivable match.*

*But no sooner had these fantasies taken hold of me than I felt a pang of betrayal. I wasn't thinking of Sarah. I was repugning my love for Mira. Fond thoughts of her would fill my idle moments on the river, and it would be her buttery brown skin rather than this sallow visage that I would continue to crave.*

> On the 10th August 1918, we embarked at Jagannath Shad at 11 p.m. as first-class passengers on the I.G.N.R. Co riverboat *Mahlong.* The only other passengers were a Mr. and Mrs. Seymour and Mr. Davies, engineer inspector of the shipping company. I had a comfortable deck cabin fitted with two electric fans.

*The* Mahlong *was a stern-wheeled, coal-fired steamship. I wondered as how a vessel of such large class might have been transported from the shipyards to the Bay of Bombay. I asked the captain, and he informed me the ship had been built in Singapore two decades ago and then navigated treacherous waters in the South China Sea.*

*The relatively commodious appointments of my cabin were consistent with the first-class booking, and the expense of that gift further indication of the generosity and favor of Mrs. H-M. I doubted she bestowed such lavish attention on every soldier she met. She had made it a point, not directed at me personally but obviously within earshot. that she would feel fortunate to have pen pals among us veterans. Correspondence addressed in care of the YMCA would surely reach her, she said.*

## Jonathan's Journal

The following morning found us running down the Hooghly River. A very acceptable breeze was blowing, and during the day we passed numerous interesting river craft. At 4 p.m., we left the river at Mud Point and entered the Sundarbans. The route then became a labyrinth of waterways. At times the river was so narrow that there was hardly room for two vessels to pass, and then it opened out into a noble waterway a mile wide. On either side was dense jungle, the home of tiger, deer, alligator, etc.

*The captain assured me the draft of the ship was sufficient to clear the shallows. I took him at his word, but the prospect of running aground on a mudbank surrounded by hostile wildlife was daunting.*

The journey was continued during the night by the aid of a 20,000-candlepower searchlight. The effect of this powerful light playing on the banks of the dense jungle was a curious sight, attracting large moths and flying beetles, with which the deck became strewn. On entering a large waterway, the searchlight would play around until it picked up a white disc indicating the route, and we then entered another narrow course.

Remarkable that Fred knows the wattage for the brightness of the searchlight and its metric. A clue like this makes me wonder if he had some engineering in his background, although my speculation that he was an accountant by training would suggest he had a head for retaining facts and figures.

## Trip up the Ganges

> After dinner, I had an interesting chat with Mr. Davies. He told me that on a previous trip they carried 1,300 natives to N. Assam who had been in France for nearly three years as a labor corps. The boat had to stop there a day for these natives to cook and eat their food. Their favourite meal was dog flesh, and at one village where they stopped, twenty-four dogs were caught and eaten. The method of cooking was to run a stake through the dog's body and keep turning it over a fire. The dogs were either skinned or cleaned out, the entrails being considered a delicacy. At the same village, they killed and ate six pigs, for which the officers in charge had to pay twenty rupees.

Fred implies the Indians ate dog but the Brits avoided it and paid for pork. Perhaps that's a generous interpretation. When they were starving in Mespot, they'd eaten their horses and mules after all.

> It was a lovely balmy night, the fireflies dancing under the trees at the water's edge gave a pretty effect, and I felt reluctant at turning in to sleep. I turned in at 11 and rose again at 5 a.m. in the hopes of getting a pot shot at deer, which graze mornings and evenings off the spring grass on the water's edge. I saw several water buck and spotted deer, and although the *serang* (native skipper) started up the boat for me on one or two occasions, they disappeared in the jungle before I could get within range.

Shooting at deer from the boat seems hardly sporting.

## Jonathan's Journal

> During the day, we travelled through waterways surrounded by dense jungle. The water was teeming with porpoises, and we saw several large fish eagles and other interesting bird life.
>
> We eventually began to feel the effect of heavy water caused by the monsoons, and we had to combat a strong current. The flood water brought down large clusters of beautiful water hyacinths.
>
> Boys were on duty day and night at the boat's bow taking depth soundings of the water, and their continuous song of "sin from midden-may" (three fathoms and no bottom) will always ring in my ears.
>
> On the second day, we ran into open country with rice fields studied with palm woods, and later on we passed extensive jute plantations. The district was thickly populated with natives, who lived on small palm covered islets. Hundreds of native canoes swarmed the river, and the children were like water eels.
>
> On the 12th of August, we entered a five-mile-wide waterway where the Ganges and Brahmaputra meet. We hugged the eastern bank passing villages among the mango and palm trees. Most of the houses were built on bamboo poles to escape the floods, which were then running under them. The frail native fishing canoes with their square sails of many colours were a pretty sight.

Fred is obviously relaxing. It's the tourist life he craved, having earned it at considerable expense of effort, fear, and suffering. Perhaps here are the stories he would be most fond of relating over the after-dinner cigars and drinks of his retirement. If Henry had been wounded in the Balkans, he might not have had the opportunity or the inclination to reenlist as Fred had done. Or it might have been too late in the war. But if Fred had been adventuring in some respect vicariously on behalf of his brother back home, he wouldn't have mentioned the letters and gifts he'd sent so infrequently. And if Henry was to be among the future admirers of Fred's chronicle, his name would have come to the fore more often.

> At midday, our boat stopped at Tarpassa for a few hours to discharge some cargo. We went ashore and visited the bazaar, which was in a swamp at the water's edge, the paths being raised on planks. We then hired a canoe and paddled through the village. The huts were built of reed on large bamboo poles several feet above the water, and they were connected with each other by bamboo walks. The women were wearing cloth, and they looked picturesque in their indigo-blue clothes. We paddled through sylvan creeks covered with water lilies and Indian water hyacinths.

Fred had an eye for the women. It's obvious from his narrative here that these locals were clothed modestly, as befitted devout ladies.

*Relaxing on the river, here on leave without the concerns or responsibilities of being on patrol, it was as if a switch were thrown in the part of my brain that summons the libido. Mira, Mira! The kind and perhaps lustful attentions of Mrs. H-M flattered me, making me think for the first time since my cherished nurse smiled at me that I was handsome and desirable. To Sarah, I was a good provider. I was sure I had her admiration, but displays of tenderness were not in her nature. Had we wanted children and made the effort before my departure, the sex might have been ritualistic, worse than having none at all.*

> Leaving Tarpassa, the going was slow, having to combat strong currents, and we reached Goalunds at 4 p.m. on the 13th August.
>
> After dinner, Gillis and I obtained a guide and went to the post office to dispatch some letters. The first 100 yards was easy going on a boat, but the remaining 300 yards was on a rickety bamboo walk over the flood water. We found the P.O. was also a hut built of reed.

Other than sending the snakeskin home, here is one of Fred's few mentions of sending letters, but not to whom they were addressed. Multiple letters. Given his enjoyment on this trip, and now that he is officially on leave with perils of warfare are essentially over, he may have achieved the boldness to brag about his exploits. These may have been little more than postcards, perhaps with clippings enclosed. He did have access to newspapers.

*I did let Sarah know I was safe and presently free of the perils of conflict. I did not honestly know how much longer my services would be required. Technically, my tour of duty could extend beyond the armistice. The mopping up in whatever theatre would be a series of tasks for some years.*

*Most of my letters were addressed to Henry. Although he and Sarah were both living in our family home, our parents having passed on before the war, I sent the ones to my brother via his unit's postal box, thinking Sarah might be jealous of all those envelopes bearing his name. If he was convalescing and had some difficulties fetching his mail, she may have been calling for it. In such case, she'd not only see how much more often I was writing to him but also that I'd taken the precaution of using his military address would betray my betrayal. Had it been deliberate, it would have been unnecessarily mean.*

*I didn't want to alienate her, but I feared on my return we would be having a full and frank exchange of views about our marriage going forward. If she had found someone else during my protracted tours, such would be understandable. If a dalliance, perhaps forgivable. If serious, I was resolved not to stand in her way. I'd have my own plans.*

> Goalunds was an important railhead for the conveyance of jute to Calcutta. There was a permanent site for the railhead owing to the continuous shifting of the river. All the buildings were of a temporary nature. The environment and river officials lived in obsolete steamers converted into houseboats anchored in the river.

Jute is a coarse fiber used for making rope, as well as the warp of heavy textiles such as rugs and upholstery. It's a revealing sign of the times and wartime logistics that supply lines of battlefield materiel and food sent to Basra had been shipped from India, including some aid packages assembled by those Brit expat ladies.

## Jonathan's Journal

> Having reached the end of our upward journey at Goalunds, we left the Mahlong at 9 a.m. the next morning, and we became the guests of Mr. Norris, the shipping superintendent aboard his houseboat to await the arrival of a downward boat to take us back to Calcutta. The Mahlong persevered further upriver.

Again, Fred was receiving special treatment, and not because he's an honored veteran. Whatever arrangements Smyth had booked for them, the respectful attention continued. This distinction would not have been lost on Fred. I wondered how much he felt Mrs. H-M's generosity had been directed to him personally. Surely, more than a few officers, many of higher rank, had passed through that YMCA.

> We spent the day duck shooting. The only means of getting inland was on the railway bridge, as the country was underwater. About a mile in, we hired a canoe and two natives and paddled along creeks and waterways that ran through partly submerged tall grass, jute field, and palms, which was a paradise for wild fowl. We got a good mixed bag of duck, teal, and golden plover also a jackal. We saw colonies of weaver birds with their ingenious nests hanging from the trees.
>
> We dined that evening off the result of our day's sport.

The fowl was edible, surely, and a prize. But hyena? Did they eat those critters too? Those scavenging predators are both fast and agile. Felling one would have been a demonstration of shooting skill. Although these fellows were used to gamey-tasting meat, hyena would have been tough and nowhere near as succulent as the roasted birds.

> The following, day we were picked up by a downward boat, the *Sherain* which took a different course to our journey up. We arrived at a small village on the evening of the 18th August and discharged some cargo. It was a beautiful moonlit night. We went ashore and walked through the village, but the numerous village dogs did not give us a good reception.
>
> The following evening, we reached the Sundarbans, but another boat running ahead of us spoilt my chance of a shot at deer. We, however, eventually overtook her.
>
> Further on we saw an occasional mugger (alligator) basking in the sun on the mud at the water's edge. I turned one large chap over with my 240 Hauser rifle after getting three bullets into its head and shoulders. We lowered a boat, but the current was so strong that before we reached our quarry, it managed to wriggle into the water.

I researched the Hauser, finding its firepower suitable for big game. Such a weapon would also be useful for protection. This was probably a crocodile rather than an alligator. Neither will attack a human unless you happen to fall into the water with it. Killing one in these circumstances would have been unnecessary unless going for its hide. It would be foolish for Fred to think he was protecting natives by culling the population of threatening beasts.

> Early next morning, we left the Sundarbans and ran up the Hooghly. The ship's crew trailed a fishing net at the side of the boat, and when it was hauled aboard, it contained an interesting variety of small fish, including a number of water snakes. The latter were treated by the crew as venomous and were speedily returned to the water. I kept the skin of one with black and yellow rings.

Perhaps Fred had wanted to bag the croc for its skin, after all. The snakeskin would have been for Henry as an exotic trophy and another souvenir for after-dinner showings in his den.

> During the trip, we lived like fighting cocks. We had six meals a day, and all the poultry was carried alive in crates. An outstanding dish was the true Indian curry, which only a native cook seems to be able to prepare.

As anyone fond of Indian cuisine can tell you, there is no single, characteristic recipe for curry. Like American gravy and Mexican mole, it's a catchall phrase for all manner of sauces. In the case of curries, a common characteristic would be spiciness, oft times chokingly so for expat tastes.

Along with curried dishes, list mango chutney, naan bread, and gin-and-tonics as habits Fred would have brought back with him. If he had developed a taste and tolerance for spices to approach that of the locals, he would have had a stronger stomach than mine.

## TRIP UP THE GANGES

We reached Calcutta in the evening of the 22nd August after a most interesting twelve-day trip, and on the following morning I called on Mr. Norris and thanked him for his generosity. In the evening, I dined with him at his palatial house on the outskirts of the city, after which we motored to the Empire Club and witnessed a variety entertainment. During the intervals, we inclined to brilliantly illuminated grounds attached to the clubhouse and imbibed iced refreshments.

I filled in the remainder of my time at Calcutta visiting places of interest. The external and internal walls of the Jain temple were covered with inlaid glass of many colours and designs, and the large fish in the temple pond were as tame as to almost feed out of one's hand.

On the 29th August 1918, we said farewell to Calcutta and left by the 5 p.m. train for Secunderabad.

Fortunately, our return journey permitted me to see country, through which we travelled in darkness on our way up. Our run down the Bengal Coast was through glorious scenery. On one side were palm-covered islands studded along the coastline, and on the other side dense jungle footing the hills of the Eastern Shoals.

The train from Calcutta to Bombay was a journey between the major ports of east and west. The logic of the logistics here must have something to do with supply lines and troop movements. As well, there must have been some reason Fred couldn't sail from Calcutta. The train would have been a ready and frequent mode of transport, and troop ships may have been deployed elsewhere. Bombay must have been a more active base of naval operations, closer to Near Eastern theatre. In any case, Fred's making the journey westward by train must have been more efficient for various reasons.

*From Secunderabad to Bombay, I was retracing my previous journey around the cape of India, the southward route skirting the shoal formed by the sea to the east and the mountains to the west. On the prior occasion, I'd chosen to sit the right side of the car, gazing seaward and alone with my thoughts. Much of the journey was a bit inland, but on the other parts looking out at the shining waters was a comfort.*

*On the way back, I once again sat on the right side so I could admire the greenery of the foothills of the Ghats. I did so because I craved the abundance of detail and variety to take my mind off Mira. Even though by departing India I wouldn't be traveling directly home, leaving this exotic land would be a profound separation from her. I had wrongly assumed that my flirtation with Mrs. H-M would make me regard my fascination with Mira as simply a reawakening of my desire for any desirable woman.*

*But the provocative image of the elegant lady faded all too quickly. The allure of Mira's eyes and gentle smile shoved her rival aside and insisted kindly but firmly on my full and devoted attention.*

Elena observed:

> This part of his journey makes me reflect on a rarely discussed sidelight of German war strategy.

On neither of his trips by rail along the shoal did Fred fear shelling by a gunboat lying offshore. That's because the German navy had no presence in the Pacific for almost the entire duration of the war. Early on, a flotilla of battleships commanded by Admiral Von Spee was patrolling the South Pacific, a presence that alarmed the Australians. However, his strategic focus was on the other side of the ocean, along the Chilean coast. There in 1914 his squadron won the Battle of Coronel against two British cruisers. Following this victory in the same year, he sailed eastward, rounding Cape Horn in an attempt to take the Falkland Islands, and was defeated there decisively by the Royal Navy.

What's missing from all this is any deployment at scale of the German navy. Their maritime manufacturing and their operations concentrated on submarine warfare in the North Atlantic and the Eastern Mediterranean. Recall that the British admiralty initially regarded the submarine as a cowardly and defensive weapon. Deployment of subs was much more decisive in World War II, and yet German battleships still weren't much in the picture. We might speculate that Germany's alliance with Japan, which had an impressive navy, was motivated by their perception of the United States as the new primary opponent with its own highly capable navy. Having the Pacific as a major theater of battle would subject the US to a two-front war. Hitler's decision to attack Russia of course brought on another two-front war, a strategic mistake that ultimately assured their defeat in the ground war.

## Jonathan's Journal

Fred's diary continues:

We arrived at Secunderabad at 4 p.m. on the 31st August, and after a fortnight stay at the Trimulgherry Depot, I left to return to Mespot with drafts of the Devons and Somersets. My rifle and pack weighed heavily on my shoulders after two months disassociation with them.

# Troublesome Personalities

## Jonathan's Journal

One might wonder about my devotion to Mum, even after she became difficult to live with. In the early stages of her dementia, you'd think she was an angry teenager. Nothing pleased her, everything I said was wrong, and she insisted on her independence. Yet increasingly and by degrees, she needed assistance with routine tasks.

How do I know so much about teens, not having fathered any? I never taught high school, but I've dealt with college freshmen who were experiencing protracted adolescence. They were in school because their parents urged them to go and willingly paid, even without a scholarship, student loan, or work-study program. These kids skipped classes then crammed the night before each exam, expecting at least a passing grade. Art history, they must've thought, was a "gut" subject, soft science. Introductory units in any department are termed "appreciation" courses. Indeed, if they could've majored in art appreciation, they would flock to it, gawking for a grade. But even in the least technical and demanding areas, the academic study of art must comprehend names, dates, and events.

Bettina Reinders was far from being a star student in my introductory-level course. In high school, she'd had some instruction in figure drawing and painting, along with a smattering of geometry and perspective. She claimed to be bored with it all, felt she knew it intuitively without coaching, but had no interest in other subjects. She enrolled in the art history because she expected an easy MFA would be a path to an easy teaching career, perhaps cheering on bored teens as they did little more than finger paint expressive messes.

I quickly learned students could be bribed with extra-credit assignments. For most of my students in the second year, I gave them considerable latitude in their choice of topics. Although her exam performance was modest, I let her know she might improve her scores by a letter grade if she took on the specific research questions I suggested. She'd already made it clear she knew more about technique than the others did. I started her off with comparing and contrasting the chiaroscuro of Rembrandt and the contrasting use of large areas of white underpainting by Gérôme. I gave her no further guidance on how to approach the topic, nor why I thought it important. The differences between these styles of layered oil painting was a subject I'd studied intently myself. And indeed it was the core of the Neo-Romantic figurative period, the subject of my graduate thesis. However, I didn't share any of this with her, mentioning I'd read a journal article that provided few details but triggered my curiosity.

Her research into the question tickled her, then grabbed her, then took hold and infected her. She became so obsessed, in lieu of a final exam for her sophomore year,

I had her submit a lengthy white paper. That assignment set the hook.

She came to know the media and pigments available to these painters during their lifetimes, fully two hundred years apart. She understood grinding and mixing, volatility and drying times, opacity and translucence, and lightfastness and long-term color retention.

When the fascination finally took hold, she couldn't resist picking up a brush again and testing what she'd learned. She spent the summer at an artists' retreat in the Adirondacks. Of course, some of the old stuff doesn't exist anymore, or at least not in comparable form, but she was able to reproduce the processes enough to feel she not only owned the styles but also had mastered control of the results.

And she did some nice work. She still vacillated between theory and practice, but rather than simply dabbling in shapes and colors, her absorption in technique got her firmly stuck in the history of it all.

Bettina was not a beauty at first glance, but after she settled into her work, her kindness and generosity showed in her face. I confess I developed an attraction for her, but hitting on students, although something of a movie trope, must not be done. I sincerely hoped she didn't see the lust in my attentive looks. Could be my rictus had an alienating effect on her, and if my admiration was at all reciprocated, the only way she showed it was to apply herself diligently to the research tasks I set for her.

---

When Mum first came to live with me, she was willful and temperamental as ever, but when she wasn't fretting about something, she was an engaging companion. I was especially glad to have her there during the self-isolation period of Covid. She was hardly an intellectual, which might have made her unbearable as a harshly opinionated peer, but she was well educated, having earned an associate degree in business years before she met Dad.

That story is a sidelight but deserves telling here. Soon after her graduation, she landed a job as an administrative assistant in a brokerage firm in Chicago. I never got the details about how she rose in the ranks, but in short order she must have gained her license, whereupon she accepted a transfer to the firm's London office. She must have been a trader at this point, a junior staff member. The reasons for her next promotion are baffling. Without possessing stellar expertise in financial marketing, she took on the role of "gentleman's woman," as it's known in the trade. It was Dad who shared this bit of gossip with me, imparting it with a wink. I wasn't old enough at the time to get the hint. I thought he was telling me she was a prize, a lady of refinement. I didn't ask him, and he didn't explain. He could probably tell from my blank look his joke had gone over my head.

I knew she still had his brokerage account with the same firm, but she never shared what it contained, only that its funds were sufficient for her needs. After she moved in, one of the air-cargo containers with her things included a box full of magazines along with a few old paperbacks. Fred's journal was in a separate set of boxes that held the more elegant volumes of Dad's collection. She never unpacked that one, and it languished until after her death in one of my closets.

The magazines were among the first things she pulled out — glossy back issues of *Marie Claire, Vogue, Country*

*Life,* and *Architectural Digest.* As I'd soon learn, all those subscriptions were current. She was quick to retrieve one from the daily mail and declined to ever throw a new issue away. She didn't read them, as far as I could tell. She gazed, fascinated, as she paged through them. I'd say it was her favorite amusement.

She kept these few books on the lower shelf of a nightstand — several titles by only two British female authors — Daphne du Maurier and Olivia Higgins Prouty. These novels were well thumbed to the point of almost falling apart. She did read them, often opening one late at night when she couldn't sleep. She'd sleep late the next day, and when I'd knock to offer her morning coffee, I'd find her propped up in bed, still asleep, the book open on her lap, and her glasses slipped down the bridge of her nose.

Her magazines were stacked high on the nightstand on the other side of the bed, and I'd often find them strewn around her feet or kicked off onto the floor.

In those early days of her stay with me, we'd go out walking together, usually along the edge of the bike path that skirts Venice Beach. The ocean area was invigorating, and the sight of the wind blowing through her hair was memorable. She'd wear her favorite Hermès scarf around her neck. Her distinctive Versace Medusa sunglasses gave her a mature, movie-star look, emphasized by her chin-up attitude. I believe she regarded herself as a person of importance, and I'm sure she played the role of "gentleman's woman" to the max.

But even when she was ambulatory and in fair health back then, there were days she didn't get out of bed. I found I couldn't lure her out with food. I'd take her a tray with coffee and toast, a sandwich and a Diet Coke, tea and biscuits, a bowl of soup and a glass of wine. Such were her preferences at the dinner table as well, when we did venture out.

Another way she'd amuse herself would be to go out for walks on her own. When first she moved in, she could manage her COPD with a pocket inhaler. Here in the marina, we're within Los Angeles city limits, and smoking inside isn't downright illegal, but it's against this building's regulations. Thankfully, both for compliance and my health if not her own, she didn't insist on smoking, even in her bedroom. She knew it upset me if she smoked when we strolled together, so I strongly suspect one of the reasons she wanted to venture outside was to grab a smoke.

When her disease progressed, I bought her a portable oxygen concentrator. It was about the size of a large water bottle, and she could wear it slung at her side by a strap, no more cumbersome than a handbag. She hated how it looked of course, but it didn't take her long to realize she couldn't get very far without it.

It would be a serious risk for her to smoke anywhere near the device, even when not using it to breathe. I read the warning literature, and the oxygen trapped in the clothes you were wearing could catch fire. Our rule was, if she wanted to smoke, she could do it while sitting on the grounds of the building, but I wouldn't let her leave with the concentrator unless I was with her.

Sometimes when we were together and she was following the rules, we'd walk as far as a mile to the dog park in Playa Vista. She got a kick out of watching the small dogs wrestle with each other. She soon made sure to carry treats in her pocket, a practice that annoyed dog guardians who frowned on her lack of respect for their diet restrictions and discipline. Chatting among the dog fanciers was the order of the day there, but that was not an activity Mum had any interest in joining.

There's a full-service supermarket a half-block from our door, and back when she needed only the inhaler at times and so she could smoke, she'd conclude her wanderings there, mostly because it stocked gourmet cheeses and fine wine — and dog treats and cigarettes.

A major turning point was an afternoon when she'd been gone far too long. She'd been growing forgetful, and her doctor had warned me she might one day forget her way home. As scholars and writers are prone to do, I'd been preoccupied with my work and lost track of the time. As daylight began to fade, I had panicked thoughts of calling the police. But instead I ventured out, looking for her first on the footpath by the beach then at the supermarket. I finally drove to the dog park, and there I found her on a bench and cuddling a fluffy Pekingese.

Even if she'd permit me to search her for cigarettes, I didn't have to. If she'd smoked, her clothes would have reeked, and her favorite perfume would not have covered it. She wisely *did* heed my warnings about not smoking while using the oxygen.

If she met and chatted up folks on her outings, she never said. In her way, she was as private and withdrawn as I was. Perhaps it's a genetic thing. Her coolness made me suspect she'd been deeply wounded emotionally, but I doubted it was because she missed my father's companionship. She never had that much of it.

On days when she might languish in her bed, I worried she was bored, which might cause her to fret. And she'd need some exercise, even if just taking those short walks with me outside. I offered to put a TV in there, but she didn't want it. Before her first cup of coffee, she'd flip on the classical music station on an FM radio I gave her.

Having never been a parent, I was new to the role of caregiver. Her forgetting her way home was indeed an early sign of dementia. Or her physician had explained to me when I told him about the incident, habitual stress can bring on a condition called *pseudo-dementia.* The latter condition may persist but doesn't progress. He suggested that, after living for so many years in the same flat in London, the changes in her environment might be upsetting, even after many months.

One day when it seemed she might be languishing and possibly fatigued, I pulled up a chair next to her bed. She was absorbed in an issue of *Architectural Digest.* Her bedroom windows faced the Pacific to the southeast, so my announcement was no news. I began, "It's a fine day. How about a walk along the beach? Remember, the pedestrian path is paved. No sand in your shoes."

She ignored my comment, still focused on the page. But when she spoke up, she wasn't talking to herself. "Now, here is something to admire. A sprawling Palm Springs 'fifties rancho home. Get this, the concept is so simple. Fresh flowers everywhere in gleaming Steuben glass. So light and airy, windows all around. And every inch of those walls covered with original Impressionist paintings." She looked up to thrust the picture onto my lap. "Look!"

"Gorgeous," I said.

Quickly, she snatched it back. "Now, what do you think of the furniture?"

"Uh, I don't know. Can I have another look? I didn't notice it."

"Hah!" she exulted. "That's the point. No one would.

The chairs and tables might be collectibles in themselves, but who cares? The concept of the flowers, the glass, and the art is so stunning that you could fill the place with castoffs from the Salvation Army, and no one would see it."

These might have been the most enthusiastic words she'd spoken to me so far. Hoping to keep her talking, I thought of the books.

"You must love those novels. I see you've got *Rebecca* and *Now, Voyager*. You must have reread them countless times."

"Women in jeopardy. It's an old formula, but those clever British ladies do it best."

"Is it any coincidence that all of your favorite books became Hitchcock movies?"

She huffed, "Now there was an arrogant Englishman. They said his favorite meal was steak medium rare and vanilla ice cream." The pout became a frown. "Tippi Hedren said he was 'ungentlemanly' to her."

Hollywood gossip column stuff. Maybe she'd read articles in those magazines after all.

"Ungentlemanly" triggered the decades-old memory. "Mum, Dad told me you were a 'gentleman's woman.' I never knew what he meant by that."

She chuckled, "You should have asked him. All these years you must've thought your mother was a prostitute."

"I was too young to think it at the time, but since then…"

"Jon, dear boy. How sad. A gentleman's woman at a brokerage is a female account executive who has but one client. The reason being, his portfolio is massive, and so is his lust."

"Oh my."

"Your father wasn't a bad boy, although he liked to think of himself that way. When we married, back then it was not at all unusual for such a woman to snare her gentleman. It was rather like the upper-class girls over here who apply to the Seven Sisters aspiring to earn the M-r-s degree. These days, an older man with his wealth might brag of grabbing a 'trophy wife,' which is rather more demeaning." She took a sip of her cold coffee. "Of course, that's what I was."

"But you must have been a wizard in the markets."

"No, no," she chuckled again. "I had the looks. And the taste in clothes. I learned how to handle the silverware. The soup course? 'I push my spoon away from me like little ships that go to sea.' I had no head for margins or short-selling or leveraging or diversification. I had nice young men from LSE to advise me at every step."

London School of Economics, the Wharton of the UK. Of course they'd have her back.

"And how much of his portfolio is left?"

She growled, "Wouldn't you like to know? Enough to put me in some posh retirement village and throw away the key." She added with emphasis, "But you do that, you'll never get a penny."

"As you can see, Mum, I do quite all right. What's yours is yours, but if need be, what's mine is ours." I wanted her to believe me. "I really do like having you here. We've both been lonely, and with things the way we are, it's not like we'll be throwing dinner parties anytime soon. And you can use your spoon any way you like."

She dropped her voice to say, "I loved him, you know. Oh, yes, I was out for big game. But even before I'd charmed him, I liked him. A man of his age and status would have a past, of course. But he was a gentleman in every sense of the word. Wise and witty. I liked him, I grew to love him, and by the time I was devoted to him, he was gone. Careful what you ask for, my boy." She glared at me. "You came in here to get me out of bed. Didn't you ever hear of Sue Mengers, the Hollywood agent who conducted all her business from her bed?"

"I hadn't heard that one. I doubt if she's still around to brag about it though. Maybe they buried her in a queen-sized plot. But what about Hitchcock? I was trying to ask you to join me in the living room to watch one of those movies on the big screen."

"Oh, I suppose I saw those. It would have been years ago."

"Let's see *Now, Voyager.*"

"That's not Hitchcock. Irving Rapper. Gowns by Orry-Kelly."

"But you said you hardly remembered."

"Directors I never cared about. Orry-Kelly dressed Bette Davis."

I would learn she could probably name the fashion designer for every famous female star of the Studio Era. It became a favorite game of ours because, even though I had no such depth of knowledge, my studies in figurative painting did touch on textiles, which today is the department at LACMA that holds classic movie wardrobes.

For a painter, especially those classicists I'd studied, capturing the look of folded silk was as challenging technically as capturing the subtle gesture of a lady's hand.

"Do we have a deal? You'll dress for dinner and a movie?"

"No popcorn," she warned. "Gets grease on the furniture without an antimacassar."

Before the screening and as she bathed and dressed, I jumped online to research the movie. I would have thought from the look of it that this was a Hitchcock movie, but she was right about Irving Rapper. The name was new to me. He directed twenty-two other pictures and received an Oscar nomination for *Rhapsody in Blue*. Orry-Kelly is credited as costume designer on more than three hundred pictures and was certainly a favorite of Miss Davis. But he could no longer give her gowns after he left Warner Bros. in 1944, after which she reportedly lamented she'd "lost my right arm."

Mum showed up for dinner in trim wool pants and a silk blouse. She still had her figure. She demanded I fix her a drink, and I was hoping it would loosen her tongue.

She was delighted with my choice. She paid close attention and sat through the movie without a word. I thought she might trundle off to her room after she'd drained her glass, but then she wanted to talk.

She was on her second dry martini, and in the dim light of the living room, the tilt of her head and her tone of voice were indeed reminiscent of Bette Davis. She smirked. "The screenwriter got it wrong about those shoes."

"Shoes?"

"She calls them *saddle* shoes, but that style has a plain toe. Bette and her designer would both know these are *spectator pumps*."

"I don't know the term. You mean those sporty shoes she wears on the cruise?"

"White shoes with colored-leather accents across the

heel and toe. When she steps onto the gangplank of the steamer after her cruise, the first thing you see is an extreme closeup of her ankles and those shoes. Why *spectators?* You don't see them much anymore, and it's not surprising you never heard of them. The style got the name *spectators* because in the twenties and thirties they became a trademark of the idle-rich male, a lounge-lizard without a job who hung out, watched ponies at the track, and sponged off his rich buddies in night clubs. The style became such a badge of dishonor that the Brits called them *co-respondent* shoes, referring to the unscrupulous seducers of unfaithful wives."

"I'm impressed, Mum. You do know an awful lot about fashion."

"Not just fashion, my dear. I pay close attention. The director might not have understood, but there would have been a reason Orry-Kelly put those on her for our first glimpse of her as a 'new woman.'"

"I bet this is more than film trivia."

"Those shoes are saying in the subtlest way possible that she lost her virginity on that cruise. Many times over. And with married men." This gentleman's woman obviously knew how the game was played.

Our evening movie became a habit, but not always on the same nights. I had her on bland food, which she complained about, but she'd sometimes use sour stomach as a reason to skip dinner.

We got into an argument over *Rebecca*. This one *was* Hitchcock. She discouraged talk during the movie, but this time she was upset with Olivier.

"He killed her!" she insisted, referring to the core mystery question whether Maxim de Winter had murdered his first wife.

"No, Mum. I thought so too. It's a fiendishly twisty plot, but in the end it was a sailing accident."

"Read the book!" And she marched into her room and closed the door.

I didn't want to insist on being right, but a search of the movie database revealed that the production code of the era would not permit de Winter to get away with murder without punishment. Even the master of suspense had to bow to the censors.

I apologized the next morning, but Mum sulked all day. I put off my plan to make her see the doctor.

Now that I'd given in so graciously, I thought she owed me one. "You know, Mum, I've really enjoyed our chats about the movies. And I'm learning so much more about you — your likes and dislikes. I knew you followed fashion trends, but I'm impressed you know which designers dressed Hollywood stars. Perhaps you'd tell me more about how a farm girl from Kansas learned so much. And, you know, stories about your family — *our* family."

"You know, Jon. You make too much of things."

# Exeter and Sarah

## Fred Speaks

IT WAS MY TWENTY-FIRST BIRTHDAY. That was the qualifying age for a man to vote, but only if one owned or rented property. I was living at home. According to the law back then, I could have been buying myself pints at age fourteen, spirits at sixteen. But Dad forbade it. Now that the war had broken out, brother Henry, having surpassed the minimum nineteen years, had enlisted for active duty overseas. Now, two years later, I also met the requirement, but Dad, with vehement agreement from Mum, would not let me go. My plan now was to assert my patriotic right of citizenship by moving out and renting a small flat with a couple of chums, all our names on the lease. Perhaps I could count on the increasing shortage of the able-bodied to help my chances of finding a job. Having thus escaped the household, I'd then not only be able to get pissed with my mates but also do the manly thing, with the option of enlisting in hopes of lighter duty if it should look as though we'd all be conscripted anyway.

I expected Mum would use the last of her margarine to bake me a cake. Instead, I got a lecture.

Henry and I called Dad "the Vicar" behind his back, even though he was only a lay rector. He hadn't the education to be ordained, but you wouldn't know otherwise from his sanctimonious bearing. He was constantly at the beck and call of the crusty priest at St. Thomas the Apostle, and he maintained a running feud with the clergy at St. Michael's, alleging the lot were "too Catholic."

He didn't know, and I wasn't brave enough to tell him, that one of our history lessons at Bishop Blackall had boldly taught the presumed origins of this rivalry, the proctor perhaps thinking such an ancient tale was a harmless bit of local color.

And it was all quite relevant to the heritage of our town as faithful subjects of the king. As far back as 1549 in a fracas known as the Prayer Book Rebellion, Vicar Robert Welshe sided with the Pope. The prevailing followers of Henry VIII hanged that priest from the church tower by the waist, where he was left to twist in the wind for three years. To the church name was appended "the Apostle" to avoid confusion with St. Thomas Becket, another popish fellow who had met a bad end four centuries earlier.

"Son," the Vicar began after an ominous clearing of the throat, "a man who is entitled to vote must have not only property but a proper wife and family."

"The law has no such provision, sir."

"I'm not speaking legally but morally. That vote of yours must count for your entire household. How else but by the responsible voice of our men will women and children ever be heard in Parliament?"

"You didn't urge Henry to marry. You let him enlist!"

In a lowered tone, the Vicar confided, "Your brother is a thoughtful man, an intellectual who, as some do, prefers the company of other educated men. I had urged him to aspire to the priesthood, but he did not feel the call. He rightly pointed to his expert marksmanship as a gift from God and a talent destined to be applied in the service of his country. I allowed myself to be persuaded. However, given his example, you can now appreciate that, whether felled in battle or cloistered with the academics, he will be unlikely to be the one to continue the family name."

Henry was indeed a crack shot, but I was not without skill. Three years ago, he and I had both served in our school's Officer Training Corps, in which marching and riflery were the principal activities. We had both served on the Blackall team at the annual Ashburton Shield shooting competition. Henry scored personal best and team leader in the full-bore targets at a thousand yards. We didn't win. Our ranking was no doubt diminished by my own mediocre scores. You see, Henry was a dead-eyed sniper, and I was so nervous I couldn't steady my hand long enough to hold the crosshairs over the bullseye to get off an accurate shot.

"Father, I don't have anyone remotely in mind."

He'd thought about this. "Might I suggest you turn your attentions to young Sarah Maltby?"

Sarah sang in the church choir. She'd captured his attention. She was well endowed with flaxen hair and rosy cheeks. I knew Dad fancied her — not in a prurient way, mind you. More like a prize heifer who might command a high bid at auction.

I pointed out, "Being married might not prevent my conscription."

"It could put you among the last, God willing."

## Jonathan's Journal

I saw the path of least resistance might gain me favor, after all. When Sarah accepted my invitation to a dance, Dad was furious with me when I returned home after ten.

"She's Deacon Maltby's daughter!" he protested.

I assured him I was enjoying her company so much that I had lost track of time. In truth, it was Sarah who begged me linger, and I left her at my insistence.

Besides her comely appearance, Sarah's father owned a stable whereby he provisioned drayage service in the town. I aspired to learn to ride.

Now, I am humbled to think I received such tender care from the daughters of St. Thomas because the patron saint of my home parish had taken Christianity to India in ancient times. It was a blessing that one of them so captivated me that she awakened my sleeping desire.

# Sailing Away and Return to Basra

## Fred's Diary, He Speaks, and Jonathan Comments

Leaving Secunderabad for Bombay by the 10 p.m. train on the 13th September, we reached a pass in the Western Ghats on the morning of the 15th. The scenery here was grand. We looked down into deep ravines with waterfalls and surrounding were thickly wooded hills. The railway took a winding course, and at one point the train was reversed to negotiate a steep descent.

We afterwards travelled through the foothills which were well watered and rich with vegetation. We reached Bombay at 1 p.m. and immediately embarked on the troopship *Egra*. Anchor was weighed at 3 p.m. the same day, and after an uneventful voyage we ran into the Persian Gulf on the 20th September. The date palms were heavily laden with dates. I looked forward to rejoining my battalion, and although Mespot was termed "Heat River and Date Palm," it had a certain amount of attraction to me.

On arrival at Basra, I found my battalion was still at Nasiriyah where I joined them on the 23rd Sept.

*Rejoining the Devons also had the consequence of allowing me to collect my accumulated mail, which for reasons known only to the command was not forwarded to me in India. Keeping it there did ensure its delivery, had I survived the perils of noncombat duty, including sickness and poisonous creatures.*

*There was nothing from Sarah. Possibly it had been too short a time since the posting of my letter and my gift of silk. I did have two letters, dated three months apart, from Henry:*

My Dear Brother,

You have been silent. Sarah fears you are dead. I suspect she prefers to believe in your demise rather than your indifference. Knowing you as I do, I expect the latter. You will mind my saying so, but you have always been something of a cold fish. Perhaps comradeship will draw you out.

I know the two of you were not on good terms when you enlisted. You had expressed to me over a pint that you were sure she was stepping out. Such may have been the case, although I had no knowledge of it, nor any since. Granted, she has never been one to share her emotions freely. She saw in you at least a comfortable existence, but then we were all overcome by events. For your part, you felt you had little reason to stay, and as you had also expressed to me, you yearned for adventure. Your foreign postings may not have met those expectations. We get so little news of the eastern campaigns.

As for the Western Front, I know you had little experience of it, but no doubt you witnessed enough to be sickened. She told me you did not speak of it. As for me, I decline to say anything at all, except that people here little credit what we did there. The Turks are fierce warriors, and yet I appreciate now they are a cultured people, betrayed by selfish rulers and a woefully outdated form of government. The Germans are crazed and ruthless, and yet we English never threatened them. Somehow, they became angry they were encircled and feared a future contest for resources.

Perhaps my time in the Balkans will have helped bring down Ottoman rule, if not decide the Eastern Question. Pray the outcome of your campaigns will help fill the void of power and deliver some peace and stability to that troubled part of the world.

Europe will recover. I have no doubt of that. Whether the Huns have any say in what follows, we cannot yet know.

I have waxed philosophical here, and I apologise. I have told you nothing of my situation. I am living here in Exeter with Sarah in your home. She has joined the WRENS and says little of her work. I believe she spends her days folding bandages, and even though it is a valuable service, I expect she does it to have friendly contact with her colleagues and their families.

I received a gunshot wound to my left hand. I can no longer play the piano. I have considered giving lessons but have not yet taken it up. We still have the upright in the parlor. It needs tuning. I suppose I could learn to do that. My pension is sufficient to feed us.

Write to her soon. The Royal Mail is faithful as ever, even if less punctual. When you return, if you choose to do so, you can make way for your reappearance with a kind word.

Henry

*Then, his next:*

My Dear Brother,

This will be brief. It amused me to receive the snakeskin, and I thank you. It was an odd gesture, no doubt to impress, but you did take some care to send it. I will accept the kind thought.

Nevertheless, your stratagem in sending the package to me in care of Devon Exeter station failed miserably. Sarah has been the one to fetch my troop mail on her trips to the greengrocers. She did not open it, but she did of course see it was from you. After some time and I didn't share news of you, she reluctantly asked after your welfare. I admitted truthfully you had included no note with the souvenir. I am sure she was doubly offended, not just that you had sent to me and not to her but that you chose to hide it from her. More personal news from you would have been likewise welcome.

Then you compounded the error by sending the silk here. Brother dear, I know you are inexperienced in affairs of the heart. You should have understood that such a gift betrays a special kind of guilt. A woman knows that a man who strays may be quick to make it up. Doing so without a tender note confirms the mystery and compounds the offense.

In the first instance, your gift to me let her know you still breathe. Your coldness may not have surprised her, but then your gift to her cut like a knife. She knows there is someone else. You and I both understand that a dalliance may mean nothing. A wife has no such confidence.

It may not matter to you, but on your return, if you do so, a fit man of your age will be at an advantage. The ranks of eligible men have been greatly reduced. Sarah is too independent of mind to seek out some old coot, and the young men are far too silly.

Henry

*My big brother's words seemed cruel at first, but on rereading I accept them as a fatherly scolding. He knows me as well or perhaps better than I do. He is right on all counts.*

*That I will not hear him play may be the saddest of his news. That I have lost Sarah is not so much news as a humiliating reminder of my vanity and stupidity.*

*The man who loves Mira is not the man who left Exeter and in leaving repudiated whatever love Sarah may have had for me.*

*I resolved to write, but I didn't. What could I say to repair the hurt? I still felt she'd betrayed me first, despite Henry's implied denial. I held to that belief, no doubt because it made me feel slightly better, if not justified.*

> On the 24th September we proceeded to Margit Basra to congregate with other troops as reinforcements for the Caspian Sea Campaign, but owing to the subsequent withdrawal from Baku, our object was disbanded.

At war's end, the British still feared Russian troops would descend on Mespot to fill the power vacuum left by the collapse of the Ottoman Empire. The Russian Revolution had overwhelmed that government in the spring of 1917, and it did not become immediately apparent that the Bolsheviks would be able to hold on to power, which they did, subsequently recalling their troops to Moscow. The withdrawal from Baku mentioned here is the abandonment of the post by the Russians.

> We had very inadequate quarters at Margit: we were packed in dilapidated tents, and to make matters worse heavy rains made our camp knee-deep in mud. Representatives were made to the base commandant, Col. Jarrow, but he flatly refused complaints for better accommodations, although the adjoining Turkish prisoners of war, labor camps, and noncombatants had good huts and got everything they wanted.
>
> Spanish Influenza broke out amongst us and made a heavy toll of deaths in the battalion. Nearly everyone was more or less affected, and the hospitals soon became full. I managed to escape it thanks

to the opportunity of being able to obtain whisky in the evenings, which proved a good preventative.

That Spanish Flu raged all over the world is less remarkable to us since the persistent and at times intractable experience of Covid. Back then, wartime had facilitated spreading of the virus. The historians' version of the pandemic places its origins in an Army basic training camp in the United States. Infected but not yet sick soldiers deployed to Europe took it there. Troop transports bringing reinforcements to Basra no doubt brought it there. Civilian transport hadn't ceased, but its volume was nothing like the mass deployment of armed forces. In this fact alone, we can begin to appreciate this was truly a world war.

> There were great rejoicings on the 2nd November at the news of the unconditional surrender of Turkey, which was soon followed by the collapse of Austria and Germany on the 11th Nov.
>
> Whilst at Basra, the battalion was detailed for all sorts of fatigues. My platoon was for some sense in charge of Turkish prisoners of war and Persian and Kurdish labor camps, superintending the loading of shells.

This reference was to unspent munitions, heavy artillery shells. Those would be loaded into trucks bound for cargo ships in port. It would be important for the military not only to stockpile weapons against unanticipated needs of future conflicts but also to keep them out of the hands of potentially hostile groups in contested locations.

## Jonathan's Journal

On the 20th of November, we tracked across the salt marsh to our old camp at Shaiba. Immediately we arrived there, and volunteers were requested to proceed to the Near East. Desirous of seeing new countries, I did not hesitate to seize the opportunity. On the 23rd of November, I left Shaiba with a draft comprising Capt. Fellowes in charge, four other officers, and 229 other ranks, for embarkation at Basra.

I was appointed Company Sergeant Major, and I had a busy time organising the draft into a company and the setting out for our new adventure.

*For reasons made abundantly clear in Henry's letters, I was not eager to return home. The promotion, which came with not only an increase in pay but also a bump in pension, made the decision easier. I was fairly sure there would be no more fighting, unless of course saboteurs might still be lurking. Although our orders weren't specific and even the destination was a matter of speculation, I reasoned my role would be largely supervisory. Even if the privations at the new posting were severe as a result of postwar shortages, one might be confident that officers would receive commodious treatment, as had been done in India.*

We embarked on the transport *Shuza* on the 9th December. She was an iron-built boat originally used by the Indian government for conveying pilgrims to Mecca. This was her first trip as a trooper, and the arrangements were bad. She packed 2,300 troops aboard, and there was hardly room for one another to move. We sailed at 6 a.m. the following morning. We did not know our destination, but it was pleasant to feel it was nearer slightly.

Leaving the Persian Gulf, we hugged the Arabian coast. The climate became warmer, and the sea was like a mill pond. The barren cliffs of the Arabian coast, which were lit by brilliant sunshine, gave them a snow-clad appearance.

During the voyage, I spent most of my time in the sheep pen on the top deck of the ship's stern. There I was able to enjoy the breeze and have a little elbow room. Every other part of the boat was packed.

This ship was headed northward to Suez, and most of the troops on board were soldiers and nurses returning home, perhaps via ships in the Med or passenger trains through France. Fred and Capt. Shorter's contingent would not be proceeding the rest of the way. Their mission would involve the "mopping up," hard work in itself.

# Egypt

## Jonathan's Comments on Fred's Diary

After thirteen days' trip, we entered Port Suez on the 23rd of December. We felt the refreshing climate of the Egyptian winter after our journey through the Red Sea.

FOLLOWING the Armistice in November 1918, the British demobilized their foreign troops gradually. For a time, Fred's unit was assigned to Egypt, where large transit camps had been established at Suez as well as the port of Alexandria. Other drafts from the Devons and Somersets were deployed right away to Constantinople, which after collapse of the Ottoman empire was officially under Allied occupation.

Fred would be joining those forces eventually, but the transit hubs were jammed. While he waited for a billet and then further orders, he was a tourist among the colossal ruins of ancient Egypt.

> We disembarked at Port Suez and each draft was supposed to take a day's rations. The commissarial arrangements aboard the boat we aboard the boat were as badly organised that, in spite of heated representations, our draft disembarked with a box of bacon and a chest of tea, which we hung on to in case of future emergency.

*Make note of our hoarding these rations. We did not succeed in retaining possession of them. The lesson to be learned, perhaps, to which any soldier might attest, is to scarf those gifts down at the earliest opportunity. Rather reminds me of my drill sergeant back in Devonshire. "You idiots, if you learn nothing, remember this. When you're on the long march, never pass up an opportunity to piss or shit or sit down."*

> We entrained at 4 p.m. and reached Kantara on the banks of the Suez Canal at 9. Here was the Infantry Base Depot for the Palestine Front, which was to accommodate us, but as the depot was full, and some other drafts and ourselves were the last to leave Port Suez. The depot could not receive us, and we slept the night in the open on the banks of the canal.
>
> We experienced a cold night in our thin clothing, and at dawn I began to look around for a warm drink. I made for some smoke issuing from the cookhouse of the Veterinary Corps line nearby. On entering, I was met by an Exeter man who I immediately recog-

nised, and I was fortunate in enjoying one of those best cups of tea in one's life.

There have been hints of snobbishness whenever Fred encounters a citizen of the Ever Faithful. These men clearly weren't just Devonshire conscripts and officers but classmates. In this context, "tea" might be a light meal, possibly including delicacies hoarded such rare and happy occasions.

Capt. Shorter was early astir to find us quarters, and we were eventually accommodated in tents attached to the British Horse Bransford Depot. Here there was a well-catered sergeant's mess, and the men received good rations and were well cared for.

We daily expected to receive orders to proceed on our journey, but on account of our being quartered outside the infantry depot, we appeared to have been lost sight of, and we spent a pleasant month at Kantara. The other troops who came with us from Mespot were only at the infantry depot for a few days and they were then sent to Salonica.

Salonica [Thessaloniki] in Greece was where Fred would soon be going himself. That port city was a major Allied base during the war and critical postwar staging area in proximity to Constantinople.

The climate of the Egyptian winter was glorious, and I took every opportunity of visiting places of interest. I first saw Ismailia a residential resort on the banks of the Bitter Lakes. The town had a large French population with nice residences and well-kept public grounds. It was pleasant to see roses again blooming in all their glory.

On Sunday, the 5 January 1919, Quarter Master Sergeant Marsh and I visited Cairo, the pyramids, and Sphinx. We travelled by rail via the towns of Zagazig and Banha. These places were typically eastern with their flat-roofed houses. The country appeared very fertile with orange groves and sugar plantations. The smaller crops were watered by irrigation canals similar to the rice fields in India.

On arrival at Cairo, we had a meal in a cafe and then boarded a train car, which took us for seven miles through the city to the terminus near the village of Mena, where the great pyramids met our gaze.

The following story about Fred's camel ride is a more eventful yarn than he has so far offered. It's amusing to think the cavalrymen might have thought they'd have any skill handling these beasts. As well, Fred has so far avoided entrapment by opportunistic criminals. Fortunately, he hadn't lost the soldier's habit of vigilance.

We each hired a camel and a camel man and rode around the pyramids and then visited the Sphinx.

Soon after starting our ride, I discovered that my camel was old and sluggish and that my camel man was mounted on a young, sprightly one. With some persuasion on my part, he reluctantly changed camel, and I had a much better mount. The man then pressed to tell my fortune, to which I objected. He became very persistent, and although I used some strong expressions to him, he muttered some twad-

> dle, which I ignored, and he asked me to pay him five piasters for his premonitions. I refused, and he became very agitated.
>
> Returning from the Sphinx, we entered the uninhabited village of Mena, and I soon discovered that I was being led into a cul-de-sac and that the attitude of my camel man became more aggressive. Without any hesitation, I turned my camel and lashed out at the man with my loaded Nilgiri cane.

Fred's weapon here is a rattan cane named for the hills of Southern India, so he must have brought it with him. He might well have flailed at the camel as he would do with a riding crop.

> I then urged my camel and galloped back to the tram terminus, leaving the man far behind, and I handed my camel to the several camel men standing nearby. I then boarded a tram car that was about to start, and in consequences of the bold impudence of my camel man, he got nothing for the hire of his camel or for his fortunetelling. I left the tramcar a little way down the road and waited for Willoughby, who stated that the individual created quite a stir among the camel men at the terminus.

It's no surprise Fred had no patience with fortunetellers, not only because he was a pragmatic fellow but possibly also because he would be heading home eventually and feared news of how he might be greeted upon his arrival.

On our return to Cairo, we made the best of our short stay as we had to be back in camp that evening.

I also spent a day at Port Said. The place did not impress me, except for the long De Lesseps breakwater at the entrance of the Suez Canal, which forms a promenade projecting into the sea.

We had some good duck shooting in the back waters of the Niles a few miles from Kantara, but we had much difficulty in obtaining cartridges.

These waters that form part of the delta of the Nile fascinated me, and on several occasions we hired a flat-bottomed boat and punted for miles through tall rushes. For a considerable distance out, the water was only two or three feet deep with a sandy bottom, and it was the haunt of numerous wild fowl.

The native method of fishing was to stake nets along the edge of a clump of reeds and then go in the reeds and drive the fish to the nets. They would then dip the fish out of the water with a small hand net.

# SALONICA

## JONATHAN COMMENTS ON FRED'S DIARY

THESSALONIKI IS a Greek port city on the Thermaic (Thermaikos) Gulf of the Aegean Sea. Fred likely caught sight of Roman, Byzantine, and Ottoman ruins, especially around Ano Poli, the upper town. Among these was the fourth-century palace of Roman Emperor Galerius, which later became a church and then a mosque.

The Great Fire of 1917 there was not a direct result of the war. Its cause was a cooking fire accident, presumably by a refugee who was roasting eggplant (how would they know?). Strong winds known as the *vardaris* and widespread straw and dry, wooden buildings fueled a blaze that destroyed two-thirds of the city and left seventy thousand people homeless. Firefighting was hindered because Allied troops had requisitioned the city's water supplies. The devastation compounded the hardships of the entire region during the demise of Ottoman influence. St. Paul's

*Letter to the Thessalonians* attests to the early influence of Christianity here.

> After a pleasant and interesting sojourn in Egypt, we received orders to proceed to Salonica. On the 21st January 1919 we embarked at Port Said on the *Kaloomba,* a first-class Australian liner belonging to the McIlwraith Line. She had excellent accommodation, and we dined in the first-class saloon with the officers. I slept between linen sheets on a soft bed, a luxury I had not had for some time.

"We" again, chumming with sergeants.

> We sailed the following day at 12:30. Entering the Greek Archipelago, we realised we were running north into colder weather. After two days, a gale sprang up, and we encountered a rough sea. The troops suffered terribly from seasickness, and many laid like logs for the remainder of the voyage. The dining tables in our mess became deserted, and attempts by my colleagues to eat the well-served meals were distressing. Fortunately, I was a good sailor, and I made the best of what was going.

Fred could keep his food down when his mates were bent over the railings, heaving theirs up. He was a proud survivor, and commiseration was not in his makeup.

> We ran along the Albanian Coast, which was mountainous and wooded. It was like entering another world after coming from Egypt and Mespot.

## Jonathan's Journal

*This was Henry's world, and the parallels weren't lost on me. He suffered privations of frozen farmland, where I was enduring the perils of desert, swamp, and jungle. I wondered which of us had the more meager rations.*

> We reached Salonica Harbour at 6 p.m. on the 21st of January and anchored about a mile off the front. All that was visible in the darkness were the lights of the town and the camps on the surrounding hills.
>
> The next morning gave us a panorama view of Salonica, which nestled under snow-clad hills. We disembarked and marched seven miles out to a camp at Summer Hill.
>
> The town, which was full of French and Italian troops, was more continental than I expected to find it. A large number of the buildings were shells, having been gutted by the great fire two years previously.
>
> Reaching Summer Hill Camp, we were allotted very derelict tents. These and the wintry weather added greatly to our discomfort. The box of bacon and chest of tea, which we took the trouble to bring with us from Egypt, were commandeered by the camp quartermaster.

*Stealing a man's bacon? And his tea? We'd carried it all this way, prized as silk. I doubt this fellow's objective was to feed prisoners of war, which was otherwise his responsibility. We were officers, but the higher ranks know nothing of fairness. By now, we should have learned to live for today. Hoarding would seem to be a bad plan.*

> Coming from the East, our blood was thin, and we

felt the cold badly. This severe change eventually had one or two fatal results in our draft.

The following day, I had orders to find 100 men of our draft to join the 3rd Battalion of the King's Royal Rifle Corps, who were about to proceed to Constantinople. I placed myself on the draft, and we marched across the hills to Uchantar. After three days in a very cold, snow-covered and uncomfortable camp, we entrained at Salonica on the 31$^{st}$ of January for Constantinople. It was raining hard, and we unfortunately commenced our journey soaked through. Tightly packed in trucks, we left at midnight on a dilapidated and worn-out railroad.

This voyage was not the beginning of Fred's return to England. From scuttlebutt if not details of his orders, he'd have understood he wasn't being sent directly home. He would guess that Salonica was not a transit point for the welcoming ports of Italy or France. However, he makes no mention of disappointment. Instead, he volunteers for the rifle corps and posting for a time in Constantinople. Was he prolonging his tour? Postponing his homecoming? It would seem so.

Running through Macedonia, we passed Lake Doiran [Dojran], the flooded valley of the Strummer and through the Rupel Pass. It was snowing a blizzard. We saw the Bulgar positions and passed by the front where my brother Henry was wounded in 1916. At many places, the railway was partly submerged, and whilst running through the Serres Marshes nine of the rear trucks jumped the line, several which came off.

It was the roughest train journey I have ever experienced. The accommodation was so packed that we had to take it in turns to lay down. There were no springs to the buffers, and the trucks continuously bumped one into the other bringing our equipment and rifles down on top of us whilst we tried to sleep. The rolling stock and railroad were war-worn by Turkish and Bulgar troops.

*If there was one person in my life I longed to see, it was Henry, and passing through this terrain stirred my imaginings of his encounters in the field. I knew he was alive from his letters. Had his injuries not been debilitating and disqualifying, he might have shipped back out as I did. I believe by 1916 they might have been willing to take him had he been eager and fit. I worried not just about his welfare but also about how much of my brother would be left to greet me.*

A fire was a great comfort where we could get fuel, which we burnt in a brazier in the truck, making us black with smoke, and we had to wash and shave in the cold snow wakes along the line. We had our cheering comfort, however, in the armorer sergeant, who carried a violin, and we passed away many hours in song.

Did the sergeant perhaps buy the instrument from a local? For a potato or two?

Macedonia is a wild, mountainous country, and the houses of the villages in the hills look like Swiss chalets.

On Saturday the 1st of February, we crossed the

Macedonian-Bulgar frontier and ran along a river with towering mountains on either side, over which hovered an occasional eagle. We passed the ruins of small towns and villages, the relics of Balkan wars.

Along the railroad, we met many Bulgar soldiers, who were pleased that the fighting was over.

We halted at a town that had a well-built appearance, and it was the first bit of civilization we had met on our journey, but the children were starving and ate ravenously the bully beef and biscuits we gave them.

Resuming our journey, we ran through miles of low-lying country, which was mostly under water and full of wild fowl. It was necessary to travel slowly and continuously. Two trucks lost their wheels, and the trucks had to be abandoned. We packed it in and enjoyed a good night's rest.

The following day, we crossed the Bulgar-Turkish frontier. Here we met the Turk. The villages through which we passed were full of children who looked picturesque in their quaint attire, the girls wearing loose trousers. The countryside looked neglected, and cattle appeared to be scarce.

"The Turk," expressed curtly, as one might say "the Hun." No mention of the adults, whether man or woman, but children are citizens of the world and greedy thieves of the soldier's affections and whatever might be in his pockets to eat.

# Her Invitation

## Jonathan's Journal and Elena's Message

I WAS GOING to breakfast on half a grapefruit and a slice of toast, permitting myself a pat of butter. I was easily twenty pounds overweight. Discipline would be the order of the day, and in exercising sobriety of approach, I'd decide how to tell Elena I missed her and fretted for her welfare without sounding like a crybaby tween.

It was seven in the morning, which would have been five in the afternoon where she was. I was sifting through scads of phishing ads and spam newsletters when her message appeared in the inbox, continuing a thread she'd started.

> Jonathan,
>
> My apologies. I didn't hear back from you right away, which of course I had no reason to expect. I am sure my news came as a shock, and I'm embarrassed I

haven't been a more considerate friend. I know you think me more than an acquaintance. Your affection does not surprise or shock me. Indeed, it is reciprocated. You may think you don't communicate, but the shortcoming is mutual. Professional close observers like me are trained to share only the minimum necessary. What am I saying? Of all people, you have a need to know!

Rocket attacks have begun again here. I had not thought Putin would dare to destroy this city, reverent as his remarks have been about how we have always been a cherished part of Russia. Stalin sent our harvests to Moscow, starving to death the peasants who farmed it. Now the cabal of oligarchs with their cowardly, hateful munitions level our beloved cathedrals and museums as if sweeping so many playing pieces from the board. And incinerate children like so much unwanted waste.

My family is not without resources. While it is still possible, I'm putting my sister and the children on a plane to Bucharest, where she has a close friend who is well-off. Stefan is still at the front, and there's nothing for us to do about that. As for me, I share your alarm for how the political climate in the States is shifting. California may be a mecca, but for how long? I haven't even checked into the complications of emigrating once again. For me, it will be complicated, for reasons I needn't explain now.

Better I carve out some blissful time, go where I had once been happy. I never told you about my school days in Florence. Will you meet me there?

Elena xo

# Constantinople

## Jonathan's Journal

It took Elena's unsubtle offer to blast me out of my hibernation. It has been so long since I've traveled that I had to refresh myself on the requirements. One advantage of living in a high-rise apartment is that you can lock the door and jet away to distant lands, and no one will know you're gone. Your mail and packages will pile up in the receiving room, and the quiet of the hallway linking residences of resting boomers will be only a whisper quieter.

I had a valid passport, obtained some years back for the purpose of attending an academic conference that was canceled because of the pandemic. I needed a new suitcase, one that free-wheels so I need not lift it often. In my day, they called the size a two-suiter, but who wears suits anymore? I admit the sight of a CEO in a hoody is still disconcerting to me.

I booked a direct flight from LAX to Rome Fiumicino Leonardo da Vinci, which was less expensive than flying into Florence. I was appalled at the cost even of coach tickets, but the shocker on Lufthansa was that every additional inch of seat room and proximity forward or to the aisle came at a handsome surcharge. Nevertheless, I sucked it up and paid for business class, cursing my craving for luxury but blaming my susceptibility to crippling leg cramps. For what I paid, not that long ago I could have bought a decent used car.

From the airport, took a taxi to Roma Termina, then a first-class compartment on the train to Firenze Santa Maria Novella. I had no recent experience with European system, but I recall a friend telling me that the assigned seating on the Frecciarossa high-speed trains required you to board at the correct car number. I heedlessly boarded the wrong one, too far aft because I was running late, and I had to wrestle my bag through the horde of passengers, squeezing my way past students wearing enormous backpacks and finding that, in these cramped circumstances, those handy wheels were of no use.

I had wisely booked a car service to take me to our rendezvous at 35 via Maggio. Elena had described it as an intimate pensione, having only a few rooms and a storied past. She had been there once but did not say when or with whom.

On the plane, besides dozing lulled by the droning of the engines, I read the next installment of Fred's diary on my tablet. I marked where I'd insert notes later. I didn't have a keyboard for it. I hate typing on those things, and dictating into your device on a plane would be downright rude.

> On Monday the 3rd of February, we arrived at Constantinople. The sun shone, which was the first we had seen for some time, and we viewed this inter-

> esting city, rising from the Bosphorous [Bosporus], with its numerous gilt-topped minarets and oriental buildings, from the waterside railhead. The Bosphorous was full of warships of the allied fleets. What a cosmopolitan crowd of people! Some wore native costumes and others fashionably dressed, but the poverty was terrible. Children offered their souls for food, and respectably dressed Turks tendered handfuls of Turkish paper money (which was then of little or no value) for a tin of bully beef or jam.

Fred's description of Constantinople is his lengthiest diary entry. He has volunteered for this duty, and it's clear from context that his role was supervisory. The challenges there were to manage the disheartened and disadvantaged citizenry, as well as encamp the masses of refugees. All while attempting to maintain the peace. Looting and petty crime would have been commonplace and mostly uncontrollable. The shortage hardships of food and supplies were made all the more severe by the devaluation of local currency for obtaining anything.

Of all the places Fred has visited so far, Constantinople is the first where he encountered the widespread suffering and disheartened national mood of a defeated country. Salonica was a preview, especially the ruins from that fire, but that city at least had benefited from Allied military presence throughout the war. Here in this huge metropolis, the cultural richness and the opulence of the defeated empire existed as a dazzling backdrop to the gloom and misery of its population.

> Two companies of the battalion took up their quarters on the Italian monastery in the city, and the other

two companies (to one of which I belonged) occupied a portion of the Faculty de Medicine at Haidar-Pacha. This college was a large building constructed of stone and iron, and Turkish medical students were in session in the portion not occupied by us. My room was on the top floor and commanded exclusive views of the Bosphorous and the Prince Islands in the Sea of Marmara.

We found Haidar-Pacha full of stranded Germans, principally sailors off the *Golese*. These German troops had, up to our arrival, full run of the place, occupying their time in the cafes with no trooper authority over them, and they sold all the German war equipment they could lay their hands on to civilians before our arrival. We quickly rounded them up and interned them in a camp.

Weapons, especially small arms and ammo, falling into the hands of the locals was as much a threat to crime directed among themselves as resistance to the occupiers.

Everything was very dear. I paid the equivalent of four shillings in Greek silver for a cup of coffee and a cake.

Our next duties were to open up the Anatolian Railway, dispatch Armenian refugees into the interior, and prevent food from coming into Constantinople from the poverty-stricken interior, as the Armenian Mission had undertaken the distribution of food to the needy in the city.

It struck me as ironic that the Armenian genocide

perpetrated by the Turks had taken place just a few years before this.

> A large guard was mounted every morning at the Haidar-Pacha Railway Station with all the ceremony of the guards at Buckingham Palace. It was an event of the day watched by hundreds of the inhabitants. Part of our mission was to create an impression, which needless to say was carried out, and the British troops won great respect.

As in India — and to a limited extent also in Basra after the decisive battles — simply maintaining a highly visible presence was a principal function of the British military. Fred seems well aware of this role and of its importance. And of course he'd been a fan of these grand parades ever since he saw the Colours march down the street and decided to enlist.

> The large numbers of refugees were a frightful sight: whole families would wait for days sleeping on the cold stone floors of the station until a train was available to take them back to their villages in the interior from which they had been ousted during the war. Detachments of my battalion were sent to various stations down the line as far as Angora and at places they had rough encounters with brigand Turks. One party of prisoners what were sent up to Haidar-Pacha was a fierce-looking lot. Some wore several silk shirts and yards of silk wound around their bodies, which were probably stolen.
>
> Another impressive sight was to witness the Turkish

> troop ships discharge their cargoes of sad humanity. A large proportion of these troops were Arabs, who had been pressed into the Turkish army, and they were brought to Scutari Barracks to be demobilised. Many of them were in rags, others clothed in sackcloth, and some were too weak to walk without assistance. These troops were herded together in Scutari Barracks and given one meal a day consisting of black bread and a basin of soup. The sanitary arrangements were bad, and many died. Those who had been discharged hung about the streets without any means of subsistence.

There's a lesson here about the wages of war, regardless of historical period. Today, peacekeeping in the aftermath of conflict will fall to UN forces drafted in rotation from member countries. Nation building is a deprecated mission, not least because it's difficult if not impossible to achieve. I recall one of Gen. Colin Powell's maxims "If you break it, you own it." The Ottoman Empire had been broken. One might argue the Allies did not set out to do it. But it was an outcome that, even before the war, they had expected to happen, with or without their intervention.

> These conditions were investigated by the British military authorities, with the result that we took charge of the various Mesopotamian, Palestinian, and Syrian Arabs — clothed, fed, and repatriated them as ships became available. It was the intention to charge Turkey with the cost of this good work when the question of reparations was considered, but like many of our other philanthropic acts during

the war, the expenditure eventually fell on the British taxpayer.

Hmm. "Philanthropic acts." Again, rebuilding war-torn countries is necessarily the obligation of the victors. The costs often involved appropriating the resources of the vanquished in compensation. However, if grabbing those resources were a primary objective of the war, cause and effect get swapped.

Scutari Barracks is an enormous building with a large square in the center. It was here Florence Nightingale nursed the sick and wounded during the Crimean War and inaugurated the Red Cross.

In our present fretting over Putin's annexation of Crimea, we tend to forget that British forces shed blood and treasure there, recognizing then the strategic importance of its seaports and pivotal position linking Eastern Europe to Russia.

Haidar-Pacha Railway Station, which is a modern and imposing building, was the German General Von Faulkenhayn's base and ammunition dump for the intended taking of Baghdad. The dump was, however, blown up by our airmen, causing great havoc, and no doubt this destruction of ammunition had a lot to do with the eventual abandonment of the attack on Baghdad. It was rather a coincidence that I should see the headquarters of General Von Faulkenhayn's operations here, which were the means of my going East.

Even as he shipped out, Fred understood the decisive geopolitical importance of the Eastern Question, a term that was on so many European lips at the time and today is tucked away in neglected textbooks.

> Two Turkish medical students with whom I became acquainted showed me over a portion of the college that was not occupied by my battalion. In the anatomy laboratory, several groups of students were at marble tables dissecting portions of preserved human bodies. Corpses were lying about all over the place under process of preservation. It was a weird sight: a hole was made in the throat and formalin injected through a pipe from a tank overhead. The body of a large Negro was among them. Many corpses were available for the college at the time. The museum was full of interest. Every part of the anatomy was preserved in glass jars: one contained the body of a child with two heads. The majority of the students spoke good English and were very sociable.

*Until now, I haven't bothered to interject. Jon is seeing through me, and it's as embarrassing as having no clothes. Granted I tend to be an objective observer — though not heartless, I insist — and one develops a thick skin from wartime experiences. Sarah would probably have said I was such when I set out, and in retrospect some aspects of my journey did heighten my sensitivity, as a sunburn inflames the skin. I carried my heartache with me. Heading home now, I expected it would never be healed. These strange sights were diverting and provided a welcome focus of my attention.*

*It's useless to offer apologies for who I am. Or was.*

> After a few weeks at Haidar-Pacha, I was appointed regimental quartermaster sergeant. This necessitated my going into Constantinople every morning to draw rations. I crossed in the crowded ferryboat, which was commodious and built at Glasgow. During the crossing, the ration party and I made a point of turning men passengers out of their seats to enable elderly women to sit down. These men passengers of many nationalities appeared to have no respect for their opposite sex, and our action was not appreciated by them.

Ah, the English gentleman's manner is summoned to the fore! It's fascinating that British national pride has always been bound up in civilized behavior, decency, and fairness, as well as implied superiority. At least, Fred believed in those ideals.

> My work was not arduous. It gave me plenty of treasure that I spent visiting the numerous places of interest in Constantinople and its environs.
>
> As I mentioned before, the city has a picturesque appearance viewed at a distance from the Bosphorous, but its dirty and insanitary interior gave one quite a different aspect.
>
> The Galata Bridge, which is the center of the city, crosses the Golden Horn and connects Galata with Stanbul. it gives a good view of the Golden Horn, which was full of old, rusty-looking Turkish warships. The traffic over this bridge is always crowded and daily affords a picturesque scene, almost every Oriental and Western nation being represented in the motley crowd.

> The Galata Tower, which is 300 feet high, was used as a naval outlook. It commands a view of the city, the Golden Horn, Bosphorous, and the Sea of Marmara. Looking down from this tower, I saw numbers of children at play on the flat rooftops. Their favourite pastime was kite flying.
>
> I visited many mosques, the largest being St. Sophia, the interior of which is lavishly decorated with costly marbles and beautiful mosaics. Turkish soldiers were billeted in its corridors.

Fred makes an error here that is common even today among Western visitors. The Hagia Sophia temple, built under Emperor Constantine as a place of Christian worship, then later repurposed as a mosque, was not originally named for a saint. *Pistis Sophia* means "wisdom" in Latin. At its inception, it was a Greek Christian church named the Temple of God's Wisdom. Nevertheless, many references to the Church of St. Sophia can be found, even among scholarly articles and on the lips of English-speaking tour guides.

> I made several steamer trips up the Bosphorous to various places as far as the entrance to the Black Sea. These trips were interesting. Leaving Galata Bridge, we steamed through the allied fleets lying in the harbour and passed the front of the Sultan's Palace.
>
> On both sides of the Bosphorous are small towns and villages. At Büyükdere were the European ambassadors' summer residences. These houses were on the water's edge. Although strong currents

run in the Bosphorous, there is no rise and fall of tide.

One Sunday, Sergeant Mitchell and I went by steamer and landed at a small village on the European side of the Bosphorous. A stiff climb inland for about three miles brought us on the crest line of the hills, which gave us a good view of the distant Forest of Belgrade, the entrance to the Black Sea with its fortifications, and the winding Bosphorous. We then made tracks for Constantinople, crossing several valleys and steep hills. The hills were barren, but the valleys fertile and mostly cultivated. Where each valley met the Bosphorous, there was a village. Wisteria which covered nearly every house was in full bloom, and the deep-purple lotus and fruit tree blossoms in the valleys were in their glory. We arrived back in Constantinople in the evening just in time to catch the last ferryboat to Haidar-Pacha.

I also visited the small nearby towns and villages situated on the coastline of the Sea of Marmara. On one occasion, Mitchell and I struck inland across some wild country. When we were within a few miles of Haidar-Pacha on our return journey, we were suddenly fired upon from a hilltop. Several bullets whizzed uncomfortably near us, and we quickly found cover. We always carried an army revolver on these rambles, but it would only have been useful at close quarters, and we were fortunately not pursued. These men were probably discharged Turkish soldiers who at that time roamed the country in search of loot.

Once more, here is the threat of weapons of war falling into the hands of resentful, starving locals.

A walk out to Konsgoundjouk [Kuzguncuk], a small town on the Asiatic side of the Bosphorous, was interesting. It was a residential town for the principal businesspeople of Constantinople. A large cafe we entered was full of Turks, Jews, Greeks, and Armenians. They were well-dressed and very sociable. One of the Turks spoke good English, having resided in Manchester for fourteen years before the war. There was a fine Greek church here, and we were shown around as guests.

At Konsgoundjouk, the Bosphorous is only half a mile wide.

I had the use of a horse when I wanted it. Our officers, chargers, and transport horses had little work to do here. I enjoyed one or two rides down the line to Malope and Pendik on a visit to our detachments. My mount was a clever Bulgarian pony, which the battalion picked up on the Macedonian front. It was very sure-footed over the rough, broken country, which was barren with no trees and little bird and animal life.

Constantinople began to wear a different appearance from the state in which we first saw it. The cafes, shops, and the extensive Grand Bazaar brightened up as goods were being imported. The rue de Pera was full of Allied and Turkish officers in their coloured full dress uniforms. The political situation was, however, very unsettled. The Turks and Greeks were at loggerheads with each other, principally over the peace terms and the handing back of the

> Mosque of St. Sophia [sic] to the Greeks. It eventually became necessary for us to take precautionary measures. Just before I left, the battalion had to stand-to for a week with machine guns mounted in the corridors of our quarters. We had to walk about armed and in company. These unsettled conditions delayed my demobilization.

Presumably, turning the mosque over the Greeks would have repurposed it again for Eastern Orthodox Christian worship. This was not done. Today, Sophia remains a mosque, although used more as a monument, and the nearby Blue Mosque welcomes worshippers.

# Rendezvous in Florence

## Jonathan's Journal

I ARRIVED at SoprArno Suites before she did. My driver generously offered to carry my bag upstairs and even unpack for me, which I was glad to let him do for a generous tip in dollars, since I had no euros yet.

The enormous old entry doors span an archway almost two stories tall and open past another set of doors to an intimate, lovely ground-floor courtyard surrounded by lush flowering plants. I took the presence of tea tables there to be a strong hint, and while Enzo unpacked, I took my Earl Grey and fresh-baked pastry to calm my nerves. I was exhausted from the flight and yet tingled at the thought of our long-delayed reunion. I wondered whether the cares of conflict had worn her down. I was sure she needed this respite even if she weren't being met by such an ardent admirer.

The pensione has just eleven rooms, and the place seemed empty except for the lovely young proprietress who checked me in and then delivered the tea service.

## Jonathan's Journal

Having gratefully drained two cups and sent Enzo off with my thanks and a couple of crisp banknotes, I retired upstairs to what I'd been told was the most lavish room in the place. It was the size of a large studio apartment back home, one room with a half bath. Most impressive right away was a pair of ten-foot-tall French-door windows facing the street side. Above, as remarkable and attesting to the age of the place, were a frescoed ceiling and gold-leaf-covered sideboards.

And remarkable for a suite that had obviously undergone renovation was a free-standing clawfoot bathtub, positioned in the corner of the room just outside the door to the sink, toilet, and bidet.

The tub stood there, elegant in its dated cast-iron opulence, like a museum piece, with no partitioning or drapery to hide the bather.

I resolved to stay alert until Elena's arrival, but I couldn't manage it. Still in my clothes, I'd propped myself up in the bed, the ubiquitous tablet in my lap. In my reading, I was getting so close to the end of the diary and Fred's ultimate arrival home that I thought I might finish before I saw her. We'd have that much more to discuss, particularly if the ending, which I had not dared skip ahead to read, held any surprises.

I dozed off.

She must have entered with exceptional quiet, because I didn't even hear muffled voices in the hallway that would have signaled her approach. While I slept, she'd been shown into the room, whereupon her backpack was set on a luggage rack.

When I awoke to the sound of running water, she was standing next to the tub and peeling off her clothes.

Startled, I held up the tablet to hide my face.

She'd been studying me to see whether her actions would arouse me.

When she saw me peeking, she said, "Is that your sketchpad, Monsieur Degas?"

"You don't mind my peeking?"

"I sincerely hoped you would," she said as her jeans dropped to her ankles.

As I set the tablet aside, I began to unbutton my shirt.

"Oh, don't you disrobe," she cooed as she lowered herself into the steaming water. "I want to do that for you."

"So, what? I watch?"

She held up a brush. "If you scrub my back, after I've undressed you, I'll do some work with the sponge."

---

She was generous with her body, which was not scrawny. Lush and pink. She didn't just lie back and expect to be entertained. She was in there, a full participant. I don't think I've ever been better cared for.

She didn't expound or narrate. This wasn't show business for her. She gave me her full self.

What was there to say? Everything, but little else mattered.

"So," she said at last, pulling the covers over her breasts, "What do you think of this love nest I found?"

"It's amazing. Did you know about the tub?"

She turned to face me. "I confess this isn't my first time in this room."

"I didn't need to know that."

"Noted, professor. But this place has a story, and I want you to hear it."

"More World War One?"

"Centuries earlier. Let's order up a bottle of Montepulciano, then I'll tell you."

She grabbed her phone and called down to the desk, after which she announced, "Senora says she must fetch it from the café down the block. She won't be up right away."

"So what about the story?"

"Wouldn't you rather go again?"

"Whoa. I confess, I was concerned about, you know, my performance. First time — I mean, first time for *us.*"

"I really don't want to hear your war stories either."

"Doesn't happen every day. Been years actually." At which, she began to minister to me, and it was evident she expected prompt reciprocation. After a suitable period of recuperation, I did my best to oblige. Fortunately and blissfully, the wine did not arrive promptly.

---

The senora arrived with two bottles, Elena explaining, one for now, one for later. While still in bed, we eagerly had one glass each then sipped the second more slowly.

"You know your Italian wine," I told her.

"My other favorite is Sangiovese. Both dry, light. Their wine has less alcohol content than French or Californian and considerably less than Australian or South African. You can have some at lunch and not sleep through the afternoon with your mistress."

"Moderation in all things. Lovely. You want to hear the story. But I expect you're getting hungry. I know I am. You could tell me over dinner."

"No, I want to share this when we're here in this

special place." She gave me a kiss, got up, wrapped herself in a sweater, sat in a guest chair, and began, "In the late Renaissance, the Via Maggio was a main street connecting the Medici's court in the Pitti Palace to the city center. Many of these buildings were palaces, rather like townhouses, of the nobility. But this particular address, its structure possibly dating back to medieval times, was somewhat scandalous. A few houses down at number twenty-six was the palace of Bianca Cappello, mistress and then second wife of Grand Duke Francesco I. The guidebooks mark that grander structure as her residence. But legend has it that this place — and this very room — is where they had their assignations, even before his wife Joanna died." She added for emphasis, "She fell down a flight of stairs, but perhaps after she'd already been poisoned."

I almost spit out my wine. "And this is romance?"

"Divorce was not a thing, my dear. especially for royalty. But, in this room, only love. They married soon after, and years later they died together. Possibly poisoned, but the academics are saying more probably malaria."

"Touching story. Vomiting into the tub?"

"Joanna was an arranged marriage. She was from the royal family of Austria. These alliances between countries by marriage were very much the order of the day, and much of European history since. Bianca was his love. He had the luxury of choice."

"You are, I must admit, the most spectacular human being I've ever had the privilege to know, this way or any other." And I added, "I mean that exclusively and sincerely."

"You are free to choose, my dear. Florence captivated me that other time, regardless of the circumstances of my visit, and as you do, history fascinates me. I was struck by all that must have transpired here but also by the character of Francis. He was interested in alchemy and physics. His *studiolo* was in the Palazzo Vecchio, where he conducted his inquiries, but he also had a collection, a 'cabinet of curiosities.' His secret laboratory, his most private place, may also have been here and not at court."

"You're thinking we are so like them?"

"There must be reasons people are drawn to certain places, even specific houses and rooms. For sure, we are both driven by curiosity. He would have been able to surround himself with sages, but he had to have his own studio. Bianca must've been very clever as well. He was the kind of man who would have been bored with anyone who couldn't keep up with him." She bestowed another tender kiss and said, "You are a sweet man."

"Perhaps my best feature," I replied, hating myself for trying to be too clever as soon as I'd uttered it.

"Francesco moved the Medici painting collection into the Uffizi Palace. We're going there tomorrow."

"More history?"

"Your field, Professor. But you've never experienced it this way!"

# Homeward Bound

## Jonathan Comments on Fred's Diary

As Elena busied herself with morning ablutions, I resolved to finish the diary. We had yet to touch on our project of mutual interest. Whether or not she'd finished it herself, I didn't want her to have the advantage of me.

And I was curious.

My background reading told me that passage back to England via troop ship through the Med took several months. They'd sail through the Straits of Gibraltar, around the stormy coast of Spain and then Portugal, then to disembark at Southampton or Plymouth.

For Fred, it was the closing episode, marking the end of five years of continuous service across three continents.

> After nearly five months in Turkey, I left Haidar-Pacha with a demobilization party on the 19th of May, 1919. We went to the Italian monastery in Constantinople,

> and I took the opportunity of sending a cable home with the good news of my departure.

Sent to Sarah, presumably. "Good news," presumptively. Possibly, hopefully. Not until now had he bothered? Other than sending those few curios and the silk home, he'd made no mention of more meaningful communication during his long tours.

> With an escort, I went to the Eastern Telegraph Office in the rue de Pera, and after dispatching the wire, we stopped in a cafe for some refreshment. All of a sudden, the place was in a turmoil. Shots rang out in the streets, people ran about in a frenzy, shutters of shops and banks were hurriedly put up, and in a short time every place was closed and the streets deserted. The whole city was in a nervous tension with these frequent political disturbances. The shops eventually opened again, people emerged from cover, and business went on as if nothing had happened.

Was this civil unrest or opportunistic criminal activity? Perhaps both? In the minds of the British command, scenes like this justified their continuous presence in the city. Local government held no authority, and law enforcement would have been erratic at best.

If Fred had been prevailed upon to stay longer, he didn't mention it. Could it be he was finally looking forward to going home?

> The following day, we boarded the *Seang Bee*, which lay out in the harbour.

> As our freighter was leaving quay, I saw Commander Davey (of Queen Street, Exeter) in a naval pinnace alongside. He came out to the *Seang Bee* and gave me a look-up before we sailed. Although there was a general and several staff officers on deck watching his departure, as he left, he shouted, "Kind regards to all at Exeter!" He sounded his siren in long shrills for over a mile.

Fred does not remark on how the commander knew of him or their roots in the Ever Faithful. At various points in his narrative, Fred's fondness and loyalty for the city is evident. He's proud to be from there and no doubt proud of his citizenship on return. An open question is whether he has some station or position to aspire to.

> We weighed anchor at 6 p.m. and ran by the Princes' Islands through the Sea of Marmara.
> Next morning, we entered the Dardanelles and passed close by the troopship *River Clyde,* which was on the rocks of Cafe Ellis. There were also many other deserted ships of the Gallipoli campaign, and it gave one a good idea of the difficulties that were experienced in the landing of troops. Leaving the Dardanelles, we wended the Island of Embros and turned north for Salonica. The sea became rough, and our old tub, which was a Chinese boat manned by a Chinese crew, gave us a rough voyage.
> We reached Salonica harbour at 9 a.m. on the 22nd of May. The weather was still cold and rough, and the mountains of the Olympus range were covered with snow. We disembarked and marched out to a reception camp on Summer Hill. The next

day, we moved to a concentration camp and then to an embarkation camp. At all these camps we were subjected to strict medical inspections.

The British Navy had centuries of experience dealing with sailors returning home, infected with contagious organisms from distant lands.

On June 1st, we embarked on the *Maple,* a small Clyde steamer. There were 580 aboard. We left at 2 p.m. and soon lost sight of Salonica, for which I had no regrets, as on both my visits the arrangements were bad and out of all comparison with the other places of military operations I had seen.

It was a glorious day and a fair sea. We ran along the coastline under Mount Olympus, the snow-clad top of which was lit by brilliant sunshine. The next day, we navigated through a network of Greek islands in the Aegean Sea and then called at Piraeus, the port of Athens, and picked up more passengers. We afterwards ran through the Corinth Canal, which is a cutting three miles long and saves a day's journey around the Cape of Greece. Leaving the canal, we entered the Gulf of Corinth and crossed the Adriatic, reaching Taranto, Italy, at 4:30 p.m. on the 3rd of June. It was an interesting voyage, and the warm balmy nights made it pleasant sleeping on the open decks.

We stayed two nights in the rest camp at Taranto. What a change had taken place in the camp since I passed through it nearly two years previously! Instead of tents pitched knee-deep in dust, well-built bungalows with every convenience had been erected and good roads made.

From Fred's narrative, it becomes apparent that the building and maintenance of transit camps adjacent to port facilities was a major logistical function throughout the war. The rules of war would have banned the shelling of these installations, although reporting of such events might not have been as newsworthy as news from the front.

> Here we had more medical inspections. They became quite a bore. The authorities were determined that troops from the East should not carry home any diseases with them, and certificates were given to everyone who was free thereof.

Reminds me of those Covid-19 vaccination cards we had to carry, presentation on demand at public events such as concerts.

> I had no opportunity of visiting the town of Taranto as it was out of bounds to troops, owing to political disturbances, but I took an interesting walk along the shore of the expansive harbour and returned inland through cornfields and olive groves.
>
> On the 5th of June, we started on our long train journey through Italy and France. We managed to form a merry party, comprising principally of warrant officers of the army and navy — twelve in all — and we secured a roomy truck with large sliding doors on either side, which gave us good facilities for viewing the country. A

> field kitchen was carried on the train, which enabled us to have our meals fairly regularly, instead of having to stop at various places to boil water etc. as we did on our journey out. We travelled on the same route as we came out, stopping at Sarenza for a day for exercise and a bath. On that Sunday, June 8$^{th}$, the Italian villages were *en fête*, and when our train happened to stop at any of these places, we were surrounded by the populace, who had a great craving for British cigarettes, which we exchanged for wine.

The train from Taranto bypasses the more arduous sea voyage past Gibraltar and around the Atlantic coast. Fred is retracing the route he took through France, soon after he'd enlisted for his second tour, skirting the Western Front.

> We crossed the Italian-France Alps in bright moonlight, which lit up the snow-clad tops and turned the rivulets into glittering silver. It was such an imposing spectacle that our merry party sat up most of the night and enjoyed it in melody. Our spirits were naturally high, as we were getting so near home.

The value and the remembrance of comradely singing! Were they too anxious and overwhelmed to sing on the way out?

> We arrived at Bologne on the 11th of June and spent the night in a rest camp. Next morning, we entered the embarkation camp, where we had our final medical examination. Everyone, officers and men, went through a disinfecting process. We had

to strip naked and put all our belongings in a kit bag. We then had a shower bath and had to wait some time shivering in a long corridor until our belongings, which had been disinfected, were handed back to us by German prisoners who were in attendance.

They put German soldiers to work delousing the returning troops. One crucial precaution would be to make sure the men and their clothing didn't carry mosquitos, fleas, and ticks.

We crossed the Channel to Dover in the *Golden Eagle* on Saturday the 12th and proceeded to transit camp, arriving there at 9 p.m. We immediately started to go through the machinery of demobilization, which lasted until 3 a.m. on Sunday morning, when I received my discharge papers. I was turned into a civilian again, and I said farewell to my rifle and equipment, which was a relief, although they had been my companions for nearly two years.

It was a glorious feeling to be back again in dear Old Blighty. The country was looking its best in its mantle of June verdure, which only England can produce. I returned to the Ever Faithful in the afternoon and was greeted by my wife.

*Sarah had been informed of my arrival by the staff of the station in Exeter. I didn't know this, and I confess I was surprised to see her. Doubly surprised, because she was in uniform, having enlisted in the WRENS soon after my departure. Admittedly, our kiss was a cautious peck on the cheek. I had earned no more, and reasons for her reluctance escaped me. All would come out sooner or later. Or it wouldn't.*

*There would be time to decide.*

I wonder at the lack of emotion here. "Greeted by my wife" seems an understatement, perhaps deliberately obscure. The fact she showed up at all should be telling, I'd think.

---

# At the Uffizi

## Jonathan's Journal

"That's a gorgeous dress," I told her. "But all you brought is a backpack."

"Silk doesn't take much space," she replied.

"They have such fashion in Kiev?"

"They do, but this is from Firenze."

"I'm sorry. I forget. No questions to be asked."

"You are a gentleman." She smiled demurely. "Shall we venture back in time?"

With a parallel perhaps nowhere else in the world, the Uffizi Gallery is organized chronologically. In the museum floor (the second), the paintings are organized chronologically, forming a U-shaped tour from the thirteenth to eighteenth centuries, spanning five centuries of figurative art.

This was indeed my area of specialty. But as she had advised me, here was a way of experiencing it that cannot be found in any textbook.

In the early period, portraits of saints were commissioned for hanging in places of worship. The earliest paintings there depict Christ on the cross. I knew from my studies, including Manchester's *A World Lit Only by Fire,* that the peasantry, and even members of the upper classes in the feudal period, had no experience of imaginative pictures other than the paintings they saw in church. This experience and mindset are so difficult for us to understand because we are bombarded with thousands of images every moment of our waking lives. For these people in ancient times, a picture of the Virgin or of a saint's bravery could be taken as literal, perhaps captured by some witness to the experience, because there was no other version for comparison. And no priest would attest to their mythological inspirations.

The Byzantine portraits are flat, two dimensional and expressionless. These are icons, not renderings. If the artists had dared, which even with active imaginations they would not have ventured, these likenesses were sober and righteous, conveying no compassion, no sympathy, inspiring only veneration.

The flowering of virtuosity in the Renaissance stemmed not only from the rediscovery of Greek aesthetics but also the principles of perspective, admitting dimensionality and realism into portraiture. These faces exuded not only austerity and righteousness but also sensitivity.

Love.

I am told some European tour guides insist that kissing on the mouth did not begin until the Romantic period in Italy. Ridiculous! If you read the apocryphal *Book of Philip,* Jesus kissed Mary Magdalene "on her mouth" whenever he got the chance.

In the medieval period, the Arab influence persisted. Depicting the graven image was prohibited, following the second commandment strictly. Only geometric patterns, as illustrate mosques to this day. No images of Jesus or saints or even of Mohammed.

Then to the portraitists who rediscovered the legacy of Greeks, picking it up from sculpture but transposing it onto canvas. Caravaggio began with a black ground, building his oiled layers up from there to reveal faces in shadows, but it was not until Gérôme and the Neo-Romanticists that they laid in faces first as masses of white. Not surprising, they worshipped rosy cheeked, ivory complexions, made all the more pallid from doses of arsenic by upper-class ladies. The virtuosity of these painters, who were my professional preoccupation, was obscured by those rash Impressionists, who thrust emotions at the viewer with their hurried dabs of color. No one until this time had ever captured the fleeting flickering of color on crests of water, the progression of daylight on cathedral fronts, the waning of light through the seasons on haystacks.

Painters were and are God's transmitters of love, though they might not be aware. Van Gogh might not have actually cut off his ear for love, but he was brave enough to capture his hallucinogenic visions of the sky in paint.

Not all of this was at the Uffizi, but it certainly got me started.

She was right. I had never experienced the span of my fascination with the history of art in this way. Genius of the gallery curators that they understood and appreciated it more deeply than I did.

## Jonathan's Journal

Near the end of our tour around the second floor, I lingered in front of a woman's portrait. I learned later that Elena had gone ahead to marvel at Caravaggio's *Bacchus,* which I knew well from my studies, and I always found the chubby little fellow downright humorous.

The woman staring out at me wasn't, in my estimation, gorgeous. She was dressed conservatively, her hair drawn back in a tight bun, adding to the stiff severity of her pose. She was rosy-cheeked with a small mouth, drawn inward primly as if in a disapproving pout.

Her sidelong glance at me was striking, her most arresting feature. It was so suspicious, even devious, that I felt a chill.

Elena came up quietly behind me, resting a gentle hand on my shoulder. "I see you've found her," she cooed.

"Stopped me in my tracks," I said. "That look. I don't think the painter liked her much, and maybe the feeling was mutual."

"Alessandro Allori," she explained. "The foremost portraitist at the Medici court. This image would have had Francesco's blessing. He's the one, by the way, who once he gained power turned his father's government offices into this museum. And her look? She wouldn't have thought it unflattering. Commissioned renderings of the Medicis were supposed to convey high rank and authority. As for the painter, it's possible he shared the popular opinion of her at that time. Her first husband had been murdered, and the gossip was she'd hired his killer."

"Who was she?"

Elena lifted her comforting hand to her mouth to hide what must've been a devilish smile. "Oh my, Professor, read the museum card. This is the *Portrait of Bianca Cappello.*"

# Parco di Monte Ceceri

## Jonathan's Journal

A LANGUOROUS FOUR-COURSE dinner at Gilda Bistro capped our day at the museum. Afterward, we were so groggy with food and drink that good intentions did not pave the way to anything but sleep.

She must've been a sound sleeper, because next morning she was dressed before my eyes opened. A goddess with gifts, she held out a steaming cup of espresso. "Get up and wear comfortable shoes. You've got ten minutes."

As I was splashing hot water on my puffy face, a car horn from below announced the taxi's arrival. She must have run down there then, given him instructions, and loaded her rucksack into the boot.

She came back up to fetch me as I buttoned up. "I'm taking you to the mountaintop, where all will be revealed."

"Sounds biblical," I muttered. I hadn't noticed her things were not in the room.

Here was her now-familiar devilish grin. "No questions. You'll be seeing it all from a new perspective."

Once we were in the car, I was about to ask where we were going when she began to chatter endlessly about the menu delights of last night's dinner. We'd drained two bottles of her favorite Sangiovese, and I was amazed my head seemed so clear.

Each time I opened my mouth, she touched my lips gently with her forefinger to hold me to my vow of silence.

Our driver took us out of the city and into the wooded hills to the northeast. The route threaded through tall pines and rocks.

So far, she had not given him a word of instruction. Somewhere near the peak, he pulled over to the side of the road and stopped. I should have guessed from her advice about shoes. I managed to blurt out, "You're taking me on a hike."

As soon as I was out of the car, she leaned it to remind the driver, "Here at two!" He nodded, she slammed the door, and he sped off.

"Give me your phone," she demanded.

I reached into my pocket for it but hesitated to pull it out. "You know, there's a limit to trust!"

The grin again. "Professor, would you rather teach or learn?" It was the shared joke about lovemaking roles, teasing me that I need not always be the instructor. I handed it over.

She strode over to a rock on the verge that was about the size of a football and bent down to tuck both our phones behind it. She looked up and pointed. "Remember that tree."

Thieves up here? Hiding the phones seemed an unnecessary precaution, especially in the off chance we'd need them for navigation or to summon assistance. But I was giving myself over to her care.

As we set out on the hiking trail, she explained that Monte Ciceri is a large area of parkland that used to be a rock quarry. Here, going back to the time of the master builders if not before, they chiseled out *pietra serena,* a fine, blue-gray sandstone used as an accent feature in many of the city's grand buildings.

We'd gone less than half a mile when we emerged from the tree line at the top of a hill, and there, spread out before us to the south, was a panoramic vista of Florence nestled in the valley of the Arno below.

I had to catch my breath.

She knew the spot. "Belvedere di San Francesco. Beautiful view. And the saint who blesses the animals."

"That's right. New vistas. Thank you."

I thought she was continuing to tease when she corrected me, "I promised new *perspectives."* But she wasn't smiling this time. She gestured toward a bench beside the path, no doubt provided for breathless hikers to sit and discuss the lessons of history. Her movements seemed so rehearsed it seemed as though she'd memorized the location of every rock along the way.

I didn't want her to tell me what lover she'd been here with.

I didn't protest, and we sat. She took a moment. Her speech might also have been rehearsed. "I haven't told you enough about myself."

*No,* I thought. *Don't.*

I smiled, hoping she'd keep it light. I got the feeling I'd been led up here to be let down. "Perhaps not in words, but you express your feelings marvelously well."

Softly, she said, "I've loved you. And I love what you're

doing." Before I could reciprocate or ask about her choice of verb tense, she insisted, "Understand, Jon, whatever you decide to write about Fred, it's all about today." Another pause while she gestured for me not to speak. "I need to… I want to… You should know some things about my background."

I told myself, *I can't let this get serious.*

"You murdered your husband?"

The callback brought a smile, but it was fleeting. "No," she said, "he was assassinated. It was in the news. They used his workname, didn't mention me."

"You were married to a spy and the other side killed him?"

"He was an asset. These days, some brown shirts wear suits. One morning, they came for him as if he were late for a meeting."

I choked. I actually struggled to take my next breath. "I'm so sorry. I didn't —"

"It was years ago, before we met, before I left Kiev the first time. I should have told you before now. But that's not the most important part of it. He was a Russian national. When I worked at the embassy, I believed in what we were doing. I was hopeful about the Zelenskyy government and the future of my country. I admired the ambassador, and after she was recalled so rudely, there were suspicions about my loyalty to the new bosses. Even though I'd been cleared, the new leadership didn't trust me. Mikhail did not hold a government post. He was a banker. He knew too much about dark money, about where it came from, where it went. I would have stayed at that job to honor him, but they might have seen me as a threat as well. I'd read too many papers above my pay grade. I couldn't stay."

## Parco di Monte Ceceri

"Then you got pulled back. But what about your sister and her children?"

"They've now made it out as well. When the war ends, if Stefan survives, I've left money for him to join them. I won't be going back to Kiev."

"Come with me and be my love. Isn't that how the poem goes?"

She wouldn't look at me. Her eyes were downcast as she said, "My husband's enemies seem to be winning. On both sides of the ocean. I want a role in the wider world, to work for the white hats, but I must try to stay safe."

"Is there nothing I can say? Not even if I swear to follow wherever you're going?"

When she looked up, her eyes were moist. "What was it that wise history teacher told you?"

"Russia will always covet warm-water ports. Must we discuss this now?"

"You realize, that lesson explains it. Then and now. Putin invaded Ukraine for one reason."

"Control of the Black Sea."

"Yes, but the crucial reason is more urgent than that. Russia has two big nuclear submarine bases. One is Vladivostok on the Sea of Japan. The other is Sevastopol, at the southern tip of the Crimean Peninsula. When their puppet ruled our country, even though Ukraine had given up its nuclear weapons, the sub station would stay. But what about the new government? To join NATO, maybe they have to revoke the lease. Putin can't afford to lose that base."

Her situation was much more serious than I'd imagined. Wasn't taking me into her confidence a sign of trust and deeper commitment? "None of this explains why you want to break up with me."

"Another thing your teacher should have told you... Where there are women, there will always be *community*. If they don't have to go trekking for miles every day to fetch water and bring it back on their heads, there will be demand for all manner of social services."

"None of this —"

"Women covet... and deserve... *running* water."

"And where there are men? What do we demand?"

She smirked. "Alcohol and prostitutes."

"Bloody unfair!"

She was serious again. "Given who I've been and what I do — and the sad state of the world — what can *I* do? What *must* I do?" She gave me a moment to appreciate that, now that she'd let me into her life, it was not an easy decision for her. I was still bewildered about how our future had so much to do with the larger issues she was fretting about. "The United Nations has an outreach program to sponsor the empowerment of women for leadership roles. Field officers identify rising stars, help them finish their studies, promote their candidacy for office, and fund their political campaigns."

*She's committed to this. And she won't be inviting me to join.*

She went on, "The driver will pick us up where we left our phones, then he'll drop me at the airport in time to get my flight to Istanbul. From there, it will be on to East Africa and my first assignment."

I wanted a seat on that plane, a bed in her tent. At least, the hope of welcoming her home.

I insisted, "You can't be doing that forever. You'll come visit, or I'll go there, and then —"

"I'll be moving around. Five countries. I won't have a phone that can be tracked. I can't even use social media.

Understand, those governments are patriarchies. I may be running from old enemies now, but I'll be making plenty of new ones, especially if I begin to make a difference."

"And you will use your talent for remaining out of touch."

She took my hand and squeezed it. "Rather like our beloved Fred."

---

When the taxi let her out at Amerigo Vespucci International Airport, I finally got that kiss.

And a sweet, lingering memory. She did not call. She did not write. I have yet to get so much as a snakeskin or a silk neckerchief.

To this day, it was the last time I saw her. I promise to forgive all if I catch sight of her again.

But I may have to wait until a woman is elected president of Kenya.

# Settling Down

## Fred Speaks

When I was on patrol with my mates, we were a tight group. However much I might have resented any of them for their jibes or stink at various times, the bonds of mutual protection held us together in the face of the enemy and in the fight.

Returning war veterans — from ancient times to this day, I expect — at first are overcome by loneliness and perhaps even alienation from society. They had a strong sense of community on the battlefield, in the barracks, in the mess tent, and around the gaming tables. But having come back, especially if they had no caring family at home, they could well become detached and adrift.

I was surprised when Sarah was there at the station to greet my homecoming. I had expected Henry. Perhaps he'd stayed back, hoping to nudge us together.

Notably, she was not resentful. Or, if she was, she didn't show it. The look she gave me was fond. Our first kiss was brief, but warm embraces followed when we cast our misgivings aside.

In Sarah, as I would soon with Henry, I had to take but a step into community. I was undeniably proud of being a valiant son of the Ever Faithful. There was our national spirit to be bucked up, brushed off, and called to attention.

Sarah and I renewed our vows with Henry looking on. The modest service was held at St. Michael's because it was her family church. Old resentments mattered not at all.

I was fortunate to secure a position in the Exeter office of Smithson Importers as a bookkeeper. I studied and earned my chartered accountancy. Our business thrived on a brisk trade with India, and when our managers learned of my familiarity with the region, I accepted a promotion to our head office in Liverpool.

I thought then that business trips might take me back there, but I developed back trouble, and travel was out of the question.

Sarah and I had two daughters and a son. In 1940, he enlisted in the Royal Hampshire Regiment so he could fight with the infantry in France. My mistake, I didn't try to dissuade him.

Unlike Fred, our Marcus was faithful about writing whenever he was able. Then the letters stopped. Only Sarah's death a year later ended her grief.

Meredith and Lillian were a comfort to me, and they found my after-dinner war stories, continually embellished with each retelling, much more interesting than the sparse versions in my diary, which gathered dust on the shelf.

I have never mentioned Mira to anyone, not even Henry, who would no doubt have been delighted to hear that I was, at least at one time, not such an old stick.

As I approached my eightieth birthday and a kind caregiver tucked me into my hospice bed, my thoughts drifted back to my days recovering on that veranda in Satara.

In my dream, Mira appeared for the briefest moment, dressed in a colorful sari and smiling as sweetly as an angel.

She clasped her hands in a prayerful pose, nodded, and pronounced, "Perchance, my love, we will meet in another life."

# THE END OF
# MY SEARCH

## JONATHAN'S JOURNAL

ON MY RETURN to my lofty terrarium high above the marina, I threw myself back into teaching. My sabbatical year was not yet over, but I sought out assignments in the evening extension program so I could stay sharp and wouldn't be tempted to drink myself to sleep at night.

I also resumed work on my book, the one about how the invention of photography both inspired the innovators of Impressionism but also all but destroyed the marketplace for meticulous Neo-Romantic portraitists like John Singer Sargent.

From time to time, I'd peek in at the Figurativo Gallery in Santa Monica, simply to get another look at the sweet lass in *An Enthralling Novel,* the one who looks so much like Elena. They'd told me this original was not for sale, but if it ever would be, I couldn't afford it. I resisted the idea of ordering a reproduction to hang at home. I missed her terribly, but looking at her face every day

# Jonathan's Journal

would be too much like turning my private space into a shrine.

She'd certainly helped me get further along in my research — and understanding of history and geopolitics — than I could have ever done on my own. But all along, I nursed secret longings for discovering the connections between the anonymous J.F.W. and my family. I held to the hunch that Mum was more attached to that leather-bound memoir than she let on. I even considered seriously whether her happening to buy it on Portobello Road might have been a cover story, a useful fiction. Perhaps it was a family heirloom after all.

I'd certainly grown attached to Fred as if he were my forebear, even though studying him so closely only highlighted the flaws in his character. He was a decent sort, a patriotic and dutiful son of the Ever Faithful, and while he was never cited for heroism, his implied return to the role of husband (and father?) helped write the next chapter in his country's contributions to the family of nations.

---

Dad had cautioned me about relying on Uncle Ted, and my mother's opinion of him hinted at some scandal so hateful she denied his very existence.

I assumed he had long since met his end. I didn't even know whether he was my father's brother or hers. Either way, I expected his generation would all be gone by now. That's why I was gobsmacked when he left a phone message at my university number requesting that I call him.

From the sound of his voice, he was indeed crusty, his health perhaps failing. But he was cheery and talkative. As if we'd been in touch only recently and habitual chums, he wanted to be caught up on all I'd been doing. I gave him an ultra-condensed version of my efforts over the last year to root out the identity and secretive personality of J.F.W. — along with the second-chance romance story of my fondness for Elena.

He was generous with his time. It was a transatlantic call, but neither of us was watching the clock. He listened and chuckled and chortled, sounding enormously amused. Occasionally, I thought I overheard his sipping and slurping.

As I wrapped up the summary of my adventures, he congratulated me on my diligence. Then, with a portentous, preparatory throat-clearing, he finally got around to announcing the reason he'd wanted to talk. "Putting my affairs in order, dear boy. Making sure it's all set down formally with inverted commas and full stops. Understand, unscrupulous pill pushers and stiff-necked tax collectors have sucked up all my ready. Sorry to say, there'll be none of that for you. However, I'm advising you, if you have no objection, I'm bequeathing you my little cottage in Somerset. It's no grand estate, but a delightful love nest with a well-kept garden. Might do you a bit of good from time to time to get away, what?"

I expressed no objection whatever. I was touched, realizing I might be the only blood relative he has left. When I expressed concern about his health, he insisted he would not be shuffling off directly. He insisted was merely charting a wise way forward.

He asked, "This soldier chap. Had your initials. Odd happenstance. Have any idea whether he was some relation?"

"No clue whatever, Ted. I hoped you would know. I'm

## Jonathan's Journal

embarrassed to say I was never sure what relation we are to each other. Aren't you Dad's brother?"

He laughed heartily. "Not at all! Only his best friend, drinking buddy, sin eater, and father confessor. Your mum didn't approve of me because I knew all his haunts, including every last one of his lost loves. About his actual family, he shared nothing whatever, and I did the same. Sorry I can't help."

"How much can we really know of history? I suppose that's the lesson."

"Listen, young man. I had a thought while you were telling this fellow's yarn. You say there were clippings pasted into that book?"

"Yes, some photos and souvenir postcards. No news items or notes. No personal information."

"Is there perhaps a photo of him or him with his mates?"

"There is one snap of him opposite the title page. Not in uniform. He's standing in his khaki shorts with knee socks and holding a pith helmet, his safari clothes."

"I'm no amateur sleuth, and forgive me if I'm stating the obvious, but did you happen to look on the back of that picture?"

That I had missed such a basic step made me feel like a child who failed the test because he'd lost the most important homework assignment.

"Ted, that suggestion is so obvious I never thought of it. Hold the phone."

I got up from my easy chair, crossed over to the escritoire, and retrieved Fred's diary from the drawer. I turned to the front matter, slid a letter opener under the photo, and pried up gently. The paste was so old, the thing popped right off.

## The End of My Search

Holding my breath, I turned it over to look at the verso.

"Uncle Ted, I'm so dumb and you're so smart. But I'm very glad I didn't think to look before now."

"Why, ever?"

"Because the guy in this picture is J. Frost-Williams."

It occurred to me that, if I'd thought of this early in the game, I might not have pursued the investigation at all. And I might have had no compelling reason to march into the library that day to ask Elena's help.

Once again, my distant "uncle" was amused, especially by his own cleverness. "Well, there's still the possibility his name was Jonathan!"

# Acknowledgments

The handsome volume of "Fred's" diary stayed unopened and unread on my library shelf for years. Like Jonathan, I often wondered whether its author had any connection to my family. My mother told me she'd bought it on Portobello Road, but there the similarity between Jon's story and mine ends. Mother never lived with me in her later years, and her sweet, generous personality was more like Olivia de Havilland than Bette Davis.

I never did find any reason why she might treasure that book other than its attractiveness as a curio.

Undertaking this novel proved to be an ambitious and complex project. My previous historical novel, *Bonfire of the Vanderbilts,* took more than a decade to research and then several years to write. This one did not take quite that long, but the marvels of online data drilling did save a lot of time.

I owe heartfelt thanks to a small army of friends and colleagues. Robin Levey transcribed the handwritten diary and researched location names. Sarah Ambrosio, Emma Graham, Jillian Pincus, Anna Tjeltveit, Trent Babbington, and Joan Cate found references and prepared summaries of military records, historical surveys, and geographical and cultural background. Beta readers offered comments on the complex structure of the narrative: David Drum, Roberta Edgar, Jay Kenoff, Susan Jones, Marvin J. Wolf, Pamela Jaye Smith, Jennifer Thompson, and Mitzi Zilka.

It would not have been possible to bring Fred's story to you without the support of Melissa Flamson of With Permission and the UK Intellectual Property Office.

The ever-diligent Jason Letts lent his capable hand to the copyediting. Lu Ann Sodano has been furiously busy booking my appearances.

Although this is a work of fiction, readers who want to delve into the geopolitical issues that concerned Jonathan and Elena will find the following books intriguing:

*The Train that Disappeared into History: The Berlin-to-Baghdad Railway and How It Led to the Great War* by Kathie Somerwil-Ayerton. There are several histories about the railway. This one is comprehensive.

*Desert Hell: The British Invasion of Mesopotamia,* Charles Townshend. Perhaps remarkably, this author claims he is no relation to Major-General Sir Charles Townshend, just as Jon fretted about any connection he might have with soldier Fred.

*Paris in Ruins: Love, War, and the Birth of Impressionism,* Sebastian Smee. How would history have been different if the Prussians had not given up on their siege of Paris?

*Spies of the Deep: The Untold Truth About the Most Terrifying Incident in Submarine Naval History and How Putin Used the Tragedy to Ignite a New Cold War,* W. Craig Reed. The author explains why the submarine base at Sevastopol is a crucial asset. As well, he claims that manipulation of oil markets and control of global shipping lanes have long been at the core of Russian strategic planning.

*Lessons from the Edge: A Memoir*, Marie Yovanovitch. Americans in the US diplomatic corps witnessed the populist transition in Ukraine and then the invasion of the Donbas and Crimea.

*Putin's War in Syria: Russian Foreign Policy and the Price of America's Absence*, Anna Borshchevskaya. Remember, Russia will always covet warm-water ports.

*- Gerald Everett Jones*
    Santa Monica, 2026

# About the Author

Gerald Everett Jones is a freelance writer who lives in Santa Monica, California. He is a board member of the Writers & Publishers Network and host of the GetPublished! Radio podcast. He holds a Bachelor of Arts with Honors from the College of Letters, Wesleyan University, where he studied under novelists Peter Boynton *(Stone Island)*, F.D. Reeve *(The Red Machines)*, and Jerzy Kosinski *(The Painted Bird, Being There)*.

*Jonathan's Journal* is his fifteenth novel.

Find out more at **geraldeverettjones.com.** Read his interviews and blog posts at Thinking About Thinking on Substack @geraldeverettjones.

# Also by Gerald Everett Jones

**Fiction**

*Jonathan's Journal: A novel* (this book)

*Harry Harambee's Kenyan Sundowner: A Novel* – Multiple awards in Literary Fiction

*Preacher Finds a Corpse* (Evan Wycliff #1) – Multiple awards in Mystery

*Preacher Fakes a Miracle* (Evan Wycliff #2) – NYC Big Book Silver 2020

*Preacher Raises the Dead* (Evan Wycliff #3) – Multiple awards in Mystery

*Preacher Stalls the Second Coming* (Evan Wycliff #4)

*Mick & Moira & Brad: A Romantic Comedy* - Multiple awards in Romantic Comedy

*Clifford's Spiral: A Novel* – IPA Silver in Literary Fiction 2020

*Mr. Ballpoint* – Page Turner Award in Fiction Finalist 2022

*Christmas Karma* – WGA Diversity Award (Screenplay) 2016

*Choke Hold: An Eli Wolff Thriller*

*Bonfire of the Vanderbilts: A Novel / Bonfire of the Vanderbilts: Scholar's Edition*

*My Inflatable Friend* (Misadventures of Rollo Hemphill #1)

*Rubber Babes* (Misadventures of Rollo Hemphill #2)

*Farnsworth's Revenge* (Misadventures of Rollo Hemphill #3)

**Stories and Essay** *Boychik Lit*

## Nonfiction

*How to Lie with Charts* - Eric Hoffer Award Finalist in Business 2020

*The Death of Hypatia and the End of Fate*

*The Light in His Soul: Lessons from My Brother's Schizophrenia* (with Rebecca Schaper)

*Searching for Jonah: Clues in Hebrew and Assyrian History* by Don E. Jones (Afterword)

Printed in Dunstable, United Kingdom